To Milly —

From the author
who makes fewer
advances than the
Iraqi army —

As ever —

March 10.

MARITAL ASSETS

by BRUCE DUCKER

THE PERMANENT PRESS
Sag Harbor, New York 11963

Library of Congress Cataloging-in-Publication Data

Ducker, Bruce.
   Marital assets / by Bruce Ducker.
      p.   cm.
   ISBN 1-877946-26-5 : $21.95
   I. Title.
PS3554.U267M3   1993
813'.54—dc20   92-31161
                            CIP

Manufactured in the United States of America

THE PERMANENT PRESS
Noyac Road
Sag Harbor, NY 11963

Chapter One

From the Journal of Charles Meredith

Point of view is all. *The parallax, the difference in an object seen from two stances, fixes that object in space. Refract the angle of vision ever so slightly and you change the world. One's destination is the North Pole. If instead of a meridian he follows the isogonic line, trusting his compass, he will end up a thousand miles south of the Pole on Prince Edward Island.*

Every reporter on the world is suspect, even a diarist sworn to objectivity. (And I have sworn to nothing.) Without what the law of evidence calls corroboration, his point of view is flat, inutile. What does that tell someone embarking on a journal? It says his efforts are an indulgence. But every private act is an indulgence, and I shall worry no more about it.

Diaries are for confession, and here is my first: I have lived most of my life without passion. And a second: I would not have minded that it stayed away but once passion intrudes, spiritual not sexual passion, it pales the remaining days. Touched by passion one must choose. Down this path lies the heart's own secret. It is an obscured path, for no one knows where it leads and whether the secret finally uncovered will disappoint, fade, migrate. To walk there one must leave the familiar avenues, set down the baggage he has carried, the clothes he has assembled to keep him warm, the lockets, trinkets, beads of his past. The extra chairs for company.

The other path is easy. It requires no sacrifice. It sits easy and broad in front of me. That it tracks according to the topography I have made sure, for I have laid it out, surveyed it, spent years in its blading, grading, compaction.

I can keep all my belongings, all my friends, and I will always know my points of identity, my longitude and latitude. This is the path that most men lucky or unlucky enough to have the choice will choose. It beckons a pleasant journey. Its only hazard is this: the thought that down the other road sounds a birdsong that no one else has heard.

Most men I think play it safe. Concerning women, as this journal will prove, I am not able to speculate.

Choice and change. The last checkers on the board.

I hope in these pages to examine—a self-examination for I am the sole intended beneficiary of my exercise—what three events in my life meant, and why in each I acted as I did. My abrupt removal from St. Alban's, my marriage, and my—what can I call it—not affair, for that quaint French term implies its Latin root of doing, and I did the opposite. Perhaps romance is the term—my romance with Claudia Abbott. These events should establish some reckoning, an outline of place and movement. The journal itself will be a pastime, like tea roses or stamp-collecting, in preparation for my retirement. For I shall soon retire from the practice. This little project will sustain my long afternoons when I have tired of reading and when publishers have returned my jottings unread or unaccepted. Perhaps the journal will grow, as Rousseau's did, seizing hold of me, compelling me to empty the dust from my pockets. These pockets contain little else.

My retirement is permissive. That is the partnership term for it. Indeed the partnership remains a collection of men and, only lately, women who have the grace not to force me out. Were profit their sole objective, I might not last until age sixty-five. Their tolerance, this very grace may explain why, among New York law firms, we have slipped from the second or third tier we held decades ago, to our present status. We are viewed by our colleagues at the bar as an anachronism, forty or so lawyers laboring at a lesser station of legal work in a city where several hundred are required to hoist a firm into the sunlight. It is not that our connections are inferior. On the contrary, we probably have a claim to more partners of social standing per capita—but let me stop. That is a comparison I find distasteful to make, even to myself. In any event, these days social distinction is reserved for those who have no other.

Our firm's decline has resulted from a failure to attract as clients the real estate tycoons, the hedge fund organizers, the corporate raider specialists, under whose banner several major city firms have been created and expanded. If anything we have gone the other way. When I joined the firm in 1954, it had seven more partners than it has today. And I suppose the rate of attrition will be somewhat constant, as remaindermen vest, trusts distribute, money goes from its situs in Manhattan to places that the young of today find more comfortable, goes west to Arizona, Marin County, La Jolla. The modern firm follows the money, opening offices as its clients emigrate. No one has asked me to do so, but I for one am too old to follow along out there. I am too old to begin dressing for the office in clothes suitable for a cruise ship.

And so, in three years, I shall be entitled to retire, and retire I shall. Under the partnership rules, I shall draw a sum modest to start and diminishing yearly. The draftsman of our original parnership agreement showed a taste for irony when he described the draw as an "emolument". The word first meant the fee a land owner paid to the miller to grind wheat to flour. The conceit is imperfect, for a miller is paid to take delivery of grain and separate it into the edible and the chaff. My work is to take a list of property—what a man has inherited and earned, has acquired through marriage, speculation and thrift —and organize it into pages of writing, usually producing far more bulk than what came in the door. A trusts and estates lawyer, as the bar calls it, or as Weemo said when I told him and Claudia what it was that I did, a fellow who writes wills.

Not that I have minded. It will be thirty-eight years this fall, and I have few complaints. When I came to the firm out of law school, I selected this field of practice. Most young lawyers rotated through several disciplines during their apprenticeship, but the men who adjudicated these things felt I was well suited for estate planning, and I was pleased to agree. My family had had a lengthy history of trusts, and, not coincidentally, had been represented by this very firm. I knew my way around bank officers, family committees, and family feuds and welcomed the assignment. I have found that the practice appeals to my sense of order, as does very little else outside nature. One brings together the facts, the desires, the jealousies, the need to hold on or let go, the yearning to get close or move away. All of that dramaturgy must be sifted through and, not discarded, instead translated into a document accounting for one's assets, looking towards taxes, considering which offspring will be able to deal with income and which will squander it. These random elements translate themselves into a plan of disposition, written, precise, without coloration or pity. I enjoy it. It is rather like raking leaves.

I start my reminiscence without regard to time's sequence. That is the autocracy of the diarist. I start as we met the Abbotts. It was fifteen years ago, at Elbow Reef. In that era the entire resort was a club. One bought in and paid annual dues. Evelyn and I had been members for years. The Club had been the idea of the chairman of a large airline, who found himself with access to the Caribbean but nowhere that he could go to find sympathetic company. He doubtless intended to promote his airline, since it was the only one to fly into this island, but I think his real motive was companionship. Elbow Reef has since opened to the public, and while the grounds are the same, it has lost that particular reserve that I enjoyed so much. We no longer visit.

The Elbow Reef Club was built on a small, gibbous island in the Caribbean. Its main house held the usual lounge and game room, a restaurant served by an unnotable kitchen but a surprising cellar, and a card room for evening entertainment. No television sets, no loudspeakers playing Harry Belafonte songs, merely eight or ten tables for bridge, mostly, perhaps cribbage or gin rummy. The main house sat on a point looking seaward on three sides, and to enjoy the evening's vista, guests gathered in the cocktail lounge or on its adjacent patio.

Thirty or forty bungalows, painted navy blue, aqua or white, stood randomly around the cove. The cove itself was a bite-shaped bay protected from open sea by a reef, so that each bungalow had, from its screened breakfast porch, a prospect of *sunrise over flat water. The cabins were linked by paths cut in the spare gorse that covered the island, each path lined with whitewashed rock and conch shells. Most of the paths were an easy walk to the main house. A few cabins were scattered up what the Club called Honeymooners' Hill, giving to their occupants privacy and a sense, I suppose, of romance.*

Beyond the grounds, wrapping around that part of the coast unsuitable for swimming because of eddies and jagged coral, lay an eighteen-hole golf course. I do not know whether it is hard or easy, an interesting course or a dull one, how it fits in with those coordinates golfers use but most people reserve for their marriages or their lives. I've only played the game there at the Elbow Reef Club, though I must admit I enjoyed it then. Not swatting and chasing the ball so much as the walk. The landscape, even groomed as it had been by man, was beautiful. The blues and reds of the Caribbean are so intense. The colors of the landscape, the hundred greens of the sea, even the plum-bruised skin of the people. To us from the temperate zone the effect is—what?—daring?

The Club had a library, with a good selection established by the charter members and augmented annually as interested guests visited with a supply of excess reading. It was a ritual not everyone practiced, but I very much enjoyed. During the year I would separate books of my own I thought suitable. Then, on my February visit, for each contribution I would affix the Club's bookplate, enter my name in the donor's list, and make out an index card.

Evelyn and I had established something of a routine at the Elbow Reef. I like to think that a place is the sum total, the culture—if that word isn't overused— of the people who have created its traditions. We visited always the first and second weeks in February, when New York was at its dreariest, and we always took the same cabin. The bougainvillea were out in full, the red of blood, of stigmata in a bad religious painting. Until the year we met, the Abbotts had visited at the end of March, to coincide with their son's spring holiday. This year he had finished high school, apparently living on his own in New

York, and so they had changed the date to meet their, not Hap's, convenience. Weemo told us these arrangements as if they were a small triumph.

It was on a day blue as a gemstone, at the flag for the eighth hole, that we met the Abbotts. I will not go into the circumstances, for they were embarrassing to Weemo, but we met. I have never been so deaf to the wooden creak of a life changing in orbit as when I met Claudia Abbott. She seemed to me then, as she does now in my mind's eye, composed, assertive, self-assured, all of which she was. And she also seemed to have as firm a grip on her life as on the club she held, so that she knew its uses. It turned out she was not an enthusiastic golfer.

We chatted. Someone, I think it was Weemo, suggested we make up a foursome to finish the round, and the friendship began. I was not surprised that Evelyn agreed to join them. She gathers acquaintances the way a hypochondriac gathers medicines. And Weemo was handsome in a mode most women find appealing. I recall thinking how clearly he wanted to be liked. He had a way of looking at you as you spoke, even when the conversation was about the grooming of the fairway grasses, as if you might say something worthy of history. It is a mannerism designed, I think, to flatter its object, and it generally works.

Claudia wore a yellow knit golfing shirt, with the emblem of some other resort on its pocket, and knee length shorts. I have never put much stock in appearances: those of us whose appearances are unnotable rarely do. But I observed the strength in her roundish face and the vitality in her green eyes. She later told me she didn't like her looks, that she had been a homely child and still thought of herself as plain, that a few magical make-up strokes were what had held me. Perhaps she was right, but not as I remember. It was a face whose energies came out at you.

That is how I remember it. But reminiscence is a fancy that does not become more precise with practice. If only it did. I can merely set down my recollections in this journal, knowing that experience since has colored them. We have been corrupted by *the movies: even our sub-consciences want scenes that play well. After the actors are through, our memory edits the events, adds background, special effects, programmatic music. When I recall this meeting a backdrop appears beyond Claudia, ribbons of breaking surf on the shallow coralheads. I doubt at the time I was aware of anything so splendid.*

Why write this at all? Why bother with the past? Simply a matter of finding where we are. The past, our deeds and photographs track our position. Triangulation, the navigators call it. It is not a question of trying to relive my life. That is one delusion, one childhood disorder I never suffered. I've had others.

One should not be an innocent at forty-seven, yet I think when I met Claudia I was. We learn late, years after, that the magician at the children's birthday party had boxes with false bottoms, entire chrysanthemum plants that collapse to the size of a grape. As children we offer up our coins and he makes them disappear until we are penniless, shrieking with surprise.

Some tricks one catches on to. All that I write about happened before I had learned Time's clever and cruel trick of masquerading as chronology, while in fact it is something quite different. There is the time that a prisoner spends in his cell, the ticking-of-the-clock time that marches forward and spaces our days and years from each other That is the time we think of when we spend it, squandering or hoarding it, pacing the floor, playing backgammon, waiting for a taxi. Those hours we have in amplitude.

The other—the choice ingots of love and feeling that we stumble across once in a very long while—that warm us and give legs to our memories, those hours are scarce indeed.

Chapter Two

The golf course at Elbow Reef was the pride of its members. The Club was regularly asked to host major tournaments and it regularly declined. The committee took equal pleasure both in receiving the invitation and in turning it down, for it is reassuring to be sought after and gratifying to disdain those who seek us out.

The attitude of the Links Committee was consistent with everything about the Club. Its kitchen was adequate. No boasts were made about the cooking and indeed complaints arose if the guests perceived too much fuss over the food. No more facilities were provided than needed, and no moneys spent on new diversions. The Club took in few new members. One was expected to like it the way it was.

The golf course was built on the site of an old sugar cane plantation, and its holes were designed to take players past the walls, the lichen-stained grey stone, of the refinery and the ruined windmill. Several fairways paralleled the beaches of the lagoon, and the aspects from the greens were to the manicured course inland and the bubbling surf beyond. Where the course traced the ocean side of the island, enormous fluffed cotton trees served as a windbreak, and green and red peppers grew wild in the bush. The island had few hills, but the course had a slight ridge in its center, a spine that ran the length of the island. A frangipani tree stood on the course at the highest point of the ridge, and on the day of the meeting of the Abbotts and Merediths, it was massed in brilliant blossoms.

The Abbotts were considering playing only the front half of the course. By the fifth hole that day, Weemo was bored with the game. If the truth be known, he was slightly bored with Elbow Reef. He and Claudia had arrived a week earlier.

Because they were on a different schedule from their past visits, he had come upon no one he knew. And to his disappointment he had not seen a single attractive woman. Except for the brunette with the curly hair. She was coupled with a tallish, balding man who looked very much like someone you'd met before. Someone you might strike up a conversation with at the Club bar. Weemo thought the woman looked much younger than her mate. Probably a second wife.

That morning Weemo noticed them in the pro shop. They were to tee off immediately behind him and Claudia, so Weemo ventured a joke about giving them enough room. She laughed and met his look. There was something incongruous about this man and wife. A skein of wool from different dye lots. They didn't quite fit. The man looked uncomfortable in his clothes. Cruise wear, it was called at the time. He seemed more accustomed to dress for the city. Yet he had an open face, passive but not hostile. He wore clear-rimmed glasses and Weemo guessed that he hadn't changed frame styles since his first pair. The woman's appearance was more interesting. She was slender, with black hair and brows and a lovely olive complexion. To Weemo's practiced eye, her coloring marked her as an exotic.

Once on the course, he couldn't concentrate on his game. Not that Claudia minded. She was indifferent to the sport, and went around because he asked her to, usually at a new resort when her husband had no one else to play with, for he preferred not to golf alone. Weemo played with a six handicap, and Claudia often felt she was slowing him down. Today he didn't seem to mind, though. He was clowning around, not playing seriously. They laughed at each other's shots. On the eighth, he had holed out before her. While she was lining up her third putt, he was fooling with the cart, driving it in loops. That was how he came to run over his wedge. He had left it at the lip of a bunker, and had rolled in a putt from twenty feet to get his par. She was inching her ball towards the hole, hoping to sink it so they might go on, and he now had the cart in reverse, doing figure eights. She heard the crunch of the shaft as her ball dropped.

"What shall we do?" she asked. "Do you want to go back to the clubhouse and get another, or play with mine?" Weemo draped the vee shaped club around his neck and grinned at her like a little boy. He wasn't at all annoyed at the inconvenience he'd caused himself.

"Negative," he said. Weemo liked nautical words. Especially on vacation. "I can't shoot with ladies' clubs. Let's just wave this couple through," pointing down the fairway where the Merediths waited to tee off, "and see if we can join up with them."

The Merediths listed to Weemo's explanation. He expanded on the story, and soon everyone was laughing. Claudia looked over at him with an uncommon warmth. It was the sort of thing Weemo was good at. People liked him immediately.

Weemo had straight hair, the color of wet hay, and he wore it in the English fashion. Or rather in the fashion Weemo understood from magazine advertisements to be English. Long, combed straight back, and parted sharply just off center. His hairline was a distinct arch across a high forehead. He had a thin, prominent nose that pointed his face at you like a pistol, aware, ready. Blue eyes, swimming-pool blue, and an athletic tan that made him look years younger than he was. Youthful, principled, accomplished—those were the attributes one might check off from a list of adjectives if asked to interpret the personality behind this handsome face. Those, and aristocratic. When he stood next to Charles Meredith, an acquaintance might be surprised to find that they were the same height, since Weemo seemed much taller. And Charles appeared to be older by far more than the five years that separated them.

The Merediths were happy to accommodate. They walked the remaining holes together in good spirits. Only Weemo was a serious golfer, and he played with an ease and diffidence that improved all of their games. Once or twice he mentioned a point to Charles, but without any air of superiority. Charles was gratified, pleased to find suggestions he could adopt. His strokes occasionally showed improvement. As they played out Weemo hit every green, and as it turned out had no need for the wedge that had brought them together.

That evening at dinner the Abbotts sent champagne to the Merediths' table, with a note that it was for club rental. Unused to a second bottle of wine but not displeased by it, the Merediths insisted that the Abbotts help them finish it off.

The conversation turned on the topics at hand. The Elbow Reef Club, attitudes towards golf, people they knew in common. The Abbotts were from Cincinnati. Charles registered his silent surprise that such a city should produce people of the evident means of Weemo and Claudia. He did not inquire. It had been his experience that if people intend you to know anything about themselves, the origin, or indeed the extent, of their assets, they would let you know.

Weemo led the conversation and everyone seemed content to let him. Four people of the leisure class at leisure, striking up an easy association and finding they shared friends and interests with equal dispassion. They chatted amiably about wines, automobiles, and favorite vacation spots, and about how they had come upon Elbow Reef. Weemo inquired about Charles' practice and mentioned in passing the name of the large Cincinnati firm that handled the work for what he termed "Claudia's company." Oh yes, Charles had said. An excellent firm. And it was.

Weemo held out his arm to see his watch. "They're showing a movie in the game room. I think I might take it in. Anyone for it? It's the only night life we'll have."

"Oh," said Evelyn. "What an unusual watch. Let me see."

Weemo beamed. He unbuckled the strap and handed it to her. Its face was a gold medal of some sort, showing four young men wearing laurel wreaths and looking to heaven. "Turn it over," he said.

Evelyn squinted and read the inscription. "'April 5, 1952. First Place, Mile Relay.'"

"The Penn Relays," Weemo said.

"What college were you at?" Evelyn asked.

"Scholastic. That was for the scholastic division."

"Prep school," said Charles. Much of the boarding school vocabulary was unfamiliar to Evelyn and, particularly when they were first married, Meredith had found himself explaining terms he had spoken since childhood.

"High school, actually," Weemo said. "I'm a garden variety high school product. I came to prominence late in life." Evelyn enjoyed the small vindication, for Charles was so often right, and she underscored the moment with a quick glance.

Charles felt his wife's eyes. He said something trite to carry the conversation over it.

"I didn't suppose it was for your retirement. You're too young to have been given a gold watch already."

"No, no," Weemo said. "Besides, in Claudia's company they don't give watches. Pen and pencil desk sets. In marble."

"Claudia's company," asked Evelyn, rising to the bait now cast for the second time. "What is that?"

"Parine Pen," Weemo said quickly. Claudia put her hand to her throat, an unconscious gesture. If it was meant to stay her husband, it was insufficient.

"Claudia's a Parine," Weemo added.

"That didn't occur to me," Evelyn said disingenuously. "That there would be a Parine. Or a Waterman in Waterman's Pen. Or a Mr. Cadillac, for that matter."

"The Watermans aren't around anymore," Claudia said. "They sold out a while ago to a conglomerate. I don't know about the Cadillacs. I think he was an Indian chief."

"No," Weemo corrected her. "You're thinking of Pontiac."

"Cadillac too," Charles said. "Also an Indian chief."

Weemo was undeterred. "Perhaps you're right. But they're not in our set. I've never seen Mr. Cadillac at Elbow Reef. Or Lincoln or DeSoto for that matter."

Weemo recovered his prize watch and strapped it on. They rose as a group.

"Hey," said Weemo. "How about tomorrow, Merediths? Are you game for another round?"

"Sorry," said Charles. "One round of golf per vacation is my quota for exertion."

"That's how Claudia feels. Evelyn? What about you?"

"I'd like to," Evelyn said. "If I won't hold you back. My game might actually improve."

"I'm afraid I'm not much of a consolation," Charles said to Claudia. "I intend to sit on the beach and read."

"My plans exactly. For which a foursome isn't needed."

"Or a wedge," said Weemo and they laughed. Weemo made an effort to keep the conversation going, to keep up the joking, but the Merediths were saying goodnight. He spoke to Evelyn to arrange for starting times. Charles and Claudia were left to each other.

"I may see you on the beach, then," Charles said as he shook her hand. She smiled at him, and he felt that she too did much in life alone. Whether by choice or by circumstance he could not tell.

Chapter Three

"I burn easily," Charles heard himself saying. "And so I'm given to these ridiculous costumes in the sun while everyone else lounges about in a loincloth."

He hadn't meant to apologize, though it came out that way. He was seated next to Claudia, both of them in ancient beach chairs of wood turned to silver in the salt air and slung with canvas striped green, yellow, orange. It was Claudia who had initiated the conversation, asking the beach boy to place her chair there after inquiring only Do you mind?

No, Charles had said. Of course not.

They joked about the size of the books they carried. Each had a massive novel, six or seven hundred pages, and Claudia expressed doubts that she would see hers through.

"I always feel the need to have one nearby. The longer the vacation, the more generations it has to cover. "

Since she had joined him, the books had remained in their laps, unopened. Charles at last set his down on the sand. They gazed at the sparkling sea as if on a widow's watch.

"I don't burn," she said eventually to his remark. "I don't tan, either. I think I'm related to the white rhinocerous. Tough, impermeable skin."

"Curious, isn't it? Our spouses both tan so well, have whatever it is in the skin that allows them to sit in the sun." Charles knew the word, but chose not to use it lest he sound pedantic.

"Melanin," she offered. She wore a one-piece bathing suit of pale green, the color of her eyes. It was trimmed with a white fringe where fabric ended and skin began, likely, thought Charles, to soften the inevitable bulge. Yet on her, he could not help but notice, no bulges showed. He felt foolish, in his long-sleeve shirt of Indian cotton, its white cuffs meeting white skin at the wrists. He wore a tan poplin beach hat, pulled low to keep the glare of the sun off his glasses, and a pair of bathing trunks he had had ever since he could remember.

"For some reason, my legs never burn." He heard his remark and caught a short laugh in his throat. "Goodness," he said. "I beg your pardon. What a fatuous topic."

She smiled at his apology. Her smile at once relieved him and made him feel even more adolescent.

When she next spoke, some moments later, it was to go from the particular to the general. "Has it ever struck you as strange that we spend hours in the sun trying to obtain the very color that keeps others out of our country clubs?"

"It has," Charles answered. "Why do you suppose that is? Is it that we are trying to capture the characteristics of the African races that we secretly admire?"

"You mean sexual prowess?"

"Sexual prowess," Charles repeated, although he would not have led off with that. "Innate rhythm, speed of foot."

"Ah yes. The natural savage. The ability to bounce a basketball, to father a tribe of children, to sing spirituals while picking the massa's cotton."

"You're making fun of me," he said, not displeased.

She pursed her lips and looked towards him. "My turn to apologize," she said. "I don't know you well enough to do that."

"That's all right. I think I like it. The fact is, people rarely make fun of me. They see me as too serious."

"And are you?"

"No. I'm not serious at all. It's my looks. I think I remind them of their catechism instructor."

She was amused by that. "You have to excuse my teasing," she said. "It's the social activist in me. Poor Weemo. I think his real disappointment in our marriage is that I've turned out to be a Democrat."

"How does that go over in Cincinnati?"

"There you go with stereotypes again," she scolded gently. Charles held up his palms and she went on.

"Like anywhere else, I suppose. So long as I don't make a career of it, embarrass anyone, no one seems to mind. To most of our friends it's like having a child in prison or a tumor somewhere inside you. Everyone knows it's not contagious, but they certainly don't want you discussing it at their dinner table."

When Charles made no response, she went on. "I'd guess, too, it helps to have money. If you have enough money you can indulge in some eccentricities. People will accept politics so long as it stays a hobby. No one begrudges how you go about it. Some of them collect antique Ferraris or commemorative spoons, and they wouldn't expect me to criticize them."

They watched a dinghy with single sail tack upwind across the mouth of the cove. A black man in pink satin shorts and a white tee shirt was handling it, making it come about at sharp angles. Charles recognized the man as Gideon, the Club's boat boy.

"And you?" Claudia asked.

"Oh, I'm what used to be known as a Rockefeller Republican. A middle of the roader. William Scranton, Milton Shapp. I even voted for Mr. Carter this time."

"I didn't mean your politics. I meant, just you."

She had placed a blue, dotted bandana loosely over her eyes. It was an odd sensation, speaking to a woman who was blindfolded, exposed, lying in the heat of a Caribbean sun that was only now opening Charles' pores. With a breathing noise he leaned forward in the sling chair and removed his shirt.

"The same applies to me," Charles told her. "A middle of the roader. I practice law, I listen to music, I read."

"Sports? Games? Skiing, tennis, guns?"

"All devised to humiliate me. Freshman year in college I discharged my last phys ed requirement—by, I should tell you, learning how to service the derailleur of a geared bicycle. After that I vowed I would never again enter a locker room. I prefer walking to running, sitting still to both. As for hunting I find it a good assumption that if, as Thomas Aquinas says, God is all things, then he's also a grouse. Better not to offend him."

He looked over at her shielded face and saw from the corners of her mouth that his comment had bemused her. He lifted the wooden arms of the beach chair and let them slip back a notch, lowering by fifteen degrees his angle of recline.

"Oh," he added, thinking of it late. "I am a bit of a birder."

"A birder?"

"One of those odd types popping up in ditches with field glasses. But I'm an amateur."

"With one of those lists of all the birds you've seen?"

"With a life list," Charles confirmed.

"An odd hobby for a New Yorker."

"Not really. You'd be surprised how many species we get in the parks. All that asphalt and noise concentrates them, drives them to refuge. And we have a house in the country. North of Danbury."

"A life of contemplation." She said it with approval. "Does it suit you?"

"Yes," he answered, gathering conviction. "Yes it does."

There was a time when he had thought of a different vocation, he told her. By his graduaton from college he realized—though his parents never said so in those words—that his family had sufficient outside income to free him of the need to make a living. The men on his father's side had been in the professions. Lawyers, mostly, as was his father. But his mother's family had been in banking during the green and golden days. Before the laws prevented commercial banks from speculation. They had done well buying and selling. For reasons Meredith had never understood, his family admired trafficking in currency, but looked down on trafficking in other goods—shoes, say, or lettuce. "Perhaps," Charles mused, "because your competition could operate from a pushcart." As he said this, the corners of Claudia's mouth again flickered.

Financial independence had led the young Meredith to contemplate what other restrictions he might be able to shed, and he decided that he would also like to be independent of the approval of others. He'd always loved the natural world, he told her. When he was a little boy and his mother was well enough, she would take him for walks through the Botanic Gardens, to Prospect and Central Parks. And there were summers in the quiet landscape around their Connecticut house. The combination led him to conclude that he would make his living as a nature writer.

"What did your parents think?"

"Nothing very much. My mother died when I was thirteen. My father was entertained at first, then distressed, but both in mild doses. My father had no expectations of me, you see, so he couldn't very well be disappointed. For graduation he bought me a portable Smith Corona and several boxes of excellent typing paper. He thought that would be sufficient. I declared on my passport and tax return that I was a writer, and so I suppose my father was right.

"I remember bragging to my college friends that I was going to elevate outdoor writing from barber shop magazines to minor literature. Whitney Tower had done it for horse racing and Julia Child would do it to a leg of lamb. That is what I saw myself doing for the townsend solitaire."

"What happened?"

"What you'd expect. I'd overlooked a few things along the way. For one, there are damn few markets for nature writing. For a second, most of the outdoor magazines are interested in how you catch small mouth bass, not in the Platonic forms of small mouth bass.

"I was undismayed. You must remember that my original goal—is that too lofty a word? Maybe, disposition—was to be a nature writer, not necessarily a published one. I had a portable machine, and a dozen boxes of erasable bond, twenty-five percent fibre content twenty pound, five hundred sheets to the box. So my disposition was confirmed. It wasn't having my articles rejected that finally got to me. It was being ignored. I share this nagging superstition that you have to get noticed to exist."

"I don't understand," Claudia said. She leaned over and began to scoop sand to bury her foot. Charles watched her. The sand piled only as high as her ankle.

"Being noticed, you mean?" She nodded and kept shoveling.

"It's what we're taught, isn't it? Render to everyone according to his deeds. Isn't that it?"

"Not quite," she said, "but you've got the drift."

"It's a deficiency of the Western mind. Or at the very least, at the heart of my disaffection in the universe. I'd do better as a Buddhist."

"Where deeds don't count."

"Where thoughts do," he answered. She seemed to accept that. She leaned across the slatted footrest of the chair and started on the other foot.

"Anyway, when the few magazines who read my submissions stopped rejecting me and simply didn't reply, I gave it up. I enrolled in law school, my father's law school, graduated without any particular distinction, and joined a firm. The very firm with which, almost twenty years later, I still practice."

The sun was directly overhead. The silence of the day, with only the rustle of the surf and an occasional cry of a gull, seemed to stop time. It also made Meredith feel that he had gone on unduly about himself. He began to apologize.

"Don't," Claudia said. "I asked. It's interesting. It's interesting to me how we end up in a place we had no intention of being." She took the cloth from her eyes and dabbed at her brow.

"Do you feel like a swim?" she asked, suddenly standing up and brushing unseen sand from her suit.

"I usually use the pool," Charles said.

"Come," she said. She tugged her suit down at her hips. "Live a little."

And with that she turned and skipped over the hot sand and into the water. Meredith watched her run through the wash and dive into the blue curl of a breaker. Beyond, yards beyond, it seemed to him, she surfaced, stroking against a neutral sea. He rose, removed his glasses and placed them in his hat. The sand was uncomfortably hot on his feet. He retied the string at the waist of his suit and walked to the water's edge. He splashed water on his arms and chest, squinting all the while at the bobbing brown speck he knew to be the back of her head. Then he was in the water, blinded by the salt and seeing dimly, stroking he knew too furiously to be efficient, but enough to stay afloat and enough to move, erratically, out beyond the breaking waves.

When he caught up to her, she was treading water, it seemed to him without effort, for she used both hands to push back her hair. Usually auburn, it was shades darker now, drenched in the sea water. Evelyn, he realized, rarely swam without a bathing cap. That was what made Claudia look so feral.

He was breathless from the swim and did not want to speak. She merely turned on her back and floated, effortlessly, watching the bare bulb of sun directly above them. Charles did the same. I haven't floated like this since I was in summer camp, he thought. It took me two entire months to learn how.

They floated without speaking. The swell of the surf moved their bodies first up then into its troughs, perhaps a foot, no more. The effect was to drain from his body any sense of kinesthesia, any sense of muscle or effort. He kept his eyes closed, aware only of the orange of the lids and the sound the water made against itself and their bodies. Once, when he feared from a deep sink that a wave might break over him, he opened his eyes. The sun spotted his retina, so that after he closed his eyes, he saw its imprint, negative now, in black against a red canvas, moving mutely across the sky of his eyelid.

When he looked to see her she was gone. Lifting his head broke the surface tension of his body on the water, and when he looked up, he felt his body sink, as if he were a scrap of paper that once submerged would not float again. He had a moment's panic, an alloy of the possibility of her loss and a sense that he was farther out than he would be without her. Then he saw her, swimming with a firm stroke towards the shore.

He turned and began to swim after her. He reached their chairs, sitting empty now and watching the shoreline like worried mothers, but her towel, bandana and book were not there. She had gone ahead.

Chapter Four

From the Journal

I can't say what attracted me to Claudia. I had met beautiful women before, and I had usually been put off by the self-consciousness their beauty inflicts on them. She had none of that. Not that she was unaware of herself or her circumstances. On the contrary, she thought about them regularly, and it was her circumstances—the financial comfort that enabled her leisure and a marriage where her presence was discretionary— that allowed us to spend so much time together. It was shortly after our meeting, the very first day as we sat on the beach, that she explained away Weemo's remarks about Parine Pen. It was not, she wanted me to understand, "her company" as Weemo kept insisting, but a family company in which she held some minority interest.

No, her sense of her surroundings was as sharp as a killdeer's ken of the field where she's nested. What I found remarkable was how self-assured she seemed. Her descriptions of her life were plainly spoken. They were observations, not intended to reflect virtue on herself, and they seemed to be free from the doubts that, I confess, had nagged me even through to middle age. We admire what we lack and I have always admired confidence. Do we have friends for their shortcomings or their strengths?

On the several mornings that followed, we sat in the same beach chairs. It didn't occur to me to wonder how easily the two couples split apart and reformed. The alignment seemed natural, like those biology slides on mitosis and conjugation, the way cells divide. Claudia and I had no interest in the games

*the Club provided, and I'm sure if anyone had asked, Weemo
and Evelyn would have said that to sit around and talk was
to waste a perfectly good holiday.*

And so we talked.

*I learned about Claudia's childhood, about the Parine Pen
Company, and to my surprise about her predicament. We asked
the beach boy to set up an umbrella to shade me from the sun,
so that I could shed my hat and shirt. Claudia baked herself
in the light, a bandana or more often a wide-brimmed straw
hat covering her face. We sat talking blindly to each other in
the mode of classical analysis. The chairs sank deeper into the
sand, but there was little other change. Our historical novels
went unread, postcards meant for friends remained blank and
unstamped, a talk I was to give on the effect of the new tax
laws on the marital deduction trust went without outline. It
was a glorious way to spend time.*

* * * * *

"I remember mostly my father," Claudia told him. "Taking
long walks in the woods behind our house, with me holding
on to a finger or two. Until he died, we still walked that way
and I've only now realized it was because when I was a child,
I couldn't grasp his whole hand.

"I was the oldest. There were two after me. My brother
Gordon runs the company. Then there was a little girl who
died after two days. Crib death, they call it. I think it hard-
ened my mother. I don't remember her saying a loving word
since.

"My father grieved too, I'm sure. But he responded by
caring for me the more. Funny how families are. In our family, the men ran the business, and the women never had a
voice. So it came to my father to go into the company, though
I doubt he enjoyed it. He liked taking walks, dabbling with
water colors, growing geraniums. Do you know there are
more than a hundred kinds of scented geraniums? Daddy
used to cross-breed them. And when he died they packed up
the greenhouses and tried to ship his whole collection to the
university at Columbus, but the truck got caught in a frost
and not a plant survived."

She leaned forward to raise the wooden foot rest. Then she squeezed sun lotion from a brown plastic bottle and rubbed the cream on her legs and chest.

"He died only a few months after I became engaged. He liked Weemo. Everyone does. He preferred Weemo to the other boys I'd dated. For one thing, Weemo was happy with Cincinnati. My father called him a 'perfectly good fellow.' I remember his saying it, even before our engagement. 'A perfectly good fellow.'"

"This was while you were in college?" Charles asked.

"The year I graduated. We would go out when I was home from school." And she mentioned the New England town that houses a prominent women's college.

"When I was at school, I dated boys from the other colleges. But at home, for the Christmas parties and spring vacation, there was Weemo. He was a wonderful dancer and very handsome. It sounds silly to say, these years later, but there it is."

"Not at all," Charles reassured her. "There are marriages based on less firm footing."

She peeked out from beneath her hat to see if he would say more, but he was lying with his eyes closed and his face up, surrendered to the sun, silent again.

"Every December and every April we saw each other. We went to parties, danced, started going around together. Isn't that what it was called? Necking a little, necking a little more. I would go back to school. We would never write. Weemo always says he doesn't like to write more than a check. Summer vacations, I'd be home for a week in June, then off to Europe. One summer I worked in a gallery in New York. I remember telling myself it would change my life, but of course it didn't.

"Then I was home for two weeks in September. Parties, regular sessions parked in country lanes at night, and back to Northampton and the stones of Florence."

"You studied art history."

"I studied art history. It was pointless for Parine women to study business, and they weren't expected to find a vocation. Besides, I guessed how uncomfortable Daddy was with his. I think he would have been happier as a gardener. "

"But in life we can't always do what we want."

"Precisely," she said with a broad smile. "The very first lesson in the Book of Common Prayer."

A cloud the width of a ribbon crossed the sun. They both sensed its shadow passing over the glazed white beach and looked up.

"It's almost lunch time. Are you ready for a swim?"

To answer Charles stood up and removed his glasses. They walked to the water's edge together. Claudia spoke of her strolls with her father down the long, cluttered lanes of the greenhouses. He always carried a pocket watch with a hunting case, and when he thought they should be going back, he'd take it out and she would blow on it and the lid would magically open so she could tell the time.

She fell silent and traced her toe in the wet sand. When Charles spoke, it startled her.

"And you were married your senior year?"

"Engaged that Christmas to be a June bride. Daddy died that March, so we postponed it until September. The papers said it was so beautiful it might change the tradition of June weddings."

"A large affair?"

"Ten bridesmaids, ten groomsmen, a half day in rehearsal, and several hundred of Cincinnati's finest. My mother and her gardens were in their glory. No one had the brass to tell me they preferred it to the funeral, but I'm sure that's what they were all thinking. They had all been there before that year, on the first day of spring."

"Funny how conventions are."

"Mmm," said Claudia. Without a further word she ran into the surf. They had developed a ritualized swim, on the pattern of the first day. She swam on ahead, he caught up. They floated face into the sun, and wordlessly she swam on. Now as he cut through the water he realized that his breath was coming more easily. After a few days he could actually enjoy this. Unconsciously his form had become smoother, so that he moved through the water with less effort. He thought as he floated by her outstretched form how open she was, how she could tell of these things in her life with emotions as bare as her white arms.

Claudia turned and swam towards shore. Her thoughts were exactly the opposite. She had told the story and left out the clues. It couldn't be deciphered without the clues. She wasn't even sure it was decipherable with them. Growing up in a family where expectations covered you like a baby blanket. She expected security, permanence, stability. People like to list what money can't buy. But those expectations money can fulfill like a mail order house. Of course, she hadn't spoken of that.

Nor had she told Charles then of the inevitable loss of her virginity one night in the leaning seat of Weemo's Nash wagon, of how that loss, private and willful, seemed suddenly to translate into a tacit assumption of engagement. All the rest had followed, almost like a pregnancy: the party and the announcement, the article in the paper and the toasts at the wedding supper. Who had decided? Had someone proposed? She couldn't recall.

They each had their reasons. Weemo was pleased, for he had made a good match, and he seemed to care for her. To his credit, the circumstance of marriage to a wealthy woman did not alter the line of march Weemo had set for himself. He continued to have ambitions only in a social sense, and none for business, politics, other endeavors. Over the years he had maintained his physique, his flat stomach and runner's legs, and his golf game had improved.

Surely Claudia had known what was happening. She couldn't recall now, but she too must have been happy with the match. That Weemo was without ambition or depth she thought irrelevant. He was fun to be with. She was sustained by that and by the physical part of their life. When those recommendations—sex, proximity—seemed too transient to support a marriage, she found pleasure in carving so effortlessly a life of the right dimensions.

She didn't regret having married. They had both been ready for it, she knew. And readiness may be all youth has. Later on she admitted to herself that establishing their life had not been difficult. True, it had seemed so at the time. But that was because the life didn't suit her, because she assumed that the life of those about her was what she should choose. Only when she found out how unsuited she was for it did she realize it was beyond, not her grasp, but her taste.

She was only now discovering the clues herself. Her son's departure had been so sharp. She couldn't say sudden, for they had discussed his plans for months before his high school graduation. Harrison's presence at home had given her life its only intimacy, and his absence seemed to mark indelibly the next phase of her life. Security without intimacy, she was finding out, was a form of quarantine.

Harrison had decided college was of no use to him. Claudia couldn't argue. He wanted to try the theater, he told her. Then let him try it. She'd hoped to teach him to be resolute, and now his resolution cut her off so abruptly. If he'd gone off for four years she would have had a gradual withdrawal from his life. Instead, she was forced to confront issues years ahead of schedule.

She washed the salt from her body in a shower the temperature of her skin. It produced no sensation. Weemo and Evelyn would be back from the course and would meet them on the terrace. They would take their usual table for lunch, under the green and blue awning. Weemo would have one or two drinks, Bloody Marys she guessed, and he would order the club sandwich. After lunch he would nap. The chef made a wonderful salad from the little rock lobster you found in the coral. It was a disappointment if you ordered it steamed, and if you expected the Maine lobster. But shredded in a light mayonnaise and served on a bed of romaine lettuce, it made a delicious lunch. That was what she would order. That, and perhaps a glass of wine.

* * * * *

Weemo declined Evelyn's offer for a quick swim before they ate. He looked well enough in a suit, he knew, but the fact was his hair was thinning, and while it still combed back quite full, wet and flattened over his face it made him look like a different person.

They got on very well together on the course. Evelyn seemed genuinely interested in improving her game, and Weemo was a good teacher. He could spot what was wrong with her swing and, more unusual he could proffer a few simple tips that she could follow. That was the secret of being a good teacher. They had only played nine this morning and talked about completing the second half this afternoon. He would pass up a dip in the pool.

He stopped at the terrace bar to pick up a vodka martini to take to the shower with him. With a twist. It was a bracing drink, best enjoyed at midday in the heat of a tropical sun. What was it Claudia had said to him last week: that he was proof that the super-ego was soluble in alcohol. What in hell had she meant? There were times when she was purposely obscure, and he took them as reproach. It wasn't like her to carp at him about his drinking.

He came out of the shower, wet a wash cloth under the cold tap, and sponged the steam off the mirror. Then he allowed himself the first draught of his drink. There in the mirror was a smeared visage. He studied it carefully. He catalogued its flaws and its points of stress—the way a mechanic might go over a car he had tended for years—and at last he approved. Not too much sun on the nose, no sign of blood vessels that were so often the occupational hazard of his brethren, eyes a little puffy but bright. All in all, he liked what he saw.

Chapter Five

William Osborn Abbott had had an upbringing that only a careful biographer could have found. He had picked up his nickname in grammar school, its improbable mixture of boyhood, intimacy and clubbishness oddly appropriate. He was an only child. His mother worked at the lingerie counter of Cincinnati's finest department store, and she knew the names and accounts of the city's finest citizens. She was certain that she had been born to her place, and equally certain that her son could assure himself every success if he would only fit in. Before William went off to his first day at school, she had taught him enough of the world to get around in it. The names of the families who represented the store's best accounts, the sections of town where they lived, where the Procter and Gamble executives lived, and how to read and write his own name. She taught him, too, when he printed his name, always to do it twice: William Osborn Abbott, and below it the abbreviation she so fancied, Wm. O. Abbott.

So while his classmates struggled to letter James or Susan in the corner of the page, he diligently printed both names, one above the other. His classmates read the shortened version "Weemo," and he liked it and dropped the full name. In Sunday school he had learned how the apostles had taken on new names upon their conversion, and he saw his *nom d' crypt* in much the same way: a declaration of his admission into a sect.

Weemo was charming, and that was his most enduring trait. Even at the age of six, he found that he could achieve as much by smiling, by seeking contact deep into the eyes of the teacher, as he could by doing the work. The smile and the warm, penetrating look came easily to him. And it was far less tedious than practicing the loops in the penmanship work book or learning the capitals of the states, far less grimy than taking the erasers down and clapping them against the schoolyard wall.

Weemo's principal skills lay close to the surface during these early years, but lay nontheless latent. They weren't as useful with his young friends as they would become. It would take a fully developed sense of sexuality to engage him, to bring out his talents. He used to listen to the Reds' games on the radio, and he knew that a great batter could sometimes hit his best against the complexities and kinetic powers of a big league fastball.

Still, Weemo worked his work. When his father and mother came to school for the fall parent-teacher conferences, dressed as if going to church, they received reports of their son's delightful companionship, his sincerity, his earnestness. They didn't hear of his vigor or the excellence of his performance, for he had found he could get what he wanted without effort.

His discovery proved even more valuable, more applicable, as he went through his teen-age years. Suddenly the prizes to be won were popularity and sexual conquest. And for those endeavors, Weemo's single strength peculiarly enabled him to succeed. Not merely was he charming; he was charming without pretense at any other virtue. He recognized his classmates as bumbling young men who had never considered how to persuade. Weemo had been practicing on both sexes, of all ages, since he could remember, and when it became of the highest importance to be accepted, he was a master. As in most of life's efforts, the appearance of success brought success. The most popular boy in class, Weemo found himself the object of scores of schoolgirl crushes, and each one reinforced his popularity. Honorably, he never abused a relationship. Nor did he engage himself in them. He feigned no emotion, and his detachment was as plain to view as the aquiline nose on his face.

After high school, with no aptitude or interest but at the urging of his mother, Weemo went off to Ohio State University. He realized that he was bored by the life of scholarship, steps too slow for varsity track, and too poor for the fraternity life—though in every other way suited, even prepared. He had promised his mother that he'd stick at the university for two years and see where that led him. Midway through his sophomore year, he had learned barely enough about the Hapsburgs to qualify as a history major, but he had sharpened his skills on the dance floor and in the back seat of borrowed sedans. Working the fraternity parties on weekends as a bartender, he'd also learned the recipes for Sazerac slings, gin fizzes, and an elaborate and excellent fish house punch.

He was affable and a good bartender, and so he was in demand. The work had its burdens. In a small and secret way, he disdained the callow boys and girls he waited on. Not that they looked down on him. He was always treated as an equal. It was more how artless they were. The mating game that he watched from behind the knotty pine bars, among the college pennants and stolen traffic signs, was being played so clumsily it offended his standards. He didn't resent them. Yet he knew that these were the people he would serve from behind a bar the rest of his school career, and from behind a desk thereafter. The prospect was not appealing. From the usual paths to success—diligence and aptitude—he felt dissuaded. Despite his appetite for the pastimes of the rich, it was clear they would not be his. Unless a break came his way.

And no break was in sight. The one book he'd read in his years of schooling that meant something to him was *Huckleberry Finn*. His father had told him if he didn't want to read, he ought at least to know one book and one play well. Then the trick would be sliding them into every exam answer. His play was *Our Town*. In the Twain book, Weemo liked both heroes, Jim and Huck. He could have been either one. He thought of himself on the bank of a river. Maybe upstream from Cincinnati, where the Licking came into the Ohio. Waiting for an abandoned raft to float by. If he watched closely, the right chance would come floating by. So far, all he'd seen was garbage: term papers, kegs of beer, and worst of all, a job in the student laundry handling other people's sheets. He was determined to get on down the river. He'd know what a raft looked like if it passed his way.

And then came the call from Dorothy Batschelder.

It came in a rush. Dorothy talked breathlessly about events that had no meaning to him. He sorted through names he didn't know and about a half dozen apologies. Someone was going to be stuck at Bowdoin longer than he'd thought because of some glee club concert or tour, and she knew it was only two weeks away, and that she didn't know Weemo very well but he'd been so nice to her at that homecoming party when her date had passed out or gone off or whatever, it didn't matter and she'd just as soon that the boy did go off if that was the way he was going to behave. Weemo slowed her down and made her repeat the message. Yes, she was inviting him to the Glass Slipper and she knew it was an imposition since he'd have to rent a suit. But he wouldn't need tails, since she was a post-deb, not a deb, and only the dates of the debs needed tails. Escorts, really, not dates. He'd only need a tuxedo—did he think he could get one? Yes, Weemo said, he thought he could. And she said that was marvelous, it was marvelous that he could go, although Weemo had said merely that he could rent a tux.

So he found himself dressing one night, while his mother cooed in the kitchen, ironing the cummerbund and tie the rental shop had provided him. Found himself putting on the boiled shirt, studs, cuff links and patent leather shoes, putting on the tuxedo, fourteen ninety-five a night, that had seen hard use. They were double dating with Claudia Parine and Teddy Barrons, Dorothy couldn't believe he didn't know them, they were our class—by which Weemo understood her to mean year in school—and they'd gone to Country Day but they'd been around forever, and everyone called him Teddy Bear or T-Bear, and he was a riot. Weemo would love him.

Weemo was ready when Barrons leaned on the horn of his Chevy Bel-Air outside the Abbott house. He refused to let his mother see him out to the car, threatening as she had to take a picture of the young people as they went off, and it was just as well. For when he opened the door of the car to introduce himself, Teddy Barrons was swallowing the last gurgle from a pint of Green Label Jack Daniels.

"Hey," he said to Weemo. "How ya doin'?" and stuck out his hand. The empty bottle was in it. Weemo took it and looked at it. "Just toss it in the street, will you?"

Weemo slid the bottle beneath his seat.

"Don't get pissed off," Barrons said. "There's another in there," tapping the glove compartment.

They called for their dates and drove downtown to the Netherland Plaza Hotel. Its grand ballroom was elaborately decorated in tinsel and evergreen boughs and holly, and everywhere depended revolving balls of glittering mirrors. T-Bear Barrons excused himself, to get a shoe shine and, as he said, to take a leak, and Weemo with his own sense of relief led the two girls into the room. He took them through the receiving line, exchanging pleasantries with the mayor of Cincinnati and his wife, the chairladies of the ball, and the chairman of the board of the art museum, for the benefit of which the ball was held. Weemo had memorized their names from the Times-Star that Sunday—the paper had printed the list of debutantes and dignitaries as if it were a baseball lineup—and engaged each in a moment of conversation that went as he had planned.

Dorothy, who had talked without pause from the moment she'd answered her doorbell, suddenly seemed unable to say a word, so he introduced himself. Claudia, on the other hand, knew everyone, even the notables in the receiving line, and treated all of them with an easy reserve that made her seem the adult and they the ones launching their social debut. As she went down the line, Weemo watched her with sly admiration. She had a way about her, warm but distant, that he liked. Weemo was a connoisseur of postures, and he rarely got to view a performance the equal of his critical powers. Claudia's was. She was a natural.

He and the two girls stood around sipping champagne. They had the same conversation with several people. Patrons and parents of the debs and post-debs told Weemo how this was all for them, by which he understood them to mean Claudia and Dorothy. The escorts whispered to him about spiking the punch and where you could get a real drink. Three different girls that Weemo didn't know asked Dorothy whether it was true that last year Malcolm Kayser and Baba Woolsey had taken a room upstairs.

The debutantes hadn't yet made their appearance. At last it was time for the presentation. Escorts and fathers went to the waiting room at the head of the long, serpentine staircase that led down to the grand ballroom. The post-debs and their dates were to come down the stairs first, lining the balustrades as they did and making a gauntlet for the presentation. Weemo crooked his arm and Dorothy took it and they found their position near the top. Each succeeding pair went two steps below. The last couple was to be Claudia and Barrons. Murmurs went through the crowd as they hesitated at the top landing. The directress in a rose organdy dress whispered fiercely from the bottom of the stairs to move it along. Finally, they began to walk down. As they passed Weemo he realized why a commotion was following their descent. Claudia walked easily, her posture and bearing perfect. T-Bear was evidently drunk, walking with exaggerated stiffness to hide or highlight the fact. And he came down without shoes or socks, his feet bare but blackened with polish. It was only when you caught sight of the glistening of his toe nails or—from the rear—as he descended the stairs the improbable whiteness of the soles of his feet that you could be sure.

Barrons seemed to vanish after that. The parents clucked about the barefooted stroll and their deprecation reinforced the view of the people his age that T-Bear had established another chapter in a book of stunts which would amuse them for years. While he kept it to himself, Weemo viewed the behaviour as silly. Here was an opportunity to live up to an almost theatrical code, in full dress and in the city's most elegant setting. Why anyone would want to screw it up was beyond him.

He didn't ruminate long, though, on the difference of attitude. Barrons' disappearance, not from embarrassment but rather to sleep off the sour mash whiskey, encumbered Weemo with the additional duty of attending to Claudia Parine. Courtesy came easily to him—his mother had seen to it. He enjoyed the prospect of being escort to two. He brought Claudia punch in tiny cut-glass cups, walked with her and Dorothy through the buffet supper served at the stroke of midnight, and asked her more than once to dance.

"You're not turning me down because you can't dance," he told her. "You've been on the floor all night. What is it? Do I have something that even my best friends won't tell me?"

"Not at all," she said, lightly. "You are doing your duty. I just don't accept pity."

"Why not? Can you buy all you need?" Weemo had been interested in her as soon as she'd joined them that evening. She was lovely, cool, sure of herself. And in contrast to Dorothy, what she had to say was sensible. He'd decided the only way to get her attention was to nettle her.

Claudia came back quickly. "I don't happen to need any pity, thank you. And don't give me that beggar-boy-meets-princess look. You can't shame me into it, either."

No remark could have pleased him more. "The lady doesn't want to dance," he answered, arching his eyebrows to show his lack of concern, "the lady doesn't have to dance. It'll keep up your reputation." So saying, he turned, with what he hoped was an ironic tilt of the head, and walked off.

They did not speak again until after the dance. The debutantes and their escorts went off to a breakfast party, but the older set—or at least this foursome—had had enough. Weemo found T-Bear dozing on a salad table in the hotel's kitchen. He searched through jacket pockets for keys. He retrieved the car and drove it around to the front entrance to pick up Dorothy and Claudia. Then to the loading dock. There he enlisted the help of the last man in the kitchen, a dark fellow with a tattoo of a tiny dagger on his cheek, to load Barrons into the shotgun seat.

"Just a minute," Weemo said to the man after his compatriot's body was propped against the door. He reached through the open window and removed Barrons' billfold from his jacket pocket. He took out two fives of the sleeping man's money and handed them to his helper. One of the girls in the back seat squealed a little frisson of delight. He started up the car and drove without asking directions to take his passengers home. Following the most direct route first was Dorothy. He walked her to the door, planted a firm kiss on her surprised mouth, and thanked her for asking him. Then to Barrons' house, stopping only briefly in a sudden lurch to shove the waking man out the far side. T-Bear stood and vomited on a neighbor's lawn, one hand steadied on the Chevy's fender, the other on the head of a cast iron figure of a Negro jockey holding a lantern. Finally Claudia. Weemo pulled into the long gravel drive that led to the Parine house.

"Thank you for the lift," she said.

"You're quite welcome."

"And for looking after me. That was sweet."

Weemo nodded. They had parked under the Georgian port cochere that marked the front entrance. Inside the house it was dark, but they could see each other clearly in the lambent glow from the dashboard and from the stars in the December night sky. Weemo looked up at the leafless elms that lined the drive, black against the starlight.

"What did you mean about my reputation?"

Weemo was immensely gratified. This would be the best part of a very fine evening.

"Never mind," he said. "It was rude of me to mention it."

"No," she said with force. "It was rude of me not to be nicer to you when you asked me to dance. I apologize for that, but you must tell me what you meant."

"Well," he said, and here he fibbed a little, for while he had heard of Claudia Parine—anyone who drove past the factory to the south of town and saw the sign, who passed by the house on the hill or who read the Cincinnati papers would have heard of the Parines—he knew nothing about her. Other than his departed date, he was acquainted with no one who did.

"You have a reputation. Surely you know?"

"I do not know," she said, sticking out her jaw a bit. "A reputation for what?"

Weemo was being intentionally obscure, suggestive. For the phrase when applied to a young woman in its most common usage of the time connoted lubricity. It was a time when sex outside marriage was considered indiscriminate, when indeed sex was rarely considered in conversation at all.

"You have a reputation. People say . . ." and he hesitated to get the most suspense he dared," . . . you think a lot of yourself."

"They do? Who does? Dorothy Batschelder?"

"People. You know how that gets around. I suppose, being a Parine and then not dancing with a fellow who asks twice just because he's not in your set and he comes from the other side of the tracks."

"Don't give me that, William Weemo Abbott. The reason I turned you down is just what you're giving me. Everybody says you're very conceited, you know. That you can get any girl to go for you and that you do it just for fun."

Weemo couldn't decide whether Claudia was ingenuous or whether she had merely hit upon a clever counter attack from the same treatise on courtship strategy. In any event he was not displeased by the charge, particularly since it had focused her interest, albeit briefly, on him. All he needed was a chance.

"I don't know why anyone would say that." In the faint light he looked squarely into her eyes. "It's not true. I'm different from the kids in your set, and I don't run around with them. And if that's what people want to take for being aloof or conceited, then they don't know what they're talking about."

"You see what happens," Claudia said sympathetically. "You get a reputation you don't deserve and then people just perpetuate it."

It was easy for Weemo to reveal himself. He was quite at ease with the person he was. That candor set him apart from the other young men Claudia knew, all those young men carrying their families' expectations on their shoulders like a wounded comrade. They had all begun to confuse what people wanted them to do with what they had done.

The couple sat for hours. The last of the moon came out and started up the sky. They talked about the people they knew in common, and Weemo amused her. He was funny, too, about the ones he'd met at the ball. He tried to guess whether the benefit chairlady took a bath or a shower and whether she invited her equally corpulent husband to join her and whether they had promised to love, honor and obey, but not to bathe. They laughed with each other until a thin grey light showed in the far sky like the crack in an egg.

When they parted, Claudia assuring him that she wasn't in any trouble because her parents didn't expect her until dawn on cotillion night and besides, they trusted her. She thought to herself that she had found an empathetic friend. And very attractive. Handsome as a movie star. Often he talked like someone in the movies. When she got out of the car, he had said, Until we meet again. That was from some Walter Scott novel she'd read in middle school or from an Errol Flynn movie. But he wasn't acting. He had this way of looking at you, right into your eyes, and you could just tell how thoroughly he believed himself. Claudia had observed enough of men to perceive the difference between his conviction and his sincerity, and she had no doubts of the first.

After that night, Weemo found himself on the List. There were Christmas parties and post-ball parties, tea dances and skating outings. Whether it was Dorothy or Claudia who had put him there, he didn't know. Dorothy's young man had come home after the glee club concert, but he turned out not to be Dorothy's young man after all. Whatever the cause, Weemo found himself invited, turning down bartending jobs to go to the same parties as a guest, increasing his need for cash while decreasing its supply.

In January, at the end of that semester, he quit college. It no longer seemed significant, and he realized that the education afforded there was preparation for a life he did not want. He was never more than a mediocre bridge player, but he found wisdom in the advice to lead from your strength. He told Claudia of his plans to leave school the first night she came back from the East for spring vacation. She tried to talk him out of it. When she saw that she couldn't, that, as he told her, he was eager to get started in the business world, she introduced him at home and persuaded her father to get Weemo a job at Parine Pen. And Weemo worked there, first as a stock boy then running a machine that tested rubber bladders, diligently and without complaint until his engagement to Claudia some eighteen months later. It was the last job he was to hold, but its term was sufficient to convince Weemo that he had not erred in choosing a life of leisure.

Chapter Six

From the Journal

We *spent a part of every day together the week that we met. The Abbotts had arrived before us and were to leave only seven days after that first morning on the golf course. It seems impossible that so much ground could have been covered in so short a time. I felt as if I were dealing again with the untested emotions of my youth.*

Mostly we sat on the beach. Claudia asked about my interest in birding. It caught her fancy and she insisted I take her on outings. In the last days we hiked the dunes to the north of the resort, long chalk lines of beaches with gulls squawking overhead and more flotsam than shells underfoot. We invented a game, looking at the debris as an archeologist would centuries from now. Many of the labels on the bottles washed ashore were in Spanish, and we decided that they had been dumped off Cuba. Most we had to guess at. For some, orange juice and Boston baked beans, there were pictures to guide us.

The bird life was disapppointing. Nothing uncommon. Petrels and brown pelicans galore, ring-billed gulls and herring gulls. On past trips to the Caribbean I'd noted several varieties of tern, a graceful bird with narrow wings and a tail forked like a kite. They pose an interesting problem of identification, since their sighting points are so few and they usually remain well out to sea. But there were none. Still, we took my Peterson's Guide and a pair of glasses, and Claudia seemed genuinely to enjoy the search. All the while Evelyn and Weemo occupied themselves with hitting balls at distant flags or across nets, with diving for pieces of coral that they would dry out, take home, and throw away that Spring.

It was on one of our walks that Claudia told me of the curious provisions of the Parine Trusts.

I had had some experience with bizarre conditions of divestment, although in modern times one does not often come across the desire to reach from the grave and dictate morality. It is a concept that happily has receded from use, in what I assume are more secular times. The prophets of our modern era, Freud, Darwin and Marx, have pointed us towards self-realization and free will, and if we fight their teachings in matters of government and biology, at least we follow their lead in the way we spend our capital.

Why do I recall the lunch so vividly? The kitchen had packed some cold chicken, vegetable salad, and a flask of iced tea into a white plastic box. We carried it in a canvas sack, along with our towels, the birding guide, and sun lotion. By that time in our acquaintance I was sufficiently comfortable with Claudia to take along a few sketch cards and a charcoal. I've always loved to draw, but I have no particular aptitude and I carry it on much as a secret vice. We discussed our tastes in music, about which Claudia was an enthusiast. We sat on the beach towels we had brought for sitting rather than bathing, and ate the chicken with our hands. I told her I was sorry there were so few specimen of shorebird around, since spotting is what we had determined was to be our activity. In her manner she scolded me for taking on responsibility for the shoreline population. I remember stealing a glance at her, as if it were a forward act. Other than lipstick, she wore no make-up, or none that I could discern. She had on a pair of tan walking shorts and a sleeveless blouse, white with a pattern of flowering lilac boughs. She wore as jewelry only a strand of pearls, day pearls she called them, smallish but lustrous and perfectly matched, tied casually in a knot that hung at the base of her white throat.

We were comparing favorite composers. Suddenly as we spoke, water came to my eyes. I was filled with a feeling for her I couldn't name and needn't write down here. It was the strongest emotion I can remember in my life.

We are judged and recompensed according to our deeds. Or so I am taught by both my profession and what is left of my

46]

religion. My quarrel with that tenet is that it oversimplifies. It leaves out our thoughts, our intentions and our pledges. And it leaves out what we fail to do.

So unaccustomed was I to the sensation, so sure that it manifested itself in my face, my eyes, my voice, that I assumed it had communicated itself to her, had leapt across the scant fifteen inches between our elbows as we sat watching the birds skim the water, and had invested itself in her. And believing silent intercourse the most apropos mode of discourse for a topic of the heart, I said nothing.

*   *   *   *   *

They sat on a small bluff, where the yellow spartina grasses stopped, and dunes tufted with a sharp green sedge sloped down to a short expanse of beach, no more than twenty yards across. The tide was falling, and as they sat and watched, each flush of wave covered slightly less of the wet sand than the wave before.

"Yes," she was saying. "At one time they were my favorites too. Mozart, Handel, Mahler. And the passionate Beethoven. But lately I don't feel I can cope with all that . . . majesty. These days I want my music more personal."

"And so?"

"And so it's Chopin, Schubert, Schumann. If I need a fix of the baroque it's Buxtehude. But more often than not, it's Chopin."

She was leaning forward, one arm wrapped around her knees, knees drawn up to her chest, while her other hand traced illegible letters in the sand. Their beach towels parallel, Charles sat on his hip with his legs to the side. He was doodling on a fibre art card, drawing a gliding gull from the underside, trying to capture the lattice work of axillar, primary and secondary feather. Shreds of clouds that might have been thrown away crossed in the sky before them.

"Charles," she said tentatively. He realized how easily she commanded attention by the quiet way she addressed people. "May I ask you something?"

"Of course."

"It's terribly rude of me, your being on vacation. You mustn't think me the woman who corners the doctor at a cocktail party to get a diagnosis."

"Something about the law?" Charles was surprised. He was using his charcoal to line in quills in the larger feathers, giving his drawing far more detail than one could have observed from the perspective shown in the little sketch. Claudia had raised a distant subject; during the week he had spent with her he had not had a single thought about his office.

"My grandfather set up these trusts. Most of the Parine stock is in them. We get distributions regularly, and the trustee —Commonwealth Bank in Boston—votes the shares the way the beneficiaries want the shares voted."

Charles waited. It was his manner, when giving legal advice, to be cautious, to anticipate the question as far ahead as possible, but never to answer it unless asked.

"These trusts, there are separate ones for my brother and me and my cousins, these trusts all distribute at the same time. Twenty-one years from the date of death of measuring lives." She looked up to see that he was following her.

"Yes," he said without sarcasm. "I'm familiar with the term."

"Well, the measuring lives were my father and my aunt. My father died first, so he didn't count. His sister died fourteen years ago. So these trusts . . ." she trailed off, inviting his participation.

" . . . Will terminate in seven years."

"Yes," she said. "Once they terminate, as I understand it, the stock is distributed to the beneficiaries and they own it and that's that. But until then, the trusts have these odd terms. Conditions of defeasance. Have you ever heard of that?"

"I have," he said with a modest smile. "Forfeiture."

"Exactly. My grandfather was a strict man. I don't think he was religious, especially, but he was morally strict. There were things men and women didn't do. Women didn't get involved in the business, men did. I think that's why my father was so unhappy. He inherited managing the business, though he never wanted to. And women didn't smoke or vote.

"So the terms of these trusts are that a beneficiary gets the stock unless before that time he is divorced or brings shame on the family by committing a felonious act. That's for both men and women. Also, if the beneficiary is a woman, if she uses tobacco."

"Those are the words of the trusts?"

"More or less. I may not have it precisely but that is the drift. I've asked the family firm about it, in Cincinnati, and they say it's perfectly fine. But they're the same firm that wrote the will for my grandfather. And . . . "

Again she trailed off hopefully. Charles obliged.

"And they represent not only you but all the people who would benefit if anyone lost his distribution through defeasance."

"Exactly," she said. Her voice warmed with gratitude. "And so I was wondering what you thought. Are those terms legal?"

"You mean, will they be enforced?" She nodded. Charles rubbed the bridge of his nose, pushing the frame of his glasses up to reach it. He had a reluctance borne of courtesy and conservative impulse to criticize another lawyer's advice and a further reluctance, borne of common sense, to give advice other than to clients. But his desire to help Claudia find the answer she wanted, to impress her overcame his reserve. And so when he spoke it was with candor.

"The honest answer is," he said kindly, for he did not want to disappoint her, "that I don't know. It will depend on several facts we don't have in front of us, including the specific language of the document. A first question is the situs of the trust— that is, what state's laws apply, when the trust was created. Provisions like these, he can't take if he marries a Negro or leaves the ministry or dresses in women's clothing, were much more prevalent in your grandfather's day than now. Some of them have been struck down in every jurisdiction as arbitrary or against some fundamental principle of society. Courts have seen others as reasonable restrictions imposed by the settlor, the person setting up the trust. We have to remember that it was, after all, your grandfather's money, and if he didn't want to give it to a cigar-smoking divorcee, why, the law might not make him."

"No," she said quickly. "I understand. And I think I agree. I have no quarrel with that if, as you say, it's enforceable."

They watched the water's edge. Sandpipers had landed and were busy pecking at the dark, moist sand that was newly exposed. As soon as a wave broke, the birds scurried to higher ground to avoid its foam. Claudia picked up the field glasses and sighted on them.

"I'd be happy to look at it when I get back to the office," Charles said.

She turned to him. "Oh, would you? I'd be most grateful and I'd want you to do it . . . ," here she searched, "on a professional basis."

"Don't be silly," he said. "It's not a large project and I'd like to do it for our friendship. I'll need the trust instrument, though."

"I'll send it as soon as I get home. I could have the bank send it, but I'd rather this remained between us."

"Of course. When you get back home will be soon enough."

Her look conveyed her thanks not merely for the project but for his manner, that he had made it so easy for her to ask. She returned her gaze to the horizon and lifted the glasses to her eyes.

"I owe you at least an explanation of why I'm asking."

"You owe me nothing. When you do," he said lightly, "I'll be sure to send you a bill."

"I owe you that much," she insisted. She was not a woman easily dissuaded from her obligations. "My parents had something outside these trusts. Plently, really. My father had been given a little of the Parine stock outright, ten percent, and he left it to Gordon and me in his will. I'm quite comfortable by most standards. And while the stock in trust is worth a lot, I suppose, if the company were to be sold, it's only recently that it's been doing well. The past twenty years, no one's bought fountain pens. Until lately. I don't need the income, you see. It's our son."

The Abbotts had referred to their child only a few times in Charles' presence, each time, now that he considered it, Claudia bringing him up.

"Not that he's acquisitive. Just the opposite. He's convinced he can live on a small allowance and love. But I don't feel I can walk away from his inheritance, and that's what this is really. It's his."

She lowered the binoculars, absently scanned the horizon to find something to watch, and raised them again on a fishing trawler a mile off shore.

"I think it's because I was adopted." Charles was surprised by Claudia's revelation, though he could not have said why. "Daddy always made a fuss over that with me. He used to say that Gordon they had to take home from the hospital because you had to take what you brought, but me they'd picked out specially. In fact I think he believed that having me around made it possible for Mother to get pregnant with my sister and brother. That was the theory at the time. Whatever it is, I feel I owe it to my father and my son not to walk away from it. My father picked me out, and he got my offspring thrown in for the same price. That's my part of the bargain. He gave me a family tree and the security that comes with it. I owe it to him to tend that tree." She looked over to him. The glare off the sea made her squint.

"Does any of this make sense?"

As much as anything, thought Charles. "Absolutely," he said.

They packed the hamper with the remains of lunch and drank off the rest of the tea. Despite his covering—Charles wore a white cotton shirt, buttoned to the wrists, and loosely woven lisle ducks—he felt the need to come in from the sun. They decided to walk back. They carried the canvas satchel between them, each holding a large loop handle.

As they walked she asked him about birds' nesting and nurturing. He didn't know much about shorebirds, he told her. He had really spent more time in the Connecticut woods than anywhere else. He'd studied them and birds of the American west. Birds he hoped to see someday. He found himself describing to her the nesting habits of the peregrine falcon.

"I've always been fascinated by falcons and hawks," he said. "I don't know why. Sublimation, probably. Someday I'll make a trip to see one. They nest in the rock cliffs of the canyonlands. I've read about these Audobon treks where you go to view them. You can smell the sage and dry branches and dust. Falcon chicks have to learn to fly from their perch in the canyon walls. They don't get many chances. The higher they start the better. If the nest is a few hundred feet up, they may get two or three tries. They'll fly out and flap, but if they can't learn to climb they had better glide to a lower perch and wait. If they don't, they end up landing on the canyon floor and sit, prey for coyotes and foxes. If they're to make it, they have to learn to fly."

They returned to the Elbow Reef and crossed under the chain that demarked its private beach. The Club used a pontoon raft as a dive boat, and as they approached the short pier the raft was motoring out of the cove. Weemo, sitting on the far side by Evelyn, spotted them and waved his fins and mask aloft. He shouted something inaudible, and they waved back.

"When we married," she said suddenly, "I didn't love him. We were . . . involved." She picked out the word as if it might be a plum from a basket. "That was the euphemism at the time for having sex. One felt sex would lead to marriage, or the other way around. It didn't much matter. And Weemo must have thought the same. I was quite proper. I wasn't one of those girls it was easy to know, as we used to say."

"He had to make an honest woman of you," Charles offered.

"Precisely. Whether we loved each other wasn't at issue. It was assumed we would learn to."

She and Charles retired to their cottages. Charles took a cooling shower, then wrote himself a note about the legal issues Claudia had raised in their conversation. He recorded the facts as she had told them, making particular mention of the words she used to describe the conditions of forfeiture. His notes would allow him to get started on the problem before he received the document. In the harsh light of a court's judgment, the words of the document were critical. The words could well control the outcome.

Claudia lay down and rested her eyes from the sun. Had she told too much about herself? When she'd married she'd hoped to find among the physical intimacies, in the proximity itself—of comb, pillows, laundry—some other nexus. Surely, she thought, there must come another bond, a revelation of the spirit. If a dog and master grow to look like each other after years, surely man and woman grow more alike. In the first years she waited expectantly. Then she had blamed herself, that she lacked the capacity to make this fusion occur. Only recently she'd begun to realize that she'd done what she could.

Now there was merely the inheritance. It was her link to family and future. Or better, she was the link. She stood with a cable in each hand, and she would have to hold on and pull if they were to be spliced together. She felt Charles had understood— he must see that in his practice, the way money binds families together. But she wasn't sure he had understood why she married. Weemo struck people like Charles as shallow. That had been true of him ever since they courted.

People assumed that because Weemo was interested only in sensations, he was shallow. But the fact was he was profoundly interested in sensation. Claudia enjoyed the thought and smiled to herself. And dozed off to a light nap as the waves hissed on the beaches.

*　*　*　*　*

From the Journal

Memory can't always be trusted. It is a silver but faulty film that cannot record an entire range of experience. It fails us on feelings. It doesn't record the insubstantial very well. The dream and the memory of the dream are not the same at all.

It would be easy for me now, writing these years away, to revise my feelings. To exaggerate them so that they seem grander, or to describe them as a trifle, or as emotions whose quality must be tested by how they endure. But I know that isn't so. I don't have to rely on memory. I know how I felt. I knew it instantly then and I know it now. My love for Claudia hit me like a stone to the heart.

Memory is a trick, a point of view. If I sketch a soaring gull as I see it, there frozen on the page people will tell me it's merely my impression. If I draw in the detail I know from anatomy to be there, people call it realistic, though no one could possibly see all that in a glance. We are ready to be tricked by point of view. It's the artist's easiest magic.

I have replayed that day's conversation in my mind over and again, the way a jury might consider the testimony of the key witness. What shadings did I miss? What have I added that wasn't there? She was calling for my help. Was she calling for more? I heard her say that she didn't love her husband when she married him. An odd construction, unless she meant to imply that she had learned to, grown to. Had she decided on divorce? Or did the protection she wanted for her son include a continuity in her marriage?

I decided my best strategy was to answer the questions she had asked, and then simply to stand ready to do more.

Chapter Seven

From the Journal

None of this, I realize, will make sense without an inquiry into why Evelyn and I had married each other. In important issues, we are not much alike. For one, I believe that people change, that gentleness can shape character just as breezes and soft rain, given enough time, can shape mountains. Evelyn has no patience for that sort of mushy thinking. She's practical, and she likes immediacy. Both traits I admire.

Why did Evelyn and I marry? I can think of no answer that reflects well on my character. Until solid middle age, by which time I had developed some facility for practicing law and an endurance for dinner parties, I hadn't been particularly successful at life's assignments. Certainly in my school days, whether they were athletic, social, or academic, I found myself a touch out of synch.

But in bachelorhood my social life had a peculiar perplexity. My difficulty with the dating process—my particular difficulty aside from my ineptitude at finding women to date and a pervasive terror at it all—was that I saw an inevitable fork in the road, each branch equally discomfitting. Having found a suitable young woman to take to dinner, one could elect never to see her again, thus renewing the search for her successor. Or one could pursue the girl at hand. Pursuit meant—if she intended it to—some sexual intimacy. The dilemna had no solution.

Not that I objected to sexual intimacy. Quite the opposite. It is God's own invention for the distraction of the spirit of the human race, for I wonder how we would occupy our time *without it and televised sporting events. But it was inevitably accompanied, at least during my courting days, with an expectation of psychic intimacy, and it was that I feared.*

I don't know much of its parallel in the wild, but the subspecie of human I have in mind—habitat Manhattan and southern New England, an occasional sighting in the tropics—that particular bird protects its inner self. Doesn't show its hand. Or much else.

And so my fear kept me from moving down that road to its next fork, from facing that next Hobson's choice. With Evelyn, we ran down the road so fast it seemed I never had time to pause. How else would I have ended up married?

Once wed, for people like me, staying married is easy. It is more than mere habit: it is loyalty. The exchange of promises creates a social contract, a peculiarly human invention that separates us from other orders more pronouncedly, more nobly, I think, than language or the transverse thumb. Socialization allows our specie to specialize, to make families, then colonies, and so to survive. At the time I valued loyalty certainly over love, which I never expected from Evelyn, and over fidelity. I hadn't thought through how the three were related.

These grand ideas—too grand for public view, for the public would prefer to think people like the Merediths stay together from lack of imagination—wouldn't suit Evelyn, I feel sure. When we married, I got a measure of affection I'd never had before. She received a reciprocal level of security and comfort. I think the trade was important to her, but not the analysis. She doesn't care about analysis.

If I were to ask Evelyn, and I never have, whether we are responsible for our own actions, she would say no. Not that she has a higher being in mind. She simply does not believe in responsibility any more than she does in immortality. Neither concept obtains to her.

That point of view is liberating. To be a fatalist and a theist is a heavy burden. Just ask John Calvin. But to be merely a fatalist, to believe that you are what you are, and no power here or hereafter will hold you to task for it, you carry around no more regret than the doe in the field. If you are Evelyn, you decide on each day's merits what you will do. To my view, the product of her outlook is an impermanence, a separation from what I think anchors us to the life around us. But that doesn't seem to her a disadvantage. Nor to me. Quite the contrary. I admire her for it. Natural selection breeds not for the depth of one's philosophy but for fleetness of foot, and chances are it will favor this very trait. Evelyn is able to move from interest to interest in much the manner of a tourist without any taste for art who finds himself in a museum. She can observe, she can see the most important pieces, the ones she's heard of, and she is sure of being out well ahead of closing time.

* * * * *

Evelyn Meredith had gone a long way on what she had. She grew up in an attached row house just over the Nassau County border from Queens. No one thought of it as New York City. As the third child in a family of six, all born within a year or two of each other to a family with a fingertip grasp on the middle class, she had received whatever share of love and attention her parents could spare. Her father worked first as a brakeman, then as a steward, and finally as a minor executive, for the Long Island Railroad. Outside of the job, his concerns were what would happened when it was over. The family listened every night to his description of benefits and pension. He died well in advance of retirement. The irony was not wasted on Evelyn, and then and there she discarded what little appetite she had acquired for deferring rewards.

He died when she was a senior in high school. Her mother was still raising children. Evelyn had taken all the secretarial and business courses offered by the curriculum, no small number since most of the graduates of this high school trained for clerical work, and the day after the mass she answered three ads in the Times. Soon, not quite eighteen, she had a job in the typing pool of a mid-size Wall Street law firm.

She earned her way out of the pool to the next level, private secretary, although she was assigned to lawyers less important than she wished. She decided that would come. But the month after she turned twenty-five, she found herself pregnant, by, she felt fairly certain, a partner at the firm. He was only eleven years older than she, but he seemed to have been forever an adult. To her surprise and delight he stood by her in her time of need, as he put it, and married her. The year was 1966.

Evelyn was a slight woman. She had the black eyes of her Genovese parents, and she worked hard to maintain a slender waist that set off her voluptuous figure. Her skin had a singular coloration, a pale, olive shade that in a less animated face might have looked wan. When she entered a room she expected men to notice her and they did. She knew she was attractive. She'd once tried out as a model—responding to an ad on a subway placard—but she didn't photograph well. Dull and lifeless, the photographer had said about the proofs and she could see it. She was disappointed, but she admitted to herself that the woman before her looked like any face on the street. In person, the black eyes sparked with the glint of a strong intelligence, but in a snapshot no life could be seen. Those who knew Evelyn differed about which perspective was the truer.

Evelyn held few opinions. Experience had taught her that opinions were overrated, that people gave to them enormous energy only to have them challeged or grow stale. Instead she felt one should wait to see what the weather of the day would be and try to enjoy it. It was this very sense of imminence that had attracted the notice of Charles Meredith, a shy and earnest lawyer at her office, that had made him ask that she be assigned to him out of the typing pool, that had at last—after months of tactics that even she thought of as coquettish—induced him to ask her out for a drink in the Waldorf lobby.

She needed only a toe hold. She realized that this fellow Meredith was reserved, that she could expect him to speak up rarely and that the rest would be up to her. Sexually she was far more experienced than he, and that, she knew, would be the winning advantage. So long as she moved slowly and did nothing to frighten or embarrass him, she would prevail. There were hazards to her strategy. She needed patience in private and luck in public. The world of four forks to a place setting was a mystery to her.

And, stroke of luck, Charles obliged. He didn't take her to the benefits, the dinner parties, the endless reunions that, as his secretary, she knew he had attended before their romance. She never questioned the change in his habits, being too grateful that she would not need to explain her background. She loved the movies, and they went to dozens. When the date was for dinner, it was to some impersonal place Charles had read about, and when for drinks a large public bar crowded with people neither of them knew. She liked it that way. She told Charles it was her way of having him all to herself.

It was in the darkness of the movie theatres that she advanced her cause. Whatever the Puritans imputed to music and dancing, Evelyn found its modern equivalent in the movies. A skilled woman could, during the course of a minuet or a main feature, send messages of scent and touch that would tantalize a bishop. Just as the nuns used to say, the stepping stones to hell. But if you didn't mind the heat and the duration, hell could be fun. In the darkness of the theatre, with everyone's gaze on the reflecting silver light, Evelyn began to inform her captivated pupil. It was done with the touch of a shoulder, the perfume of a wrist, the occasional and fleeting brush of breast on arm.

Soon Charles had moved out of his capacious Central Park West suite, shared with a bachelor friend from college, and had taken his own place. That was not at her urging, since in a house with five brothers and sisters she had developed a pragmatic sense of modesty. It was Charles' own need for privacy. There, in a handsomely furnished two-bedroom apartment overlooking the East River, they made love in earnest enjoyment of each other.

They were married in a small civil ceremony, held in a private dining room at the mid-town club of Charles' college. His ex-roommate and a friend of hers from work served as witnesses. They invited several guests for champagne. Charles had arranged for the reception. A party, in Evelyn's experience, was laden with food, noise, wine. Here there were barely enough hors d'oevres to see one through to dinner, and Evelyn decided that starving one's guests was another inexplicable affectation of the rich. No family attended from either side. Charles' father had died. Charles' brother was many years older. They'd never been close, and the brother had long since moved to live year 'round at a resort off the Georgia coast, where he handled investments by telephone. Evelyn's mother was still living just beyond the Queens border, in the same house where Evelyn had been raised, and would have come despite the rushed circumstances and the absence of a priest. Evelyn had not thought to invite her.

There followed a honeymoon, her first trip outside the country, to the British Virgin Islands. Her husband, she discovered, liked to sketch sea birds. Standing in an elegant tile shower, water cascading down upon her and slatted jalousies open to the sky, she miscarried. It was over so quickly, with only the slightest cramping and blood, that Evelyn wasn't sure it had happened. Later, back in Manhattan she visited her doctor to be certain. And submitted herself to a routine operation and hospital stay to make sure that, now without a single salubrious reason left, an unwanted pregnancy would not happen again.

Charles was disappointed in the news that they would not be able to have children. Other than that he was quite pleased with married life. Evelyn tidied up after him and fussed about him, and he enjoyed the ministrations. He had first gone away to boarding school when he was twelve, and from kindergarten through his graduate school had attended classes with only males. He was gratified that his circumstances could change so. At first, his wife was put off by most of the social invitations they received, and that discomfort enabled him to decline them. He found that he far preferred staying at home, poring over the latest issue of Audubon or Scientific American, to evenings out. His repose was short-lived, for as Evelyn warmed to the idea of a social life, she began accepting invitations and giving reciprocal parties, and Charles found himself busier than before.

For her part, Evelyn was happy. She never worried about whether she could acclimate—she knew she could. Until she met Meredith, she hadn't been sure she would have a chance to use what she'd learned so far. Financial independence wasn't important to her, but money, money to spend whenever she wanted, was. Charles was kind to her, and the worst she could say was that he wasn't much fun. If he made jokes, she never understood them. She soon grew inured to his methodical habits. Early in their marriage, she discovered as she lay in bed that he brushed his teeth in a precise rhythmic pattern. Both tempo and time were constant, as if it were the rhythm signature of a dance band. Did he know? Had he hit upon a pattern that covered all his teeth, and adopted it for the rest of his life? Whatever it was, she lay waiting for the four-by-four shuffling of brush over enamel. At first, the idiosyncracy of it all infuriated her. But the marriage had benefits for her. She was a practical soul, and she learned easily to take comfort in the fact that his foibles were insignificant and, as long as she made them so, irrelevant.

*   *   *   *   *

The last night of the Abbotts' stay at Elbow Reef coincided with a local holiday. Every year the island marked the anniversary of a revolution or a decree of self-determination, dim in significance. Whatever reforms had been introduced, the several intervening regimes from the full range of the political spectrum had long since supplanted them. The current administration was avowedly socialistic, although, as Charles told the Abbotts, in all the years he had been coming to the island, there was a constancy to the poverty of the towns one passed on the drive to and from the airport. From the numbers of ragged children in the street it wasn't possible to tell which political philosophy was in power.

The Elbow Reef always celebrated the day by flying the flags of the nation and its Caribbean neighbors. Now seated at what had become their table in the dining room, Charles and Weemo argued over one flag in particular. Was it Texas or Cuba? Claudia sided with Charles, and the debate was dropped.

A small dance band had flown in from Nassau especially for the occasion. They played Rodgers and Hart, Irving Berlin and Victor Youmans tunes. The dress code for dinner at Elbow Reef was publicized as appropriate. That meant jackets and ties for men and dresses for women. This evening the guests turned out in their finery. Claudia wore a green silk paisley gown, backless, and a thin gold chain hung with an aquamarine pendant. Evelyn, her tan now at its peak, wore a strapless gown of organdy, white or more accurately oyster, and fitted, with a vee of brilliant purple in its center pleat. Curious, thought Charles. In birds and reptiles it's the males who color for mating, but in primates it's the females. Does it come from a higher intelligence, he wondered, or from coming down from trees and nesting instead on the drab plain?

He himself had put on one of the three ties in his suitcase and the single linen blazer he brought on these trips, now wrinkled where his arms bent. Weemo was more in the spirit of things. He wore lemon trousers and a rust-colored jacket the salesman had told him was that season's fashion color: burnt sienna. Weemo took a sportsman's pride in the story of shopping for his clothes and finding the season's color. He had tracked it down and bagged it.

Weemo danced with both women. When he and Evelyn returned from a Latin number, Claudia complimented them.

"You make a lovely picture," she said. "You could have been in a painting."

"Who do you suppose would have done it?" asked Charles. "Winslow Homer worked around here, but you couldn't have gotten him in from his fishing."

"No," Claudia said, sharing his joke. "Not Homer. Perhaps if Aubrey Beardsley had come to the Caribbean. "

"How about Gauguin? He wouldn't have painted any of the natives. Just Weemo and the ladies."

The foursome had seated themselves together, as they had most of the week. A bottle of Taittinger rested in a silver plated bucket on the table. Weemo had insisted that since tonight was their farewell, they never be without a full bottle of champagne. He plucked the bottle from its icey water and filled the glasses.

"Ahh, the hell with that," he said, unsure of whether Charles was poking fun. "What's art? Pretty pictures. The parsley on the roast. Give me the meat on the platter," and he grinned around at them.

Charles found himself drawn into the discussion as if it were a serious matter. Why, he could not tell, but he was defending art. He felt somehow it was up to him. Midway into the conversation he lost heart, let the argument die, and was hoping everyone else would too.

"That's Charles," announced Evelyn. "He fancies himself an artist, you see. Draws flowers and birds. What's wrong with being a lawyer, I don't know. Or for that matter a rich man who is the grandson of a rich man. It's really funny. He'd like it if everyone thought of him as an artist. Me, I'd be mortified. And we'd never get asked to a nice party."

Claudia passed a tray of conch fritters and the subject was dropped. Later, as the tray went from Charles back to her, she caught his eye with a look of amusment and astonishment. He nodded to her in their innocent conspiracy.

When the first bottle of wine had been finished and the appetizers eaten, they rose as a group and filed through the buffet line. There were several kinds of fish, watermelons scooped out and filled with fresh fruits. There were salads of egg, potato, rice, arranged in the shape of the island itself, and tables of pastries and sherbert. The band played "Say It Isn't So," up tempo, and Weemo sang its words happily as they walked by the serving tables, men ladling food on their plates in response to a turn of the head.

Seated again, they poured most of a second bottle of champagne and toasted each other.

"To a great and new friendship," said Weemo. They clinked glasses.

"Now," he continued, having downed most of his drink. "How shall we perpetuate this? I have a wonderful idea. Why don't you all come out to Aspen this summer?"

Claudia looked at him, holding her napkin in both hands before her. She thought to correct Weemo: engagements made under beery spirits on the last night of a vacation had too much the tang of pledges exchanged in a shipboard romance. It would be a rendezvous all might awaken to regret. But she enjoyed this serious man, and if they wanted to visit Aspen that August, Aspen would be more fun.

"We have a smashing house on the mountain overlooking town. Claudia has a place and her brother is building one. We used to share ours with Gordon but he's building his own. Ours is far too much for us, and Hap won't come out this year, I'm sure. What do you say? You and Claudia could go to concerts and stuff, Charles, and we could all climb the mountains and bike and golf."

Charles realized with disappointment that they'd planned their vacation.

"We usually go to Connecticut for part of the summer," he said.

"A dreary old house," Evelyn interrupted. "With hooked rugs and slanted floors and not a thing to do. I think we go because it was left to Charles."

"Then the last weeks we've reservations for the Outer Banks. In August. Chinconteague Island."

Evelyn grimaced conspicuously. "Birds," she said.

"Actually," Charles said, thinking aloud, "there's probably better birding in Colorado."

"There," said Weemo, triumphantly. "There, you see? All these years going to Connecticutt and chasing birds and you thought she just loved it. Well, come on. What do you say? We'd love to have you, old man, and it would give Claudia someone to listen to the music with."

Charles sat silently and allowed Evelyn to answer.

"It really sounds like fun. We wouldn't stay with you though. Couldn't we find a house to rent?"

The subject was left without resolution, but the Merediths agreed to consider it and the Abbotts agreed to help them find a suitable rental. They exchanged addresses and telephone numbers. Charles realized that he had previously given Claudia his business card, so she could send him the trust documents. He reddened slightly at his concealment, innocent as it was.

The band played. Weemo began to sing.
"Red sails in the sunset,
Red sails in the sea,
Red sails in the sunset,
Red sails in the sea."

"Those aren't the words," said Evelyn.

"It doesn't matter," Claudia said. Weemo went on. When he got to the release he sang louder.
"Red sails on the window,
Red sails on the floor,
Red sails on the window,
We'll go sailing no more."

"I think he ought to learn the words," Evelyn said.

"It doesn't matter," Claudia said laughing. "Does it, Charles?"

"No," he said and he smiled. "No, it doesn't."

Weemo got up and danced by himself. When he returned he had another bottle of wine. Charles protested.

"Don't be silly," Weemo said, filling Evelyn's glass. "You all shouldn't care," Weemo teased. "You both can sleep in. Me, I have to get up for six o'clock mass before we fly back."

"Do you, Weemo?" Evelyn asked and her eyes opened wide with concern.

"Don't believe him," Claudia said. "If he got inside the doorway of a church, it would collapse on him."

Evelyn realized Weemo was kidding. She found it odd that he would feign piety for a laugh.

"For a moment. . . . ," she said in a small voice. Her eyes lost focus. "That's why I asked. I used to be a practicing Catholic." Her words ran together.

"You must think we're all apostates, then," Claudia said. "I admire that. The conviction it must take to keep up one's faith."

"Don't," said Evelyn and she waved her hand vaguely. "Not to be admired. They just try to scare the pee out of you."

Charles had never heard his wife discuss her religion before, and was as surprised at that as at the mild crudity. He laid both off to the wine, and spoke up. "Now, Evelyn," he said. "The Roman Church has been around for centuries. It has some redeeming features."

"Oh, Charles," Evelyn observed flatly. "You made a joke."

Charles went on. "What I mean is this. The Church watched over everyone, told them what to do. You couldn't have several wives in succession. Or husbands. So everyone simply had them simultaneously. Now we don't think that's right and we frown on infidelities. But it's quite proper and Protestant to go from one bed to the next so long as you go to divorce court in between."

He was pleased with his observation. It didn't matter that the effect of the wine deprived him of a worthy audience. Both couples invoked the late hour as they rose from the table and said their goodbyes.

In the morning, the Abbotts took the Club's motor launch to the airport at the far end of the island and caught the only flight of the day to Miami. From there they had a non-stop flight to Cincinnati. That morning Charles sat in his beach chair by its empty mate. On a yellow legal pad in his lap, he wrote an outline of the research project he'd undertaken for Claudia. Then he opened the large novel, scanned the description on the flap, and settled in at last to read its first chapters.

Chapter Eight

From the Journal

I *often find relief in the end of a vacation and my return to the office. There is the accumulation of mail to be sorted through, assigned to categories, dealt with as a client matter, a firm matter. It's a pleasant task, supporting as it does one of my favorite illusions of making order from chaos. If you kick apart the elaborately constructed hive of the carpenter ant, the ants proceed to repair it without alarm, at the same speed they had been going about its enlargement. In so much of nature, the process is what is important.*

My particular practice has few sudden movements. Estates progress through probate like barges through a canal. Waters are lowered and raised, locks flooded, gates opened and closed. The lawyer's job is akin to the tugs and the mules, guiding the assets through, adding a pull for the tight spots. There were several matters in the planning stage, wills and trusts that I had to draft. None of their progenitors had died or decided on a different plan in my absence, and the tasks waited for me now. I took up at my desk where I had left off.

There were changes in my behaviour. I don't think they were perceptible to anyone but me. One of the luxuries I allow myself is driving to work. Since I live in Manhattan and office down-town, many consider my conduct evidence of a latent instability, but I enjoy it. I garage my car a four-block walk from our apartment, by the East River. The walk is a pleasant one, even in inclement weather when it forces me to confront elements I can't control. The morning's radio tells me whether my route will be over the Drive or down Second Avenue. I depart and return a good hour after the conventional rush hour. And I have an accomodating relationship with a twenty-four hour lunch counter next to the uptown parking garage, so that I have a full mug of steaming coffee ready for me when I drive off, one of those magnetized plastic mugs designed to sit on the dashboard and covered to prevent spills.

It's an important part of my day. I have never heard a better sound system than the one I have installed in that car. When I arrive downtown, I often sit, the engine turned off but the power on, and allow the selection on the radio or the tape to play through. And to that extent, my conduct changed. Now, upon my return from Elbow Reef, I found myself in my car in its extravagantly expensive parking space by the Battery while I played a second tape and finished the coffee, thinking of nothing but the music. After the trip to the Caribbean, as often as not I played Rachmaninoff, Chopin and Schumann, allowing myself for the first time to listen to the complexities and color in music I had regarded until then as nothing more than sentimental.

Another curious thing. One of the few pieces of advice I can recall from my father, who gave advice to clients as a profession and to his family as an avocation, was to keep my shoes shined and my watch running on time. Did he say it to me because, tongue-tied, it was one of the few personal things his father could find to say to him? In any event, I began to skip my regular appointment with the bootblack in the lobby at our office building. Perhaps I was redepositing in my bank of labors the small withdrawal of time expended over my automobile concerts. It was not as if I fell into disrepair, but these tiny variations were noticeable to me, like the dimpling of the surface as a mayfly alights on an otherwise still pond.

There were two tasks I had identified as a result of my talks with Claudia. I undertook them myself. Were I to have assigned them to an associate, I would have owed my partners an explanation of a new client. I preferred to keep Claudia's matters to myself.

The first task involved legal research, to determine under what circumstances a clause such as Claudia had described to me, forfeiting a remainder interest in a trust because of divorce, would be enforced. I couldn't reach a conclusion until I had read a copy of the trust itself, but I got started on the issue. I enjoy research, the stacks of books, trying to extract from the cases enough lines of logic to sketch a picture. Senior lawyers are supposed to be occupied with more important concerns, so I don't get to do as much of it as I'd like.

The second task turned out to be quite easy. That was to find out whatever I could about the Parine Pen Company. There was very little. It was a privately held company, estimated to be the third or fourth largest manufacturer of fine fountain pens in the industry, but one that had had hard times in the recent few years. Gordon Parine's entry in Who's Who gave me nothing new. I could find no financial data about the company, but the general press had done a few stories on whatever happened to the fountain pen, and from them I extracted a rough history of the company that was Claudia's inheritance.

In a word, the company suffered from obsolescence. Once a healthy force shipping internationally, it had refused until recently to follow the market into ball point pens from their appearance after the Second World War. By the time the company had tooled up to make a new product, the ball point market was controlled. The leaders were not writing-implement firms, but specialty firms that through mass distribution had changed the nature of the purchase from a luxury item to a throw-away, a cheap item that had nothing to do with status or who its owner was. Parine, run by Claudia's father until his death and now by her younger brother Gordon, finally entered the field, but decided to do so with a high-priced, highly designed product in an attempt to renew the public's esteem for a fine pen. The public was apparently having none of it.

In the more immediate past, the last two or three years, the company's fortunes had improved. One article talked about assembly plants in Mexico and Europe. And there was a renewed consumer interest in fountain pens as nostalgia. Parine Pen was a mixed bag.

The legal issue had, to my surprise, a specific answer. It was not the answer I had hoped to find, and its very certitude—I could find no cases offering hope of a minority rule—diminished my eagerness to see Claudia again to tell her of my efforts. But my eagerness was to be dulled even more by the absence of news. Claudia had said that she would send me the documents when she got back to Cincinnati, but weeks went by and I heard nothing. Had I rushed into a romance like a schoolboy, imagining there was more in her questions, our talks, than she had intended? Was what had happened no more than a middle-aged reprise of a summer's flirtation, and now, back in the comfort of her own surroundings had her feelings changed about the trust and its significance in her life?

Not hearing, I put the issues and the thoughts of her out of my mind . To the extent I craved an extra-legal project to fill my time, I turned to researching an article I had intended to do about fruits in the Nile Valley. The grey New York winter gradually gave up its grip, and the freezing sleet warmed to a drizzle. By mid-April, I had stopped looking through my office mail for the package from Cincinnati, had determined that the issue had passed. I had returned to my routine, with the moderate and private exception of the tapes of Romantic piano music.

I was thus caught up sharp when, returning home for dinner one evening, I was told by Evelyn that we had a note from Claudia. It hadn't occurred that she would write to my house, or that she would address us both. The note, on handsome paper with a blue monogram and border, slightly mannish but otherwise elegant, inquired after us and reminded us to plan an Aspen visit. It listed some telephone numbers of rental agents, and promised her help. The Abbotts would be there the entire month of August and it would be delightful if we could be there for all or a part of it, too.

As an afterthought, a message was addressed to me.

"I'll be in New York early next month. Could you save me an hour or so, Charles, perhaps on the second, to discuss that legal matter I mentioned to you. Let me know if not. Otherwise, I'll ring you then."

Evelyn and I discussed the invitation, and, each deferring to the other the final decision and having signalled by inference and interpretation our mutual desire to accept, determined that *we would. We cancelled our reservations at Chincoteague Island. I knew my motives and I assumed I knew Evelyn's as well. Chinconteague was too remote and pastoral for her tastes. Evelyn wrote a note in kind to the Abbotts, to let them know we were making arrangments for two weeks in Colorado. At my request, she added a postscript telling Claudia that I was looking forward to seeing her at my office on the second of May.*

* * * * *

By eleven o'clock on that day, Charles Meredith wondered if he had made a mistake. In readiness for a call from Claudia to make an appointment, he had cleared his calendar. That act in itself was no imposition, for his practice often included long periods without the need for conferring with clients. And this day, he had scheduled only a meeting among his firm's estate practitioners, their monthly meeting to discuss assignments, and after that a haircut.

At eleven-thirty, the switchboard operator rang to tell him that a Mrs. Abbott was on the line. It took only the salutations and explanations of the intervening time to recapture their past warmth.

"Can I come down there and take you to lunch? Or will I disrupt your entire day?"

"Where are you now?"

"The Colony. Sixty-second and Park."

Charles knew it, and knew a pleasant restaurant within a block's walk. They arranged to meet at one, Charles asking for a margin of time in case midtown traffic held him up.

In fact, he was early, and Claudia was there, sitting demurely on a straight-backed chair opposite the long bar that filled the restaurant's front half. They were shown to a table in the rear. Claudia chose to sit against the wall with Charles opposite. They were inches from tables on either side, and although Charles searched there was no more secluded seating in the place. Charles suggested that they leave their business until after lunch, nodding to the progress of the diners on either side. Claudia understood him to mean that they might be alone by then.

Claudia wore a black dress with a small floral print. Charles asked and she assured him that they were indeed hollyhocks,

and he apologized for squinting. The dress had a high, ruf-
fled neck, around which Claudia wore her day pearls.

They each had a dry sherry. She ordered a salad and he
the antipasto. The restaurant held itself out as a trattoria,
though its location in prime space pushed up the prices beyond the range of a street cafe. Still, Charles heard himself
explaining, the food was simple and good.

He looked up from his plate. "Why do you always bring
out the fatuous in me?" he asked with a self-conscious laugh.

"I didn't realize I did," she said. "I thought that was your
charm showing."

They declined dessert and ordered espresso. As it came, a
couple at a neighboring table got up to leave. Charles waited
a moment and brought up the subject he assumed she had
mentioned in her note.

"I've done some work on the legal questions," he began. "I
had told you it would depend on the document and the law of
the state of the trust. I no longer think that's so true. The law
for once seems clear." He realized he had unconsciously in-
flected his voice to express sympathy, regret for the news he
was about to impart. He attempted a more neutral tone.

"As you can imagine, a provision such as this in a substantial trust is . . . unusual. The cases are few and far between,
and most of them are ancient. Reaching beyond the grave to
control the marital conduct of one's grandchildren is itself
an antiquated practice. It may be because today we realize
how fast mores change, while our grandparents felt more
assured about the longevity of right and wrong.

"The courts have felt that certain conduct, like divorce,
shouldn't be encouraged by payment, and so they have said
no. You can't write a trust compelling that. You can't make a
gift conditional on getting a divorce. That's because social
policy, as expressed in the law, favors marriage. People may
not," and here Claudia smiled thinly to acknowledge his droll
remark, "but social policy does. Marriage brings order to
the holding and passing of property. And that's why every
jurisdiction—every state—that's considered a clause like the
one in your trust has upheld it.

"Now, we've looked at the law in every jurisdiction, and
found cases in only eight states. And none in Ohio. So, if
Ohio is where this question would be litigated, technically it
would be what lawyers call a question of first impression. But

with eight states on the other side of the issue, I couldn't advise you to litigate it."

Claudia looked at him steadily.

"By enforceable you mean that if I were divorced, a court would rule that I'd forfeited my share of the trust."

"Correct. The court is supposed to enforce the intention of the person who created the trust. We start with the right of private property: it was your grandfather's money, to do with as he pleased, unless what he does is illegal or against some basic societal goal."

"Like the freedom to choose."

Claudia's tone was sarcastic.

"I didn't make the laws, Claudia. And I didn't choose to marry Weemo."

He wondered as he spoke if he were not too forward. His words went well beyond his professional role, and presumed on their friendship. She took no offense. Instead she retracted her rebuke. "I'm sorry. That was harsh. Thank you, Charles. You've done a lot of work for naught. I'm grateful."

He shrugged off the remark. "I should still take a look at the document. Perhaps there's some other language we could use to argue our side, or perhaps the forfeiting clause isn't as specific as you remember."

"It is," she said, opening a large purse and taking out a manila envelope. "I brought copies of the papers, but I don't want you to have to do any more work."

He held out his hand and she put the envelope in it.

"It won't take me long. We've come this far, it's worth glancing over the language."

It was the passing of a key. It would open the intent of James Parine, Claudia's grandfather, what he thought about love, marriage, fidelity, property. Odd, Claudia thought, the relationship between marriage and property. She'd accepted it as a tacit premise. Had groomed herself as an award, by the right person to be sought and won. And then placed on the mantle. Title to be shared in joint tenancy. The idea hadn't seemed so mercantile to her at the time. She trained herself for the very posture, had kept her complexion fresh, her conversation modulated and well informed. Once the game was over, she would be looked after. The recollection made her shudder.

Meredith motioned to the waiter for the check. While they waited Claudia mentioned Aspen again and urged that he and Evelyn come for as long as they could.

"The music is wonderful. My kind and yours. And without company I go to all the concerts by myself."

Charles assured her they would be there.

They went out into the chill sun. A damp ocean wind was blowing and it cut through the light clothes of those who had dressed for spring.

He asked if he might walk with her back to the Colony. She accepted. They walked, shoulders almost touching, talking loudly enough to hear each other, but at a volume made discreet by the street noise. To a passerby, they would have appeared a couple, an unmistakeably well-to-do couple, dressed in a style almost too stolid to be called a style, its design independent of the length of hemline or width of lapel. Their dress was matched by their manner: no laughter too harsh, no anger too virile, no jealousy that could not be purged.

Weemo, Claudia was saying out of nowhere, did not like changes. Particularly in others. He wanted things to go on just as they were. "Not that there is anything wrong with continuity," Claudia said. "But it ought to depend on what keeps continuing.

"I don't think he would mind it if we had an affair," she said, although Charles understood from her tone that she did not mean her remark as coy or provocative. "He would mind if we flaunted it in his face, if we forced him to look at it. For then he would have to choose. To confront one of us. As it is, my behaviour complements perfectly his desire for equipoise."

Charles considered her words. He had early resolved to help Claudia however he could. Her legal problem happened to be up his alley. It was what he knew how to do. But her remarks seemed to call for more. Perhaps he had misjudged her. Perhaps provocation was precisely what she had in mind.

"Being well matched on that level is not all bad," Charles said. His fondness for recognizing complexity before seeking order, his lawyerly impulse to gather facts, played against him. Claudia's remarks were ambiguous, he thought properly so. And he understood Weemo's bent for stability. That, he translated into a real sense of marriage as a state, not a circumstance. A state of physical dimension.

Claudia didn't reply immediately. She was unsure of his meaning. Did he intend to reassure her or was he saying something about his own life? When she did answer, she had decided his meaning didn't matter.

And with her next words, the moment passed, the opening, into which Charles' feelings might have glided, closed like the tunnel of a wave.

"Try living with it," she said. "A man who won't engage about art, literature, politics. That's one thing. Different from you, but liveable. But a man who doesn't get involved with the people he professes to love . . ." She trailed off. "It's hard not to resent that. . . ." She looked to the sky over Central Park as if the word she sought would be written there.

". . . that balance."

They arrived at the Romanesque portico of the Colony Club. She waved the doorman off, and he retreated back inside the lobby to allow her to complete her conversation.

"Would you do me one other favor?" she asked. "I'm going downtown tomorrow, to see my son. I'd thought I might be telling him some important news. I want to see him while I'm in New York anyway. I know it's a lot to ask, but will you come with me?"

Charles agreed readily. She wrote out an address in the East Village for him, where she said she would be by eleven, so perhaps they could meet at noon. They'd all have lunch together. It had been so nice to see him again. So far they had had several conversations and Claudia had never mentioned the word divorce. To Charles it seemed that, in light of his resolute if unhappy response to her legal questions, she would not do so. But Claudia proved him wrong.

"I've thought about divorce regardless of the trust. Why spend seven years in a loveless marriage? But it's my family's inheritance. And besides, I find the process so dreary. Announcing yourself to friends. Their concern, their solicitude, their pity. What will she do? Will he keep the house? Who initiated it, do you suppose? Afterwards, she gets invited to lunch, he to dinner."

Back at his office, Charles called for the file containing his work on Claudia's trust and the Parine Pen Company. With the language at last in front of him, he might need to consult his notes on legal precedent. Then, with a carved ebony letter opener Evelyn had insisted he buy in Kenya, the handle the full figure of a nude woman, he slit open the manila envelope and removed the trust document. It was flimsy by modern drafting standards, only some twelve pages long. And it didn't take Charles long to corroborate what Claudia had said. The language was unambiguous. Claudia would be entitled to a distribution of the corpus at the expiration of twenty-one years after the death of her aunt, unless prior to that time she as the beneficiary "shall have legally separated from or, shall have divorced, or have been divorced from or by, his or her spouse. . . ." He glanced at the last pages: the situs of the trust was indeed Ohio, where no court, his work in the library had shown, had decided the question. But he knew the conservative procedures by which law is made. Courts uncover law; they don't create it. It wasn't reasonable to hope that Ohio, particularly that state sitting as it did in the midsection of the country's moral stripe, would take a position different from the existing precedent in other states.

Meredith put the document aside. But his training as a lawyer, generating neither innovation nor, often, enthusiasm, had produced in him an involuntary thoroughness. If he had undertaken to review the document, he had better read it. He picked it up again. In a half hour, when he had finished, he knew that his lunch with Claudia tomorrow would be more disturbing than today's.

Chapter Nine

From the Journal

It might have been a mistake for me to agree to meet Claudia at her son's apartment, preoccupied as I was with my news. I don't know what her motives were in inviting me. It was certainly not a social accommodation, since neither the young man nor I would have sought out the meeting. For myself, I agreed out of an idle affability that too often places me in circumstances I'd rather avoid.

The visit was not uncomfortable. It was over too quickly for that. But I found Hap Abbott, or Harrison, as he sharply instructed me he preferred to be called, a brittle and distrustful young man, with shaggy blond hair in need of a washing. I guessed that before I arrived, some words might have been spoken between him and his mother. He neglected to introduce me to his young woman, who throughout our brief stay sat on a corduroy couch and thumbed through an old issue of Variety. They were both aspiring actors, they were both uncommunicative, and they were both, I feel sure, enabled in those idiosyncracies by allowances from home.

Claudia tried to bring her son out, to find points of common interest for us to discuss. But Harrison remained indifferent, and was sedulous only in his desire to show that neither his parents nor their friends mattered to him.

I was relieved to vacate the grim apartment, a one-bedroom flat with a kitchen wall behind a raised wicker screen, as soon as we could. It upset me to see Harrison's incivility towards his mother, and I told Claudia so. She defended him, so kindly that it convinced me of her resolve. She urged me to understand that *different children had different ways of separating from their parents, and that this was his way. For some reason—was it jealousy, jealousy of her unconditional affection?—I wouldn't accept that. I responded that he was separating at every point except the hip pocket, where the wallet was kept. The remark was meant to be sardonic, but Claudia, if she was stung at all, merely smiled amiably and took my hand in hers. I realized how different our perspectives were. I thought her son ill kempt, spoiled, unmannerly. And I was not wrong. But Claudia was watching for other signs in him.*

Just so our perspectives were different at lunch. The news I brought her I felt was a disaster. Speaking as her lawyer. I didn't allow myself any other point of view, because the job I had undertaken for her was to consider her legal position. Perhaps I take my oath of admission to the bar too seriously.

As her lawyer, I considered the news an enormous disruption, a fissure in how I thought my client had constructed her future. Claudia seemed more curious than distraught. Perhaps she had not constructed her future with the architectural detail to which I was accustomed, or perhaps she had and didn't like what she saw. In any event, that day I realized, contrary to what I wanted to believe, that I didn't yet know how she thought. Not at all.

* * * * *

When Claudia arrived they were still in bed. Harrison slipped on a pair of jeans and opened the door. He didn't pull away when his mother offered her cheek but brushed his lips to it, and allowed his own cheek to be kissed lightly. His girlfriend, embarrassed, excused herself and went into the bathroom to dress. Harrison hadn't mentioned his mother was coming that morning.

Claudia unpacked the bags and boxes she had brought. She just assumed he would need things, setting up a new apartment, so she'd stopped at a housewares place on the way down. There was a can opener and a coffee machine, a set of mugs, some chrome-plated bar tools. She had thought to choose adult things, things that would show she accepted, encouraged his new status. If Harrison recognized her effort he didn't acknowledge it.

She inquired of his life and health, told him how healthy he looked. The girl came back and Claudia asked her about job-hunting and living in New York. She responded and they talked brightly for a while about the theater and what they each enjoyed. The conversation seemed to make Harrison more sullen.

Claudia rose from the kitchen chair she'd been seated on and walked about the room. It was dreary—cracking plaster walls showing light rectangles where the former tenants had hung pictures—and she had to stop herself from pretending otherwise. It was, she realized, exactly what Harrison wanted. In New York, a touch squalid, his own.

"Would you like some lithographs for the walls?" Claudia asked. "We have all sorts of things at home we're not hanging, or something from the gallery down the street."

"Oh, Mom," the boy said. "That gallery's for the tourists. No one around here buys that crap. A thousand bucks for some jerk who throws paint from the top of a ladder."

"Then something from home." She was going over what was stored in the basement in Cincinnati but couldn't think of anything suitable. There were prints of the English countryside they had had in a breakfast room, a series of hunt scenes she'd finally gotten out of the front hall.

"This is my home," the boy said.

"I know," Claudia said. She was lost for the moment in her inventory and so missed the edge in his voice. "Those tsunami drawings. They'd be perfect."

"Damn it, no," he shouted. Both women were startled at how loud his voice was in the small room. "I don't need anything for the goddamn walls."

"I'm sorry, Harrison," Claudia said.

"It's just like being back there. There you and Dad gave me shit all the time about homework and haircuts. Now you just want to give me more shit."

"I'm sorry, Harrison," she said again, this time with a note of sternness.. "You have to allow me a little time to change. It's just that, I've been mothering you since you were born. It's hard to stop, even when you clearly don't need it anymore."

The boy relented. He was unused to attacking his mother and wasn't sure whether he'd gone too far.

"You're always in there like a switchboard operator. Arranging my life for me. I don't need that. I don't want it. I just want to be by myself. Why is that so hard to understand?"

The question tugged deep inside Claudia and made her smile. She fingered the pearls at her neck.

"That's not at all hard to understand. What's hard is for me to change the way I act about it. Give me a little time and I'll try to do better."

In the silence they heard the pinging of the water's boil. The girl got up to take the kettle from the stove before it started to whistle. They occupied themselves with the pouring of tea into a pot, its steeping and its serving. Charles arrived. If there had been a crisis, it had passed. Claudia invited the young couple to join them for lunch, and Harrison declined for them both. He gave no reason. By the time she and Charles said goodbye, the boy was calm but no more cheerful.

Claudia told Charles of her words with her son as they walked. They strolled across Twelfth Street towards Avenue A and at the corner she took his arm. The shops reflected the impermanence of the neighborhood. Used clothing, most of it studded or sequined or tattooed, head shops, astrologers, galleries selling angry, modish art. Meredith told Claudia of something Freud had written. It is only cultures in transformation that are unhappy.

"Are you thinking of Hap?" she asked.

"I hadn't been. I'd been thinking of here, where he lives. But perhaps him too." They walked on. The day promised to be warm. There were ginko trees along the sidewalk. Around their roots someone had artfully planted mosaics from the detritus of the street. Slices of beer cans, pop-top rings, chips of glass and vinyl. Some were symmetrical, and in one, they formed the letter K, Budweiser caps against a field of brown bottle shards. "Besides," Charles said. "He wants to be called Harrison."

She nodded as if he had said something profound. She was thinking of pulling those two cables together, her past and her son's future. It suddenly seemed much harder.

"When he was born," she told him, "his father had his name all ready. Harrison Parine Abbott. He presented it to me with two dozen long-stemmed roses and an assortment of magazines. I was quite breathless about having this baby and never gave a name much thought. The Harrison he'd found as a surname on his mother's family tree. I think Weemo thought it sounded patrician. Weemo likes things patrician. He's not at all self-conscious about it. The Parine was an obvious choice. He liked them in combination. They made a nickname, like Weemo's, with the first name and the initial.

"So," and she let out a little sigh. "So we called him Hap from the start. He never much liked it. I wonder he didn't change over before now. It never mattered to me what we called him. I only wish Weemo would have given as much time to raising him as naming him."

They agreed to lunch in the neighborhood, since Charles needed to be back at his office and Claudia was catching a mid-afternoon plane. From the facade, the restaurant looked adequate. Inside it was cozy: they found themselves seated in an oak booth, large plants set upon the booth dividers, overflowing their pots and giving off a mild fragrance of spice.

"You seem upset," Charles said as he hung up her coat. "Are you worried about your son?"

Claudia looked at him a full moment. Her thoughts were elsewhere.

"You're very observant, Charles. And kind. I am worried, but I don't think it's only Harrison. I think it's me as well."

He slid into the booth and sat opposite her. "I'd really expected to be helping him with his courses and fraternity dues. This leaving the nest may be easier for human chicks than falcon chicks, but I'll bet it's as tough on the mothers."

Charles nodded. He knew nothing of parenting directly. What he'd observed from his own father and could recall from his mother he dismissed as not useful. His mother had died during his first year away at school. He was thirteen. Even before she was rarely around. He remembered most the nurses who cared for her, a succession of grim women who rustled when they moved about. And the large lead crystal decanter in the dining room. He'd occasionally meet his mother in the dining room, when the nurse wasn't about, and she would pour a large water glass from the decanter. Then they'd have the same little joke, about her secret cure. "Mustn't tell nurse," she'd say, and he'd smile back.

Claudia was speaking of her son. "He may be ready for this," she was saying, "but I'm not."

"You're ready, I'm sure. It's just that we'll take on any problems we can find, especially those of people close to us, before we'll look at our own. We only take up our own when we've nothing left to do."

"Do you really think we avoid living our own lives?" she asked.

"Yes," he said. "I think I do."

"How very sad."

A handsome young woman handed them menus. She wore a white blouse crocheted with two figures in the likeness of Adam and Eve. "We're out of the tempeh melt," she said sorrowfully. Charles reassured her and Claudia laughed a silent laugh. They ordered conservatively; radicchio salads, a loaf of zucchini bread, almond sodas.

He waited until they had been served to begin his news. When he started, his voice modulated to what he would consider the voice of a physician with a terminal patient. So much of life, he had discovered, was in the anticipation.

"It wasn't until I read the entire trust that I realized the problem," he was saying. "I'm particularly sensitive to it, I suppose, because we handled a similar case involving a New York estate. Almost the identical language."

"You're talking about something other than the divorce language, I gather."

"I am," he said. "Your grandfather's trust was set up in a very different era. Things like temperance, divorce, adoption were significant issues. Moral issues. They turn up in devises of property and they seem like anachronisms. But they're there, and courts tend to do what the settlor wanted. Even if times have changed."

"What are you saying, Charles?"

Meredith took his fork and moved the vegetables around on his plate. The meal was really quite good.

"Your grandfather left his estate in three trusts for his three children, your father and your aunts. Then he instructed that it be used for their children, and that twenty-one years after their death—your father and his sisters'—it be distributed to the heirs of his body. That is the exact language he used. 'Heirs of the body.'"

"Meaning," Claudia said, "the children of his children."

"Meaning," Charles nodded, "the children of his children. The natural children. Not the adopted children."

82]

"What are you saying?"

"Just that. The words are all-important. Those words have been construed to mean blood descendents. Like most states, Ohio has passed a law saying that adopted children are going to be treated exactly the same as children born to the family, what we used to call natural children until we got sensitized to the connotation. So there is that statute. But courts have held that where someone writes in the language before the statute was passed, as your grandfather did, the statute doesn't apply. In other words, your grandfather's trust appears to give all of the rights in the stock now held in trust to the non-adopted children of your father and aunt."

Claudia didn't respond immediately. She tore the heel from the bread loaf, split it in two, put half on his plate and half on her own. The waitress came by to ask if they needed anything else and Claudia asked for a butter knife. Then she turned to Charles.

"You mean that in seven years, when the trust is distributed, not only do I no longer get half the current income of my father's share, I get none of the distribution."

"On the face of the trust, that's what I'm saying."

"And this threat of forfeiture, the keeping my marriage together until my interest vests, there's been no need to do that? Nothing vests?" She spoke in a measured voice, as if she were discussing the salad dressing.

"Again, without more research, and on the face of the trust, yes. That's what it appears."

"What do you suggest we do? Is there anything to be done?" The waitress brought Claudia a second knife. She took her bread from the plate and broke off a piece. Then, holding that piece deliberately with the tips of all the fingers of one hand, she spread enough butter for a mouthful.

"There are several questions. One is how well thought through are the Ohio cases. Could we reverse them. A more fundamental question is, does your brother know about this? No one, I gather, has ever mentioned it to you?"

She shook her head.

"It's possible no one knows, but unlikely. It's less likely that it would get through probate without being caught. There are too many professionals in the trustee and probate process for it to slip by. But if he doesn't know, he might be more receptive to negotiating an interpretation and agreeing to allow you your share. How do you and your brother get on?"

"At arm's length," Claudia replied without hesitation. "Gordon is the male line of the Parine family. In command, bull headed, infallible. So long as I don't question him about running the company or increasing his perks and salary, he tolerates me."

"There are other facts we need. When your grandfather died. If it was after 1932—the year of the Ohio statute . . ."

"It was."

". . . we could argue that he died with the awareness that the language he put in this trust would be interpreted to include adopted children. The basic rule of interpreting language is to determine the intent of the person who wrote it. But that's also the greatest fiction, since the person isn't around anymore. We have to create a radio play to show what he was thinking."

Their waitress cleared the plates and suggested desserts. They ordered only tea, a ginseng blend that they were surprised to find they liked.

"I don't know what to say," Claudia looked at him directly as she spoke. "The Parine stock has always been a mixed blessing. Like one of those legendary diamonds, where the owners seem to be cursed. I don't believe all rich people are unhappy. I know that's a popular American myth, and I don't buy it. Owning the company didn't give my father any happiness. I only thought the security of that stock, it really is worth quite a bit of money you know, would allow Hap— Harrison—to do what he wants to. At least one of us . . ."

Charles was prepared. Here was a chance for him to help. Skills that for years seemed arcane or irrelevant to the way people lived their lives were finally just what was needed. He closed his eyes and imagined—did not see again but imagined—the spot of a sunball on his eyelid.

"Here's what we'll do," he said. "You find out for me as much as you can about your grandfather. Whether there were other wills or trusts, whether he ever expressed a view, in them or anywhere else, about adoptive versus natural children. What firm drafted this and whether they have files. They often do. I'll get to work on what it would take to convince an Ohio court that this language wasn't thought through, that 'heirs of the body' was used as a convention, not intending to cut off Claudia Abbott. Most jurisdictions agree that if the author of the will had used 'children' you'd be scot-free. 'Heirs' and 'issue' are supposed to denote more of blood lines. It's a silly construction. Obsolete. Maybe we can convince a court.

"Also, think about your brother's reaction. Will he fight us, go along with us? If not, will he be willing to negotiate some financial compromise? Don't bring it up, but think about a strategy. We can talk this summer in Aspen."

Charles' plans seemed appropriate, reasonable. Claudia agreed to them. They said goodbye and parted, he hailing a cab for Broadway and Wall, she insisting that she would walk for a while.

In fact she walked all the way uptown. It took two hours and forced her to take a later flight. But she never thought of the distance. Her rage obscured it, a rage at fate, at her grandfather, at herself. How was it that property could continue to control her life, determined as she had been to sort the two out? Weemo would be for fighting the language, she was sure of it. Gordon? No telling. He might oblige her, broadly grant her her half of the inheritance, which surely he didn't need, and reinforce her subordination in the scheme of things.

It fired her fury to think of it. It was an affront, an attack on her right to be in the family. This was putting her out on the street, not penniless but in some more fundamental way. Her family was who she was. Her father had always told her that.

So the two could not be separated. But she didn't want to ask Gordon for anything. She would do as Charles had suggested. She would gather the material Charles needed, and then, this summer, they would see.

*   *   *   *   *

Gordon Parine was also thinking about Aspen. The president of Parine Pen was thinking that might be a good place to spend the spoils that had befallen him.

At the end of the Second World War, Parine Pen was a leader in manufacturing fine writing-instruments, with a strong market share. But the disposable postwar world had almost done it in. Within ten years of their introduction, everyone switched to ball points.

When the change hit, Parine Pen wasn't ready. Andrew Parine was then the company's president. Although he was the son of the founder, the very man who had created the trust that now concerned Charles Meredith, Andrew had none of his father's financial skills. Faced with a business in crisis, he grafted his geraniums and avoided the office. At forty-five, he suffered a heart attack and his board replaced him with a professional manager. His children Claudia and Gordon were then college age, too young for service. Andrew died the next year. Parine pen was barely alive.

Because for half a century the company had conserved most of its earnings, it could now weather some losses. But not indefinitely, and a manufacturer of an obsolete product has poor prospects. Yet new management held on. Without a plan and, some said, without a hope they held on.

And then, two years after Gordon Parine became the fourth president of the company, Fashion turned her head, glanced over her shoulder, and focused her luminous eyes on the forgotten fountain pen.

A law of business thermodynamics holds that a company in motion cannot remain in motion without new energy, new capital or luck. Parine had had no energies or income for years. It had maintained its patents, its inventory, and its lines of distribution. Just as its momentum was giving out, tastes changed. The fountain pen made a comeback in the late sixties, as buyers sought to imitate styles of a simpler age. Articles in *Connoisseur* and *Women's Wear Daily* documented the fashion, and fueled by the journals of high taste, pens moved from curio shops to Madison Avenue's antique row.

Good fortune fell upon the company like a mountain shower and changed more than its balance sheet. The income beneficiaries of the trusts, Gordon, Claudia and their cousins, saw their annual distributions rise. None of them had been deprived before and, other than Gordon, none used this fortuity to enhance an already ample style of life. But the rise in values quickened the cupidity of the beneficiaries—for in financial matters men and women often leave logic aside: when the number of diners is constant and the pie grows, appetites increase proportionately.

And there were changes in the life of Gordon Parine. When he had graduated from college he had assumed he would be made president of the company. But the board, following his mother's wishes, overlooked him. Her husband's experience had been sufficiently unpleasant that she wanted to spare Gordon a morally forced indenture. Disposed since childhood to antagonism, Gordon took her protectiveness as a slight. It was one in a long line: his family had always ignored him, had squandered their attention on his sister, for her beauty and intelligence.

Gordon decided he could wait no longer. He organized his sister and cousins to vote their shares for a new board, then got himself elected as president of the company. He resolved to make good. When the company began to prosper, Gordon decided causation and not happenstance was the reason and gave himself credit. More, he gave himself bonuses and elaborate perquisites. Now handsomely compensated, he grew in the estimate of his own skills.

Gordon Parine expanded the base of the company by entering into a European joint venture to license products abroad. He built a profitable assembly plant in a small Mexican city. He believed, because it had worked for him so far, that if you presume success, success will happen upon you. The day his accountant told him he had entered the highest tax bracket, he traded his Mercedes sedan for a Bentley. And since he was partial to vacation houses, he determined to build himself a fitting house in the Colorado Rockies in which to estivate.

Chapter Ten

From the Journal

Astronomers and physicists speak of the point of singularity. It is that point where an object disappearing into a hole occupies no space and has an infinite density. The term came to me as we flew the last leg of the journey that started at Sixty-seventh Street two doors east of Park Avenue and now carried us over a mountain range called the Sawatch and into the valley that held Aspen. In the enormous spaces of the American west I began to feel that I had no dimension, that my ability to be measured was shrinking, condensing, in the vast and open air.

I had never been to Colorado, and while I have seen the Alps and the Rockies from the air, I was not prepared for the sensation of crossing fourteen thousand foot peaks with what seemed no more than a thousand feet to spare. I am not comfortable with heights, and I concentrated on watching to forget my agitation. We flew close enough to see pick-up trucks raise red dust on the mountain roads, close enough to see the black squares of mine shafts opening into the sides of the hill. That depth made the height more pronounced, and finally I had to look away. I've experienced the same sensation flying into a harbor like New York, when the plane suddenly crosses over the top of a ship and the perspective steals one's breath.

Evelyn too looked out the window, but with pure excitement. Her eyes glistened and she squeezed my arm each time the plane crossed the top of a peak as if her effort were needed to lighten my weight. Ever since I met Evelyn, I have thought her eyes were the most remarkable of any I know. They are large and *dark, and ever on the verge, it seems, of filling with tears. Even when she is happy, her eyes suggest a pathos that appeals to me. More, that holds me.*

The plane made its last banking turn to align the runway. I felt as if I might be spilled from the cabin, spilled into this slender valley like one more stone, to be rubbed smooth by the river that cut through it. To go from the towers that man builds to nature's underscores how specialized man's are. Only he has a purpose for them. I'd been taught as a child that all God's creatures have a purpose. As we prepared to land in western Colorado, that Sunday school lesson occurred to me, and I wondered whether, for man, any use exists but those he makes for himself. It is an undigestible thought, and I put it behind me.

When I travel I regularly bring with me a writing project and again on this trip I had brought more than my trepidation. I had begun an outline of a story I wanted to do on the fruit of the Garden of Eden. The hypothesis was that the fruit of Genesis was not an apple, as the myth had it, but more likely a banana or a plantain. If you assume any literal truth to the Old Testament, the Garden is widely thought to have existed somewhere in the upper valley of the Nile. Most scholars place it between the Tigris and the Euphrates. And that is not apple orchard country. Through botanical readings I'd found that the ancestry of most fruits is indistinct, but the plantain is a relative of the banana and has always grown in that part of the world.

I had also brought the inconclusive results of my research for Claudia. And a fierce appetite to see her again. I wondered whether my feelings were produced by her nearness or by my imagination, and I hoped that in the next two weeks I would be given opportunity to find out.

The plane came down among peaks whose caps were covered with snow and whose flanks were covered with sprawling houses and swimming pools. Aspen sat like a gold coin in the corner of a wallet. Mad money. As we taxied to the homey terminal, past a fleet of private jets larger, I would bet, than the air force of most free nations, I caught sight of the Abbotts

standing at a chest-high hurricane fence, waving at our plane.
I was gratified that in falling into this hole, I nonetheless con-
tinued to occupy space.

* * * * *

The four friends exchanged greetings and even Charles found himself hugging and hugged. Weemo poked fun at him for his seersucker sports coat and linen tie, assuring him that this was not Martha's Vineyard and that he'd have no further use for it. The Merediths retrieved their luggage inside the small terminal and Weemo brought the car around to fetch them.

More precisely, the jeep. The Abbotts kept an old Willys at their mountain house, painted bright green and looking nothing like its eleven years. The women sat in back and Charles by the driver. All but Weemo carried luggage on their laps.

Weemo insisted they do a quick tour, and he drove them in the open jeep, cheerily calling out the sights. Downtown and on some of the side streets traces of the original Victorian mining town remained. The rest of the architecture—what wasn't modern—struck Charles as self-consciously aping that trace. They drove up Red Mountain, a bare knob facing the ski area, where large houses perched. Weemo pointed out Claudia's and, further up, at the crest of the hill, a stark modern house like a layer cake that was Claudia's brother's. Then back to town, to the quiet and charming West End, where, close enough to the music tent so they could hear an orchestra rehearsing as they disembarked, sat the small salmon-colored frame house the Abbotts had found for the Merediths to rent.

Weemo showed them around the place. He was in high spirits, and rushed through, always one room ahead of them. When he had opened every door and cabinet, he brought them to the kitchen. He was agitated, excited.

"Go ahead," he said to Evelyn. "Open it."

"Open what?"

"The refrigerator."

She looked surprised, but she obliged him. Inside there were foodstuffs of every description: sliced hams and smoked turkeys, cartons of delicatessen cole slaw and salad. And six or seven bottles of a good Champagne.

"Weemo didn't want you to starve," Claudia said. "He's spent more time shopping for your visit than he's ever spent shopping before."

The foursome walked around one last time. The Abbotts had also equipped the house with hiking maps, the music schedule, and Charles noted with a hidden smile, Peterson's Field Guide to Western Birds.

They decided to dine separately that night, Charles asserting that he was tired from the trip. The discussion turned to the next day's plans.

"I'm on a hike," announced Claudia. "Several of us are doing Castle Peak. It's a long walk, but it's supposed to be spectacular. Who wants to go?"

"With ropes and ice picks?" asked Evelyn.

"No," and Claudia laughed. "It's merely a hike. But we'll have to leave at sunrise—that's six o'clock— and we won't be back until mid-afternoon."

"For the more civilized," Weemo said, "I am leading an assault on the local course. Eighteen holes, flat ground. No pitons. Then a cold beer and a sandwich."

"That's for me," said Evelyn. "Especially the cold beer."

Charles hesitated. He did not look forward to an exertive two weeks, following Claudia not through the surf but over cliffs and ice fields.

"A hike, you say." He sought reassurance.

"That's what I'm told," said Claudia. "I've never done it. Nothing more than a long walk uphill. We can go at our own pace, and if we don't like it we can turn back."

He very much wanted the time with her. He agreed and their plans were set.

* * * * *

Promptly at six the next morning, a rendezvous Meredith met without effort since he'd awakened on New York time, Claudia pulled the jeep up to his house. To signal he'd heard he blinked a porch light. Then he donned a light windbreaker and went out into the new morning. It was the only challenge of the day he would meet easily.

The sun rose red and pink into a cloudless sky. They gasped at the beauty of it, Claudia reaching over from the shift knob that stuck up from the floor and patting his hand. At a parking pull-off by the side of the road just as they left town, she braked the jeep to a stop. There, a group of three or four waited. They sat on the fenders of a second jeep and drank steaming coffee from the plastic nesting tops of a thermos. One of the men came over and asked Claudia if she was for the Castle Peak climb.

"That's us," she said with enthusiasm.

"Our guide's in that car," the man told them. "Why don't I ride along with you and we'll follow them." So saying, he went quickly to the other group, let them know the plan, and returned. He wore a cotton sweater over a denim shirt, hiking shorts, and fancy kletter boots over rag socks. Charles, in jeans and sneakers, eyed him suspiciously.

"I may be in over my head," he said. Once again, Claudia reassured him.

The fellow swung a rucksack off his back and climbed in the back of Claudia's jeep. The first car struck out at a good pace, and they followed in pursuit. The valley floor was in darkness, but long planks of sunlight lay over the top of Independence Pass like a gangway.

"My name's Slatkin," said the man who had joined them. His voice rang with eagerness in the quiet dawn. "I've never done this before. Climbed a mountain, I mean. I'm looking forward to it. Jeremy Slatkin."

Charles turned and smiled weakly. "I'm Charles Meredith," he said. "And this is Claudia Abbott."

Jeremy Slatkin extended a hand over the seat back. He was wiry, dark, forthright. How, thought Charles, can anyone be forthright quite so early. He had black, curly hair, and a bushy moustache, squared off in the Groucho tradition. Charles guessed Slatkin was past forty but a few years his junior. He was short, perhaps five-seven, and the tendons of his neck showed when he turned his head. He looked like someone who would run up the hill. As if to confirm his fitness, Jeremy said, "I'm from California. Los Angeles."

Charles nodded glumly, turned in his seat and peered ahead in hopes of seeing the sun. He hadn't realized they were traveling west.

* * * * *

The jeep with Claudia at the wheel disappeared into the darkness of morning. Weemo stood at the window, watching it go. He could see its headlights as it made its way to the house the Merediths were in, and see it move down the highway towards the west. Smiling to himself, he picked up the phone.

"Hello," the voice said. He couldn't tell if she'd been awake.

"We've both been abandoned," he said.

"Oh, hi."

"I thought of you, alone in bed, and couldn't resist calling."

"I'm glad you called."

"Are you? Wonderful. I thought you might need some protection. There are burglars out this time of night."

"I could certainly use some protection."

"Go downstairs." Weemo visualized the house he had found for them, its front door facing the street, its side entry to a mud room for skiis, well protected from sight. "Go downstairs and unlock the side door and the mud room. Then go back to bed. We'll send one of our men over shortly."

She giggled. "How will I know he's not a burglar."

"Oh. You'll just have to ask to see his credentials."

"Mmm," said Evelyn. "Won't that embarrass him?"

"Not if he's the right man."

When Weemo arrived the side door was ajar and the light was on in the inside hall. He had ridden his bike over, because it would give him a reason to be seen out and about and because it was faster than walking. When he closed the door behind him, he heard his own breathing. He thought the entire escapade romantic, the stealing out in the dark of night, entering another man's bed with his wife still in it, even the wheezing of his breath that now, in the confined space, was the only sound he heard. He waited a moment, and breathed deeply, until he recovered a normal rate. He didn't want to appear winded.

Then he walked noiselessly up the wooden steps. She was lying on her side, facing the door.

"Are you the right man?" she asked with a sly smile.

"Oh yes," he said. "I certainly am."

* * * * *

"Igneous," the chap from the Colorado Mountain Club was saying. "Most of what you see there . . ." pointing across the valley and naming Snowmass and Capitol Peak, ". . . is igneous, the very bedrock of the earth's crust. What we're on, Castle, and those . . . ," pointing to neighboring crags, "are Permian rock, stratified. You can see the difference in the way they crumble. Igneous swoops gracefully from point to point. Permian is sedimentary. It's layered, from deposits when it was an ocean floor. It tends to shatter and split. It doesn't make for good traction if you're climbing it. It doesn't hold the hardware.

"Volcanic thrusts caused this range. This whole valley, in fact all of Colorado, used to be the bottom of an ocean floor in the Pleistocene period, but the continental plates shifted, the mass that is now North America got pinched, and this upthrust was the result. The sea ran dry."

The group of seven had assembled on a long col that was the shoulder to Castle Peak. They had driven both jeeps through Castle Creek, over the old timbering road and past a mine shaft to where a boulder field began. There they got out, checked each other's gear, and listened while their guide summed up the earth's early life in fifteen minutes. As they stood, the sun appeared. By the time the guide was through, they were standing in the sunshine, and sun bathed the mountains around them in the rose light of dawn. The red was reflected in the sandstone cliffs around them and in the dirt, a chalk-like, reddish dirt that had washed down as the cliffs eroded and that puffed dust when you walked on it. The peak they intended to climb was out of sight, behind the long shoulder they stood on, but across the way they could see the rock tops of Pyramid Peak and the Maroon Bells.

Claudia came and stood at Charles' side. He realized she was shivering.

"Why are you shaking?" he asked her. The mountain air was thin, and while the sun shone through it Charles wasn't sure it could retain any heat, even the heat he reluctantly yielded.

"I'm chilled," she said. "By the morning."

He put his arm around her and carefully grasped her far arm.

"Do you mind?" he asked her.

"Not at all," she said, and her body relaxed against his.

* * * * *

Inside the curtains were drawn and the spare light that penetrated, that came around the window shade and seeped into the room, lit the lovers softly, dimly, so they could barely make each other out.

She lay on top of him, both of them facing the ceiling. He told her to lie still, to be his shadow. She rested lightly on his skin, perfectly framed by his outline. Her hands rested on the backs of his hands, framed by his, and her fingers rested on the backs of his fingers. She watched his hands move and with them hers. He talked softly into the ear that nested by his mouth, his lower lip brushing her ear, the helix of her ear, the fleshy curve.

"Now you'll see the pleasure I feel," he told her. His fingertips brushed her body, almost not touching. They skated over her and if her skin had been water they would not have rippled the surface. "You'll feel the surprise and the pleasure." The tips of their fingers in tandem, the fingers of four hands, roamed around her, as she lay stunned to silence. Slowly the fingers went over her body, traced her sex, then his, then returned to explore her face. Then his.

"My God," she said in earnest. "My Christ. What are you doing to me?"

Weemo knew full well. He continued his exploration. He felt her thrill to the game and it was that thrill that he could produce, that was his particular and peculiar talent, a talent he knew was undervalued except by those it served.

*   *   *   *   *

Their group was convivial. Charles liked Slatkin immediately. He was clever and self-deprecating and, sensitive to Charles' apprehension about the hike, lagged back to walk with him. Then there was the guide, an athletic fellow in his thirties who was an accountant with a large firm. A young couple from Texas led the way, in fact hit the trail so early neither Charles nor Claudia got their names. They each carried an elaborate pack that they let be known was filled with camera equipment. Finally there was a lanky grey-haired man named Molderer, who spoke with an Austrian or Swiss accent and who was in Aspen to deliver a paper at the Institute. When Charles asked him his field, he said, "Mathematics," and added with a twinkle, "but no fair asking me any questions. I walk in the mountains to forget that."

The trail was definite, a path trod across the fragile alpine tundra. The guide asked them all to stay on it, since the high country did not recover easily from a stray footprint. The mosses took years to regenerate, so by staying to the path, he urged them, our visit does no harm. The first leg of the trail wove a serpentine path through a pinion forest. There were only a few wildflowers left, the guide said. June was the best month for them. Charles and Claudia pointed out to each other the ones they saw. The guide went up and back from one hiker to the next as a dog might happily do, never tiring. He heard their comments and took their questions and named the flowers for them. The yellow, he told them, are cinquefoil and the whites, arctic gentian and sandwort. And there, he pointed to the mulch of a pine floor, the columbine. They stopped and marvelled at it.

"It's beautiful," said Claudia. "A little orchid. The sculptured shape is so satisfying. It asks to be held."

Charles agreed. While he was reticent by nature, in the thin air he spoke even less. He was having trouble breathing. Slatkin realized it and spoke to the guide, who slowed down the party without any mention.

Other than Charles, everyone maintained an easy patter. Molderer told them there were fifty-four peaks in Colorado over fourteen thousand feet. Eventually he hoped to climb them all.

Claudia gained enthusiasm with the altitude. She found herself lightened by the thin air, as if it were gravity and not oxygen that was in short supply. She watched the others. Some people like Molderer and Slatkin seemed to thrive in it. Slatkin especially seemed quick to adapt, strong and sure in his step. Poor Charles was having a tough go of it.

They emerged from timberline at about ten thousand feet. Now they were in a landscape without shelter or relief. They crossed a field of large boulders, many the height of a man. The traverse required a series of balancing moves. Sometimes one could lean against a rock and step from one rounded surface to the next, but as often one had to take a small leap, alighting on the new perch and leaving it for the next. Charles was becoming increasingly winded. No one else seemed to be affected.

At the guide's insistence, when they had crossed the field, Charles sat and rested. The guide passed a water bottle among them. The couple from Texas had gone on.

"It can be tough at this altitude if you're not used to it," the guide said in an attempt to put Charles at his ease.

"Charles just arrived yesterday," Claudia offered in his defense. "From sea level."

"That really makes a difference," Slatkin agreed. "You do this every day for a month, why, you'll be carrying us up." They all smiled. Charles was thankful for the laugh. He didn't want his condition to sap the fun from the day.

"Have you done much hiking?" the European Molderer asked him.

"Only when I was young," he said. "Only in my youth." It was an exaggeration. Charles had never liked exertion. At summer camp he avoided the organized hikes, staying back to stencil the outlines of leaves on to construction paper.

"Ah, our youth," Slatkin said grandly. "When we lay our plans, the foundations for our lives, and the wives of our friends."

Charles was surprised by the bluntness of Slatkin's manner. But if he feared for Claudia's sense of propriety, he needn't have. She was amused by the remark, and she encouraged him.

"Why, Mr. Slatkin. You sound like a cynic." She was affected by the vastness of the spaces around them, felt their expansiveness and the freedom of the air.

"It's Jeremy," he said. "In Southern California it's a misdemeanor to call anyone mister. Not cynical, I don't think. Perhaps realistic, with a splash of overexposure."

"Too much sun and avocado," Charles said. He was recovering. He rose to his feet and they resumed the hike.

Now they climbed a long slope of loose scree, scrambled over rocks that gave and rolled as they went up. Look below you, the guide cautioned, to make sure you're not kicking the mountain down on someone coming along behind us. But the mountain was theirs, the day was theirs, and when they looked around at the mute peaks that surrounded their goal, they could have been the only people on the face of the earth.

As they ascended Charles felt increasingly worse. His shortness of breath remained—he could never seem to get any air in his lungs. He became heady, dizzy, and began to feel a sense of forboding about their safety. They stopped for lunch. Everyone else ate heartily. The guide questioned him and reluctantly he described his symptoms.

"Altitude sickness," the guide said. "A sense of ill-being and light-headedness. If it doesn't get better, let me know and we'll take you down."

Charles had no intention of spoiling the trip for the group. He had formed a spontaneous loyalty to these people, common among those who undergo an ordeal together. For it was his perception that the outing was an ordeal and that they were in some unspoken danger. He forced down half of a granola bar and an orange. Food didn't seem to help.

The climbing party crossed a rock-strewn couloir. The guide pointed out the morain, where the glacier had stopped, deposited its loose rock and debris, and receded, leaving a long U-shaped valley down to the Roaring Fork River below. Usually Meredith would have loved this experience, and he scolded himself for his inadequate body and his inability to keep up. Still the foreboding and the dizziness continued.

As the hike sapped Charles' strength it nourished Claudia's. She and Slatkin walked easily ahead, the guide and Molderer next, Charles last. She found the altitude liberating. Might she climb high enough so she would float away, so she would fly?

They arrived at the single stretch the guide had warned might have some peril. Before one got to the final approach, he had told them, there was a long ridge. It was perfectly easy to cross, being the width of a sidewalk without, this with a wink at Charles, without New Yorkers to jostle you off it. Anyone who would feel more secure, anyone who wanted to, he'd belay: rope up to himself. So long as you paid attention, though, there was no danger.

They stood at the mouth of that rubbly path. The guide was saying something about safety. Charles had envisioned a sidewalk, a lane of smooth cement leading to the summit much as the yellow brick road in the movie. What he saw was a knife edge, serrated by boulders the size of beachballs, and falling off on either side a thousand feet into bluish air. In his mind's eye, he saw the entire party floating down, one by one, a long rope attached to the first and all of them going over the edge like a link of sausages. And then he fainted.

Molderer had been standing behind him and caught his body by the armpits. They lowered him to the ground. The guide propped Meredith's feet up, pulled a metallic blanket from a rucksack to cover him, and vigorously rubbed his hands. In a matter of seconds he opened his eyes. The ring of faces that looked down at him, outlined against the ring of mountains, made him think of Mount Rushmore and he said so. There was a murmer of laughter and relief.

The guide wanted Charles to retreat to a lower altitude but felt obliged not to leave the Texas couple alone on the summit. Claudia volunteered to take him down, and Slatkin and Molderer insisted on coming along. Charles protested weakly—not that he was insincere, but rather weak—and they were resolute. Molderer said that he would come back later to climb this peak, now that he knew the way. He had been doing several a week, he told them, and had heard that this needed a guide because of the ridge. Now that he'd seen it, though, he knew he could do it alone.

Slowly the party of four descended. By the time they were in the trees Charles had fully recovered. Nausea was replaced by embarrassment, but his companions relieved him of it by assuring him that he had had a common experience among climbers and that it boded well. He was now on his way to becoming a serious mountaineer.

"But I deprived you of getting to the top," he insisted.

"Nonsense," said Jeremy. "You know what they say about the bear who went over the mountain. Tops are tedious. Am I right?" he asked Molderer, who agreed.

"Besides, you know what we'll find there?" Slatkin went on. "Tensing and Hillary. Doing a car commercial."

Charles insisted that they come to dinner that night with him and his wife. He included the Abbotts, of course, because they were planning to dine as a foursome. Molderer declined, citing some official function. Slatkin, whom they had discovered was single, accepted. They arranged to meet that night at the Merediths' house in town.

Claudia drove Charles back to his house and made sure he was well enough before leaving him alone. She thanked him for including Jeremy Slatkin. "It's a way of keeping the day from ending," she told him. "Jeremy's presence will be our souvenier of the climb."

Evelyn and Weemo, back from golf, were also pleased to have a newcomer joining them. Charles insisted on cooking the dinner at their little house. It was fully equipped, he pointed out, and had a charming dining table in a cove room that might perfectly fit five or six. His motives were not singular. He felt an uncommon remorse at the day's happenings. Halfway up the mountain he had sensed that the outing might feed a particular curiousity he had developed about nature's more remote places. To date his interest had been in the lush, the occupied, the fecund. He recognized that some other message might be found on those high peaks, and he wanted very much to get there. Too, a quiet dinner might give him a moment alone with Claudia, which to date he'd barely had. Less than five minutes in a bounding jeep leaving town. And finally he enjoyed cooking. It was solitary work. It was precise, utile. Not unlike the drafting of wills.

Evelyn and he shopped, while Weemo, for his contribution, organized the kitchen and bar and set the table. He looked forward, he told Charles and Claudia, to meeting their mysterious Levantine.

Jeremy Slatkin proved the perfect complement to their group. He was witty, fun-loving, gregarious. He told them over cocktails that he was a private investor. That meant, he said, he'd been lucky more than once in a row, and now he got to live by his wits.

They were sitting on the screened porch of the bungalow as the sun set. Charles was in the kitchen, preparing an elaborate spaghetti sauce.

"How dramatic," said Weemo. "Don't we all?"

"No dear," Claudia said softly. "Thank God the Abbotts don't have to live by our wits or there's no telling how we'd eat. We live by our capital."

Slatkin noticed the space in conversation and deftly filled it.

"I enjoy business," he said. "But not as a steady diet. Three or four hours a day is all I can do well. After that it's like a tourist's overdose of cathedrals. You find you're merely trudging through Gothic halls."

Claudia saw that Slatkin could fend for himself. She left him with Weemo and Evelyn and went to the back of the house where Charles was dicing a clove of garlic to put in the sauce. He was unconscious of her. On the gas stove, over a low heat that shone blue in the dim light of the kitchen, an enormous skillet bubbled and spat. He chopped and manipulated the garlic with a great flourish, the way he imagined a television chef might. All the while he was singing. "Seems Like Old Times." Charles knew the words and while his tenor trembled in the upper registers and gave way to breathiness in the lower notes, his voice was quite true.

When he turned, she was leaning against the door jamb, smiling at him.

"What are you smiling at?" he asked, grinning.

"You," she said. "I'm smiling at you."

He didn't respond. Instead he watched her for a moment, turned back to the stove. He knew he needed to talk to her about the Parine trusts and his work, but he chose not to do so then. They said very little. The fragrance of the sauce filled the room. When it was ready, he told her and she assembled the others at the table.

The dinner was festive. Slatkin had brought several bottles of an excellent wine and they drank all but one. He made everyone laugh, with an easy, lambent wit that was telling but not familiar. It was as if he had known them all for years, and known how they teased, flattered, taunted each other. By the end of the evening, he had been included. He had entered the elipse that was their particular course. No one could be sure whether he had joined it or been pulled into it by their gravity. But by the end of the evening they accepted him as if he had been there all along, like the moon that now rose behind Ajax Mountain, that they saw, each with his own thoughts, as they stood on the screened porch of the rented house and said goodnight.

Chapter Eleven

From the Journal

I welcomed the introduction of Jeremy Slatkin into our little family. He was a lively addition, and as a bonus, a student of serious music. It was the music festival that brought him every summer to Aspen, just as, when he'd lived in the East, he had spent a month each year at Tanglewood. He told us that the next day, as he, Claudia and I walked down the gravel path towards the music tent for a mid-day, all-Bach concert.

The tent was a blue and white construction, designed Jeremy told us by Eero Saarinen. It sat in the middle of a broad meadow—they call them parks in the west. The hills that surround the tent act as sounding boards. The music bounces off and percolates up through the mountain air, and many people sit outside the tent on blankets to listen to the concert. The entire setting was one of informality and openness. I had never been to a Bach concert in walking shorts, I observed. "More's the pity," Slatkin said and to my surprise I could already agree.

It seemed that Claudia and I might never find time alone, and so as we walked the tree-lined path towards the tent's entrance I touched her lightly at the elbow and asked if I might have a word with her before we went in. My tone was not quite sotto voce but unmistakably confidential. To his credit that was all that Slatkin needed and he went ahead to secure our seats. I wonder now whether I could have foreseen the role he was to play, when his conduct at the time seemed so remote and—the very word tags me as an ingenue—decorous. I told Claudia that I had looked at the adoption question, but my research had been inconclusive, that I could not predict with certitude whether a court challenge to the language might succeed. And I suggested that there was no reason not to inquire how her brother saw the trust's odd provision.

She listened without expression. "Let's put it to Gordon, then, shall we? He's invited us for drinks this afternoon at his Red Mountain manse. You and Evelyn must see it. It's one of the local sights. I thought I'd ask Jeremy to come along too."

I was surprised by her lack of guile, mistaking it for ignorance about the ways of the world. In fact it marked not ignorance but impatience. She was only now deciding to change the construct of property and legalisms that structured her life and locked her into it. Her eagerness caught me unprepared, and I suggested that broaching the subject with Gordon should be carefully planned. If he didn't know about the different interpretations of the will, we should plan for his possible reactions, think it through. She said, no, that she wanted simply to raise it and see what he said.

"I've really got two fences to jump, haven't I? If I divorce Weemo, then it doesn't matter about this adoption question, does it?"

"True," I answered. "But look at it another way. If Gordon concedes the adoption point, or if you beat him in court on it, you might want to consider waiting seven years and taking under the trust." She nodded at my words, took my arm and steered me into the tent. We filed in with the crowd. Jeremy was standing in the middle section, waving us to the seats he had saved. I thought the subject was closed, but as we neared our row she spoke to me in the hushed tones people assume before concerts or church.

"Six and a half," she said. "Besides, Charles, there have been developments from our talks on the beach. They make me think even a six-and-a-half year wait is too long. We'll put it to Gordon this evening over drinks."

We settled in by Slatkin for the Fourth Brandenberg. Although it is a piece I particularly enjoy, during the first movement its familiarity let me ponder what developments Claudia *had in mind. She hadn't said developments* since *our talk. She'd said,* from.

But by the slow movement my thoughts had washed away in the grandeur of the music. The second half of the program was equally beautiful, a liturgical cantata the name of which I can't recall. It doesn't matter.

In combination, the resonance of the music we heard that afternoon and the imprint of the mountains, like the spot of sun on the inner eye, turned my thoughts to a single focus. I forgot about my article on the fruit of Eden, about the vagaries of James Parine's trust, even about my own nagging discomfort about fitting into a world that seems to accept far odder shapes.

The music—it doesn't matter what it was, but I should like to find the name of that cantata—was so manifestly the most sombre, the highest articulation of man's efforts. I do not mean that my thought was the commonplace observation of man's insignificance. Mine was doubtless as trite, but it was the opposite. If you wanted to converse with God, wouldn't you need to create a language? And Bach had done just that, created a language worthy of the attempt.

And yet how inadequate. Exalted, yes. Majestic, echoing in the human ear with universal intimations. But no more successful than the whir of a kitchen blender, the honk of a taxi.

After the music and before the encore, I left my friends in the tent and walked in the meadow. The afternoon light had begun to polarize, so that as one looked north the sky took on a blue so deep it seemed not to end. Not even with the stratosphere. And my single insight, as I walked away from the thin voice of a violin followed by the rumble of an appreciative audience, was this: that the sounds of the world's beings push out the voices they seek. The sounds of God's creatures, their matings and machines, cries of labor, joy, grief, rush to fill the vacuum of the hum of nature, the hum of the absence of sound.

* * * * *

Every year, one grand new house is the focus of Aspen's attention—for extravagance here is a tribal sacrament—and this year's was Gordon Parine's. When the Merediths arrived, the rest of their party was there. The house had been pointed out to Charles that first day on the tour with Weemo, but still he carefully followed Claudia's instructions, crossing the bridge at the bottom of the hill, bearing to the right and easing around sharp-angled switchbacks, keeping the gas flowing lest the rental car stall on the steep grade. Each curve revealed the backs of houses set into the mountain like perches, so that their facades faced Ajax Mountain, with its groomed slopes, and the hatchet-shaped peaks of Pyramid, Hagerman and the twin Maroon Bells. Claudia and Weemo's house sat at the foot of the mountain, around the first curve.

Claudia had told Charles to drive until he was blinded by the reflection. In fact the sun was setting when he got to the new Parine house, but the figure of speech Claudia had used was telling. The Parine house glowed, its glass wings stretched on the top ledge of the mountain like a raptor ready for take-off.

Gordon Parine met them at the door. That he bore no physical resemblence to his sister was not illogical, since he was a natural child and she adopted. Nevertheless, Charles was surprised at the difference in temperament their appearences suggested. Gordon was rubicund, with a reddish complexion and brick-colored hair that went to orange, while Claudia's red highlights went to brown. The contrast could not have been more extreme. Gordon's complexion and body type were beefy, excessive. His skin seemed sensitive to light, and the high flush of his face was due, Charles guessed, not entirely to sun. He had fat hands, and his forearms were thick, like Popeye's, but not muscular. His arms extended from the rolled-up sleeves of a khaki shirt, and they were covered with downy yellow hair.

His behaviour similarly set him apart from Claudia. He was at once gruff and outgoing, as if those traits were struggling within him to win and only one would prevail. He took Meredith and Evelyn by the fleshy part of the arm, one in each hand, and all but carried them through the enormous living room onto a deck overlooking a swimming pool and the whole town of Aspen, guiding them lest they were too feeble to navigate the deep pile of the carpet on their own.

"I'm in a good mood, Charley. I just settled a matter with my neighbor there that's been in my craw." He nodded beyond the deck to a simple log shack across the way. It sat directly in line with their view of the mountains.

"A local character. Does odd jobs for my sister. I've finally settled with the old bird." A Spanish-looking woman in an apron appeared and took their drink orders. "Owns that property, looks like a dump. It's a damn eyesore, and I'm going to tear it down," Gordon said. His ardor suggested that he might mean that very afternoon, with his bare hands, as soon as he had finished his Campari and soda.

"Well," said Charles. The phrase came out as an astonishment.

"Congratulations," Evelyn said, sensing the victory in Parine's tone. It was the right comment, and as a reward he turned his attention to her. Charles slipped off and joined the Abbotts and Slatkin. They were talking to an attractive young woman with long brown hair. She was introduced to Charles as Gordon's wife. She wore a cranberry jogging suit with "Jocelyn" stitched in script on the chest, and wrapped around her tanned forehead she wore a bright pink band, like an Indian squaw.

"Nice place," Jeremy was saying. "Be it ever so humble."

She told them of its planning, its construction, its furnishing, and the long and—only today—victorious fight to get rid of their neighbor's house. "Gordon wants his house to be perfect," she said. Jeremy and Claudia told of their plans to lead another mountain expedition, but at a reasonable altitude, and invited everyone to go along. Claudia said to Charles she especially hoped he'd come. He agreed to. Weemo and Jocelyn declined. Weemo said he was enjoying the golf courses too much, and Jocelyn said that she liked to run up mountains, and that once you've done that, walking wasn't fun.

Another round of drinks was served, the same woman passing a tray of pretty hors d'œuvres. Jocelyn volunteered to lead a tour of the house, and several guests set off with her. Charles stayed behind purposefully, hoping that Claudia might too. Instead, a pleasant alternative, he found himself alone on the deck. He walked to the corner of the decking, where a hummingbird feeder hung from a miniature post and boom. It was built of the same cedar as the sun deck. He looked around. Three other feeders were installed symmetrically at the corners of the railing. Each had a plastic tube with yellow knobs at the bottom formed to look like petals. Sugar-water, colored red to attract birds, filled the tube. Around the contraption as Charles watched, two birds fluttered and fed. He believed they were either the Rufous or the Broad-tailed, and muttered to himself for not bringing his book. The Broad-tailed would go on his life list. He observed them carefully. If you could spot the sighting points, you stood a better chance of making a positive identification when you got the guide in hand. In bird-watching, one never had too many facts. How would one draw them, he wondered, their flight? The conventional way is to blur their wings, just as the wings look to us. A high-speed shutter could catch them as if they weren't moving. Neither picture was accurate, he thought. What had John Audubon done?

Gordon Parine came up behind him. "Are you a bird watcher," he asked in jest.

"Yes," Charles replied. He was startled but did not turn. "I like birds."

"So do I. Medium rare." It wasn't Gordon's laughter that induced Charles to yield his watch, but rather the familiar nudging of his arm. He felt it would be rude to continue to ignore Parine.

"Claudia tells me you're a hot shot New York lawyer."

"Hardly a hot shot. Just a lawyer."

"What field?" Charles realized suddenly that he was heading for an important conversation, and on his host's terms. It was the second time that day he'd been caught off guard by a Parine.

"Trusts and estates." Charles said the words as if they were an admission. His tone invited the next question.

"And you're doing some work for Claudia?"

Had she told him, or had he guessed? In either event, she had wanted the subject raised, and this, Charles consoled himself, though he knew it not to be true, was as good a time as any. He wished Claudia would return.

"I am. I've been looking at the trusts your grandfather set up."

"Ah, yes. The famous James Parine Trusts. The bony hand of the great man pointing the way from the grave. And what do you make of them?"

"What do you?" Charles asked.

Parine took a draught of his highball and smacked his lips before answering. He was several inches shorter than Charles and looked up at him, but there was nothing deferential in his posture.

"The trusts speak for themselves. Isn't that what you lawyers say? The language speaks for itself."

"That's what we say when it's accurate. When it's clear that the author of the language made his intent explicit, when he anticipated all the circumstances."

Gordon Parine regarded him. His eyes showed humor but his face locked in an expression of quite a different, sombre sentiment. Meredith was unsure whether Parine was on to the issue that he had discovered. The man's next words dispelled any doubt.

"Well, Charley. That's exactly what we have, isn't it? 'Heirs of the body.' Couldn't be clearer."

Charles considered his response and decided to say more. "Clarity might depend on what the draftsman knew at the time, what your grandfather told him. A lot might depend on your lawyers, the ones who drafted this trust."

"Oh, no. Not my lawyers. Parine Pen's lawyers. If you want to speak to my lawyers, you'll have to look up these fellows." And he removed a business card from the pocket of his safari shirt and handed it to Charles. There was printed the name, at once recognized by Charles, of a New York lawyer. One who could not, would not have disclaimed the title of hotshot with which Gordon had teased Charles.

"You're represented in this?" Charles asked.

"I am."

"Then we shouldn't be discussing the matter. I should take this up directly with . . ." and he looked at the card though he knew the name on it, ". . . Mr. Stillman."

Gordon gave a slightly theatrical bow. Charles turned again to the rail and changed the subject.

"Your view from here is marvellous," he said. "Really quite perfect."

The others returned from the tour, exclaiming on the beauty of the house. Gordon seemed genuinely pleased. Charles signalled Claudia to the side and told her that he and Gordon had spoken. "We should meet," he said. "The game is afoot."

Tomorrow, she told him. They would take a walk by the river. An easy walk, not another climb. And she would bring a picnic. She'd invited everyone. Jeremy was coming, but not Weemo or Evelyn.

They said their goodbyes to Gordon and Jocelyn Parine and left the glass aerie for their own houses.

The next day began like all the others, cloudless and blue. But by eleven o'clock, the hour appointed to begin the walk down the Roaring Fork canyon, a black cloud had appeared from the northwest, from behind Gordon Parine's privileged mountain, and an icy rain had begun to fall. The telephone rang in the Merediths' frame house. Weemo was inquiring about other plans. The freak storm had ruined golfing, and the few indoor tennis courts were taken by those who had heard the weather report. Apparently it was snowing in the mountains, snow or sleet, so everyone was in town. Charles suggested the art museum: it had a retrospective hung by Leo Castelli, the famous gallery owner, with many of the great moderns Castelli had discovered. To Meredith's great surprise, Weemo agreed. Evelyn too.

But the Abbotts didn't show up. Charles and Evelyn toured the show. Slatkin walked around with them. Claudia had decided to stay home and listen to music. Weemo met the Merediths as they came out of the museum to tell them. He was going into town to do some shopping. He assured Charles that their river hike was on for the next day.

Though in fact it got postponed again. That evening, as Charles and Evelyn sat by a cracking fire and the last of the rain fell outside, Claudia called.

"Charles. Did you watch the news?" she asked hurriedly.

"No. I didn't think there was news in Aspen."

"I turned it on to get the local weather. For the hike. That's where I heard. There's been an accident. A man slipped on the Maroon Bells. He got caught in the snow, climbing alone, and fell. He's dead."

"How awful," said Charles.

"It was that man Molderer," she said. "The one who was on our climb. Do you remember?"

Yes, Charles remembered. It seemed so unlikely he asked whether Claudia was sure.

"Yes," she said petulantly. "Yes of course. They said he was a mathematician. From the University of Chicago. Here for the Institute. There's a service for him tomorrow at the Community Church. The large redstone one off Main Street. Do you know it?"

Charles said that he did. They rang off. Charles could make nothing of the news. Molderer was only barely in his circle of acquaintence, and he found himself touched more by astonishment than by grief. He called Slatkin, who also had heard the news on the radio, and arranged to meet him in front of the church for the service. He suggested to Evelyn that she go along, but she declined, pointing out what Charles knew, that she had never met the man.

Chapter Twelve

Perhaps it was the chill in the rain that had fallen the day before. Perhaps that caused it. Whatever it was, when Charles arrived at the squat redstone church the next morning for the funeral, he sensed the woody smell of autumn. The sky had been washed clean to a brilliant blue, and as he looked beyond the church, in the unfiltered light the heavens seemed to be glazed with a porcelain surface. He wore the coat and tie Weemo had teased him about that first day in Aspen. The congregation were of all ages, and they dressed in every manner from black suits of mourning to jeans and climbing shoes.

Jeremy was waiting for him at the entry hall. They went in and walked up groaning wood steps to the main nave on the second floor. Charles remarked on the crowd. Most had their faces set against any sociability. Had anyone known Molderer? he wondered. Was he no more to everyone there than a day's climbing companion?

The church was laid out in the English style, two aisles making for three blocks of pews. Many people were already seated. An organist played a Haydn piece Charles knew but could not name. As he and Slatkin stepped forward, a young man in a navy cotton suit handed each of them a folded sheet. On the inside left page was a blurry photograph of Molderer and, crudely printed opposite, the program for the service.

"There," Jeremy said in a whisper. "There are two seats over there."

They were shown to the back pew. A couple arriving late forced them to slide in from the aisle. To Charles' mind, they had the worst possible vantage. Had they kept their place on the aisle, he might see her come in or, when the congregation

exited, see her leave. That was more likely. From a station by
the aisle in the rear one could watch the entire crowd exit.
The woman who had just settled beside him reached down
and swung out the bench, and she and her husband knelt.
Jeremy sat quietly, reading the pamphlet. Charles stretched
his neck and examined the crowd. It was of no use. He could
not distinguish the backs of the well-groomed heads from
each other. Perhaps, he thought, if he studied each one. He
began in the pew in front of him, his eyes alighting on the
hair of each woman until he decided it wasn't she, then moving on. He had completed an inventory of three pews just
this way, when the minister came forward and as a person
the congregation stirred and rose.

The service began. It was the funeral service from the
Book of Common Prayer. Charles had sat through it a dozen
times, maybe two. When they stood for the first hymn, Come
Thou Almighty King, he continued his inspection. His height
gave him a slight advantage, and by rocking forward on his
toes, he was able to see several pews further on.

"'Come and reign over us, all o'er victorious . . .'"

Charles heard Jeremy's deep voice and it caught him up
in unconscious song. He looked down to find the hymn book
in his hand, opened, but to another page entirely. It didn't
matter. The verses came back to him from some cubbyhole
of memory.

Some one who knew Molderer spoke, described him as a
brilliant theoretician and a great humanist. Then the minister spoke, about how we should take this most antic event
without complaint, but with grief. Charles exhausted his efforts to find her.

A second hymn was sung. Once to Every Man and Nation.
Again he was conscious of Jeremy's voice, of the pleasure in
it. He noticed one or two heads turn, and he sang more
loudly, as if to participate with his friend and save him any
embarrassment. It wasn't necessary. The congregation sang
all four verses, Jeremy right along, alternating between the
melody line and the baritone.

The Lord's Prayer, then a short benediction, and the service was over.

The crowd was filing out. First was a young man wearing
a grey worsted wool suit, Charles guessed a relative, come out
to Colorado to claim the body and accompany it back to its

burial. The young man wore a white carnation in his lapel. Charles watched carefully, but Claudia did not appear. Only the last three pews remained. He turned to Jeremy.

"Remarkable, isn't it?"

"What's that?"

"How well behaved we all are. How we file out in order, without instructions. It's part of the ritual. Like driving in lanes."

Jeremy smiled as if he had been thinking the same thought. "It's part of the Anglo-Saxon triumph in the world. The imposition of order, civility in the face of death. Have you ever noticed how the English love their queues? At a Jewish funeral or a Greek, people are wailing. They grieve, they shriek. Here people are waiting patiently to exit, and they'll line up at the parish house reception for coffee and a piece of pound cake. Wonderful thing, civilization."

They were standing in a line that wound down the church's outdoor steps. At the bottom the minister and the relative were receiving people, briefly shaking hands and exchanging one of several comments.

"That's my favorite hymn," Jeremy said. "'Once to every man and nation comes the moment to decide.'"

Charles looked at him for a full moment. Lately he was hearing hidden messages in everyone's words. Did Jeremy intend a message in his?

"How did you get so good at Episcopal hymns?" he asked Slatkin.

"Went to a church boarding school. In Rhode Island. My parents wanted me to learn manners. Besides, it was an easier curve than where the Jewish kids went."

It wasn't until they were in the street, walking in the sunshine, that Charles mentioned her.

"I thought we'd see Claudia." The remark brought a glance from Jeremy.

"No, she told me she wasn't coming. She felt she really didn't know him, and she said she doesn't like false grief. I told her there were other reasons to come, but she said no."

The two men walked together in silence. Charles' rented house was only a few blocks to the west. He assumed Slatkin was walking to a parked car, but he didn't ask. He was happy to have the company. As it turned out Jeremy owned a house not two blocks from where the Merediths had rented.

"Charles . . ." Jeremy's tone was uncharacteristically tentative.

"Claudia told me yesterday about the legal issue. About the work you've done for her and your conversation with her brother."

Meredith pursed his lips but said nothing. Slatkin, sensitive to the gesture, responded.

"I hope you don't mind," he added.

"No," Charles said, not entirely truthfully. "I don't. I'm just a little surprised that she would share the problem with you. I mean," he added quickly, "it's a recent friendship."

"Claudia's at sea," Jeremy said. "She's trying to make large decisions and, of the people around her, half have a vested interest and half she's just met. That's why she's seized upon us as her advisors."

Charles noted Slatkin's use of the plural pronoun. Though he hadn't thought on it, he too was a recent arrival in her life. Why would she not select Slatkin as readily as a confidante? It was not in Charles' nature to resent the expansion of that status, even though that status represented his only intimacy with her.

"I gather you're considering a law suit to address the issue," Jeremy said.

"Yes," Charles answered. "Yes, I am." Slatkin was one step ahead of Claudia in his surmise, but clearly of the two he knew more of the world. "Why? Do you have any views?"

"I'm not a fan of lawsuits," the other man said. "They rarely accomplish anything, unless you're after money. And then it has to be a lot of money. The only person I know who used a lawsuit to win his lady fair was Robert Schumann. He had to sue Clara's father to prove he was worthy. The father had forbidden the match, and Schumann sued. It always seems to me a little . . ." and Slatkin paused for emphasis, a favorite mannerism of his," . . . indirect."

They had arrived at Meredith's house. Charles asked Jeremy in, but was declined. He thanked him for his words, and Slatkin turned and walked back in the direction they'd come from.

When Meredith entered the cottage, he found Weemo Abbott and his wife in the kitchen. They were readying themselves for a bicycle trip of several miles. In the front yard were parked two mountain bikes, equipped with wide tires, heavy tread for off-road use, and an elaborate gear system for hilly terrain. Weemo had bought them last year, he told Charles, but Claudia never cared for cycling. They had prepared a lunch which, as Charles and Weemo spoke, Evelyn stowed into a bright orange backpack.

"A bit overdressed, aren't you?" Weemo asked him in a friendly tone. The comment was one Meredith expected of him, but he had no reply ready. He knew it was meant as a joke, but he didn't care for jokes at others' expense and he viewed this, however mildly intended, as directed at him. He liked Weemo. That he considered him shallow and his marriage to Claudia an impediment to her happiness didn't prevent him from liking the man. And so his response was made in words calculated not to insult Abbott but to let him understand that the way Charles dressed was no concern of his.

"I've been to a funeral service."

Weemo raised his eyebrows, closing the subject.

"Love to have you join us," Weemo said.

"No thanks. I'm going to read, do some scribbling, just unwind."

Evelyn put plastic wrap over two or three mixing bowls and replaced them in the refrigerator.

"There's crab salad and melon balls and a fresh baguette of bread for lunch," she told him. "Sourdough. We didn't know your plans so we got extra." She fetched a cotton sweater from their bedroom and tied its arms around her neck. It was lavender, and brought out the paleness of her complexion. She saw Charles watching her, and was touched by it. She came over and, standing on tip toes, kissed his cheek.

"We'll be back for cocktails," she assured him. "Claudia called to ask whether you wanted to go to the concert this afternoon. Moderns, she said. I forget who. And then we've planned to go out to that dude ranch tonight for a cookout. Sound good?"

"Yes. Sounds good," Charles said. "I'll be fine. You go ahead."

They boarded their bikes and pedalled slowly out of town. They were on their way to a side road only a few miles from Aspen that turned to the south and followed a creek on a gentle ascent some fifteen miles into the forest. There stood the remains of an old mining town, in a broad park among cottonwood trees and red willows. It was a favorite picnic spot of Weemo's. He had ridden there often before.

They talked of books as they rode. Not of any particular book, but of the fact of them.

"I don't know how he can stay indoors and read on a day like this," Evelyn said. "I've never found a book as much fun as a ride in the countryside."

Weemo agreed. "I find books tiresome. Of course, most people won't admit that. They think they are supposed to like them. I find them tiresome, and I didn't have to read a lot of them to make up my mind."

Weemo breathed deeply and felt exhilarated by the air and by his observation. Evelyn was so good for him. And she loved athletics as much as he did. The perfect companion. Interesting about women, he thought. Pacing was important. When he ran track he avoided pacing. He liked the four-forty because it was a dash. His high school coach always called it the longest dash. All out and hope to make it to the wire. You didn't have to worry about pacing. But in marriage, even in an affair, if it went on too long, pacing was important.

Early in their romance, that week at Elbow Reef, he had cautioned Evelyn to try not to exaggerate their relationship. Don't try to make this into something it's not, he'd said. And she had understood him exactly. It was so refreshing. She had what he considered a man's view of these matters.

His affairs were important to him, and he would never think of giving them up. He had always put effort into them and had, he felt, given of himself. But he also recognized in his private moments how transitory were their benefits, and how inevitable their tedium. One went from panting to yawning. Bicycling in between helped.

* * * * *

Charles took out the food Evelyn had left behind and fixed himself a light lunch. When he was finished he washed the few dishes in the sink, electing that over the dishwasher whose noise he disliked, and wiped them dry with a cotton towel depicting various butterflies. He spread the towel on the kitchen counter to let it dry and looked at its pictures. He knew the names of all the butterflies it showed.

Then he telephoned Claudia. Yes, she had called about the concert but also she wanted to see him. They hadn't had any time, she agreed, and they had so much to talk over. He got in the rental car and drove the mile or so to her house.

The Abbotts' house, just up from the base of Red Mountain, was from a different era than Gordon Parine's. It had been built in the early years of Aspen's post-war boom, at a time when many owners of great wealth thought that its best display was Protestant simplicity. Claudia wanted a structure akin to the Adirondack cottage she remembered her father owning, plank construction with green asphalt roofing and screened porches. Her house was the Western equivalent. Screening wasn't necessary, since at eight thousand feet there was little distress from insect life. But the rest of the house fit her recollection. It was a wood structure, tongue-in-groove boards left unfinished and stained, not painted, with a dark oil. The rear of the house was set into the mountain, and there were the service rooms: laundry, furnace, storage, all cold cement and windowless. In the front, because of the cant of the hill, the living room stood some ten feet off the ground and was supported by large pilings, the girth of telephone poles. The house fit neatly into the hill, as if it had been carved for the foundation. To the west, where the land leveled slightly in a natural bench, a flagstone terrace had been laid, surrounded by a wall of square cut redstone and a barbeque pit the size of an upright piano.

Claudia was waiting for him on the terrace. She wore tan shorts and a sleeveless blouse, and sunglasses against the high sun. He recognized the pattern of lilac branches on her blouse from their first week together.

She poured him a tall glass of iced tea, and served it with a sprig of fresh mint. They sat on padded lawn furniture, both facing the sun.

"I want to tell you my thoughts," she said. "But first tell me what you've found out. And what Gordon said to you about the trust."

He started talking. To his great joy, they soon lapsed into that privacy of conversation they had enjoyed six months ago.

Now that he had more facts before him, he told her, he was no more able to predict the outcome of the issue than before. The question of whether an adopted child is included within a class designation in an inter vivos trust—one created before the maker's death—is, as he had said, a question of the intention of the maker. Several conclusions could be drawn. In Ohio, the state whose law would control this issue, it was clear that historically the phrase her grandfather had used, "heirs of the body," excluded adopted children. Before her grandfather's death but after the date of the trust, Ohio had passed an adopted-child statute, similar to laws now in every other jurisdiction. It said that, unless a will or trust explicity excludes adopted children, they are to be treated the same as natural children.

Now the questions: first, did her grandfather or the lawyer who wrote the will know what "heirs of the body" meant, or did they simply take the language because that was the form of document they used? Next, did they know that the law was changed before James Parine's death, and thus intend that their language be interpreted to gather all grandchildren together? Another complication. Claudia was adopted after the date of the trust but before her grandfather died. Could any evidence be found—letters from the grandfather, conversations with the lawyer—that showed his approval of her, his affection towards her? We needn't find anything special, Charles said, merely equal treatment. That would show that he didn't distinguish during his lifetime among his natural and adopted grandchildren, and that he didn't intend to distinguish after death.

"We'll really have two arguments," Charles told her. "One is pretty legalistic, and I have to tell you I don't like it. We would argue that the term 'heir' means one who is entitled to a gift. The law is pretty clear that you're not an heir until you become entitled. So we would argue that when the potential gift to an adoptive child as an heir occurs at a time in the future, like this one, then the law at the time of the gift should control rather than the law at the time of execution.

"But that's a bloodless argument, and it will be rebutted by the other side—assuming there is another side—saying we're distorting the intent of James Parine. Far better if we could find evidence that James Parine, if he were standing in court, would say to the judge, I've always intended to include Claudia. I want her treated as I treat all my grandchildren."

"Then that's the argument we shall use," said Claudia.

"The difficulty with it is proof. Unless you can find more than you've sent me so far, we'll have to get evidence from the lawyers who prepared the trust. And, as you know, they are the lawyers for Parine Pen."

"And for Gordon," she added.

"Curiously, no. Gordon has hired special counsel for this question. An excellent firm. It's a canny move. He wants the Cincinnati firm to have the appearance of independence in case their testimony is necessary to show what James Parine meant."

"But Gordon is their major client. Surely any judge will see that."

Charles was noncommittal. "The judge may. There's nothing to be done about that. The real question is whether that firm's files contain anything that will help us, and if so, whether we will be able to find it out."

He then told her word for word of his conversation with Gordon. It was clear that her brother not only knew of the language but had explored its ambiguity with Mr. Stillman, his lawyer.

"You didn't ask Gordon, Charles, whether he would in fact oppose me on this?" Her tone was remonstrative, less like a client's than a schoolteacher's to a favorite but forgetful pupil.

"I didn't. I thought we should talk first. And I think that propriety indicates I should deal only through Mr. Stillman from here out. I know him, and I can call him directly."

As he spoke he saw a flutter in the tall pines below. Noticing his start, Claudia rose and went inside. She returned with the pitcher of tea and a pair of field glasses. She refilled his drink and handed the binoculars to him wordlessly. He put them to his eyes.

"Only a junco, I think."

"I've spotted several of them," she said. "I've only just put out seed to see what else we can attract." She pointed down the hill to a rough-cut tray feeder mounted on a greying stump.

"I haven't spotted much in town," Charles said. "We have a family of magpie in back of the house. The loud birds scare off the smaller ones."

He handed her the glasses and she scanned the horizon.

"I see no need for you to call Stillman from here," she said as she looked. "It's your vacation. But I would like to know what they say."

"Bear in mind, Claudia, that we must act to prevail. If we do nothing, the trustee has the right to construe the trust literally and, in seven years, preclude you from the distribution. The burden will be on us to go into court, in Cincinnati with Parine's lawyers probably testifying for Gordon, and prove that you're entitled."

"I understand," she said quietly. They sat in silence for several minutes. Down the valley to the west, clouds were forming from the afternoon's thermal convection. It seemed to happen daily. Clouds gathered in darkening masses and threatened rain. Most evenings they blew over, leaving the night sky clear for stars.

"You mentioned developments," he said at last.

"I've thought a great deal of our times on the beach at Elbow Reef," she replied.

"As have I."

"I can't tell you what they've meant to me. What is the word?" she asked, pausing but too briefly to allow an answer. "Happiness is silly. Peace is better, I think, or satisfaction. Not only from knowing you. From seeing myself with some perspective. It's as if I passed over this little rill, not a mountain, just a wrinkle in the landscape. And now I'm on the other side. I've gone from thinking that life was too long to thinking it's too short. All these years I've worried about my son and my husband and what they needed. Suddenly I know I have to determine what I want and then get it. That sounds so elemental, I wonder you sit and listen to me. Does that sound odd?"

"No," Charles said, though he wasn't sure what she was asking. He glanced at his watch. If they were to go to the concert, they ought to be leaving. He was content to stay.

"It's curious, isn't it?" he said. He looked out at a spectacular scape of rock and sky. "Life's paths seem to take us further and further away from the center. Like the veins in a leaf. We find ourselves in a destination so remote that we've never chosen and we can never retrace our steps."

Claudia didn't respond for a while. When she did, her words were exact. "We don't have to retrace our steps to change. We merely have to change."

Charles lay back in the chaise. His eyes were closed to the sun's disc and he watched the yellow-black image of it on the back of his lids slide out of view. He thought briefly of his skin's sensitivity but did nothing about it.

When Claudia spoke again, she dropped the note of chastisement from her voice.

"You remember our talks about the peregrine falcon, Charles. You told me how they learn to fly. Some of them don't, I suspect. You were too much a gentleman to tell me about those. I'm just getting ready to dive off the cliff. It's got a bit of terror to it.

"Does any of this make sense to you?" she asked earnestly.

"Of course," he said. "It makes elegant sense." They sat silently, as they had on the beach. With his eyes closed, he might have been drawn into the sun, its heat. He'd been told that at this altitude, the air filtered out less ultra-violet light and he imagined he could feel those rays. As if he and Claudia were floating. Would they be drawn to each other like leaves on the surface of a pond, drawn by some indiscernible but compelling force, a capillary attraction?

"Do you think it's true we're going to crash into the sun?" he asked her.

"Mmm," she said. "What a lovely way to go."

"And do you think God's hand will reach down before we do and pluck off the righteous and the just?"

She laughed softly. "Will He? Or will He make the sinners reboard a different earth, and let the righteous and the just fry to a sizzle? Then we'll have to go around twice, and those beer ads will be wrong."

"I think we make too much of Him," she said after they had sat for a minute or two in silence. "Everyone talks of predestination and God's watchful eye. What makes us suppose He's interested in us? It's terribly presumptuous. More likely that the universe was caused by God's sneeze, all this spinning off in an absolutely haphazard way. Merely because it's left in perpetual motion isn't evidence of His caring. It's no more logical than saying that an orderly God would have cleaned up His own mess and started over again."

"I suppose we should be grateful He didn't have a tissue," Charles said.

They sat a few moments more. The concert would have started. Neither seemed interested any longer. Charles, realizing from the heat on his face that he was susceptible, rose to move to the shade. Once he had stirred, he determined it was better that he go on home. They agreed on the time and place for their evening's entertainment. It was a cook-out, Claudia said. And a square dance.

Chapter Thirteen

Their group of five—the Abbotts, the Merediths, and Slatkin—arrived at the Double Bar S that evening in festive spirits. Jeremy started them out with a mock inquisition. Whose brainless idea was this outing? Was this some part of rogue theme park? "The very idea of corn on the cob," he said archly, "is infra dig."

Amid the laughter no one would confess to thinking up the evening. So he started a competition to design the shabbiest vacation outing. Soon they were hilarious, more from laughter than wit. A limousine tour of Graceland. An Orlando luau. Weemo's entry won by acclaim: a Holiday Inn tour of the Stations of the Cross, including a complimentary mai-tai.

Despite their protests the evening was a success. They met at the stables. There five docile horses and two accomodating wranglers awaited them. They mounted and rode a short mile through a thick and verdant meadow. Their pack moved through a grove of aspen, and the wafer-thin leaves trembled from the weight of the horses' passing. Even Jeremy made the ride, despite his protest that horses were illegal if unaccompanied by a jockey. "I don't understand," he said to a young man from Durango who was the head wrangler. "I don't understand all this cowboy affection for a beast which isn't funny or edible or toilet trained."

Beyond the grove was a clearing where a campsite had been struck. There, they dismounted and watched the sun trail behind the peaks. The sky was clear of cloud and dust, and the sun went down without color, disappeared as if it had been doused. A second, larger group arrived, eight couples with name tags. The men had won a sales contest for a national auto parts company. Jeremy talked to everyone. He compared notes on restaurants in Joplin and asked a South

Dakota couple about the condition of the Corn Palace in Mitchell. Steaks were pan-fried over an open fire. There were corn and spuds cooked in the coals, baked beans from an iron kettle, beer and sweet red wine.

The wranglers picked Jeremy to sit at the head of the long picnic table. Claudia and Charles sat half-way down, facing each other. Weemo and Evelyn came through the line last and sat on stumps by the fire.

Jeremy had had enough small talk. He engaged his dinner partners in a discussion of cultural totems. The idea went around the table, and everyone was to voice an opinion on whether the West was a place or an idea. A woman from Laguna Beach, sitting at his elbow, wanted to know what he meant.

"Why would anyone want to eat ash in his food and sleep on the ground?" he asked her.

"I'm sure I don't know," she said. "I thought a totem was a pole."

"A totem is a thing that shows our attitudes," someone else said, and the woman from Laguna Beach asked Jeremy if that was right.

"On the nose," he said. "It shows your attitudes. Which produces which, I can't say, but your attitudes and your totems are intertwined."

"Give me an example," said the woman.

"Take menstruation." Here Evelyn turned from her perch by the fire and regarded him as if he had turned into soured milk.

"In some societies, it's considered unclean. In orthodox Jewry the women take a ritual bath afterwards, before they can rejoin society. While the Benin tribe think that's when a woman is most desirable. That's when you must have intercourse to stop the flow. If you don't, she'll bear a child." He looked to the woman from Laguna Beach. "I take it from your expression you side with the Jews."

Claudia spoke up. "It's simply not something we've often considered, Jeremy. I don't know that I've heard it brought up as campfire conversation before."

"Ah," Jeremy said. "Around our campfires conversation was always, Look out, here come the cossacks. Should I apologize?" he asked Claudia. From the way he spoke to her they might have been the only people there.

"Only for us," she answered, the firelight reflecting amusement and admiration in her eyes.

Afterwards the wranglers fetched the horses. Claudia stood by Charles, waiting to mount. She held her large bay mare by the reins. Since the sun had splashed out, stars had emerged from the darkness like blooms. The longer they looked up, the more appeared. Claudia shivered.

"Are you chilled?" he asked. He longed to be by her, to have his arm around her as he had that morning on the mountain.

"No," she said. "Just scared."

Charles was confused. She seemed at ease around horses. "I'm sure you could walk down if you'd rather."

Claudia was indulgent. "Not of the ride, Charles. I'm scared that this won't happen again."

They mounted and rode down the trail in groups of three and four. At the main lodge they joined up for a square dance. The owner's wife, a brawny woman with a neck the size of a calf's and a trace of a German accent, picked Jeremy as the only single male for her partner. They danced every dance, reeling and stepping, allemanding, ducking for the oyster. They were all winded, even Weemo and Evelyn, as they waited by a large, moss rock hearth in the lodge for the haywagon to take them back to where their cars were parked.

One of the ranch's countless dogs, a muddy yellow animal resembling a retriever more than anything else, wandered in amongst them and took their attention. He was an old dog and large, his head as big as a football. He circled to find a comfortable nest on the Indian rug by the hearth. He screwed closer to the ground, never quite settling his haunches, all the while groaning in complaint. It was as if he expected the floor to change its contours better to fit his shape. When no change came, he gave a sigh and settled down, instantly asleep.

Someone said the square dance was really the minuet, someone said the American pioneers had invented it, but they were too tired to argue. Weemo rose from the couch he and Claudia were on to stir the embers in the fireplace.

"It doesn't matter," Evelyn repeated. "Dances don't have ancestors, anyway."

"Neither do people, anymore," said Weemo. "Or at least it doesn't matter if they do." He stood, looking into the fire in what Claudia knew was both an unconscious and a theatrical pose. He held the poker and watched the fire reflectively.

"You sound regretful," Charles said.

"Yes, I am, I think." Weemo rapped the poker to knock the ash off a large log. The fire flared. "You can't get around breeding. That's what the wrangler was saying about horses and I think it holds true for people." It was unlike Weemo to take a strong position. Charles, unused to hearing his convictions, assumed he was merely making conversation.

"I don't believe it," Charles said. "You're having us on. No one pays any attention to lineage anymore. That went out with Tuxedo Park and the Four Hundred."

Jeremy responded. "Bravo, Charles. Spoken like a true aristocrat. You see, you're unconscious of class. It's what makes you so unmistakably classy."

The genuineness of Jeremy's statement, and the complicity it imported between the very two people who happened to be the object of Weemo's petulance, prompted his next words.

"Good old Charles and his self-effacement." Weemo's voice was stern. "Well, unfashionable as it is, I'm one who speaks up for breeding and history. Families are important. It's foolish to deny it. Foolish and crypto-democratic. It's important to know your past, to keep an eye looking behind you if you want to know where you're going."

"I suppose that's true," said Claudia, "if you happen to be in a rowboat."

The host came in and announced that the haywagon was ready. It was not too soon. Yet if there were harsh feelings among the friends, they were not remarked upon.

*   *   *   *   *

From the Journal

Considering my reflective disposition and the journey of thought on which I had embarked during those weeks in Aspen, it strikes me now as extraordinary that I have no greater recollection of poor Molderer's funeral than I do. The fact was, as Claudia pointed out, we didn't know him well, and I suppose I was moved to attend as much from a tourist's idleness as from a sense of loss. Still, he and I shared an afternoon's experience together, and he showed kindness, what's more a gratuitous kindness since he had nothing to gain, in helping to bring me down the mountain. I wondered briefly about haphazard fate. Whether, had I not been along, had not needed aid in the descent, he would have climbed Castle Peak that first day, not the next. And so whether he would have been a day's further along in his schedule, and whether he would have been off the fatal ridge and on safe ground the day of the storm.

My musings did not come, I think, out of any sense of guilt, but were instead a function of my inquiry into the way causes and effects intertwine. Is there a vast electronic circuitry that flashes binary signals at each nexus, blinking on and off and looking like the night's stars? Generating the night's stars? Or is it, as Claudia said, a giant sneeze? In any case, I have long since stopped wondering about it, and about Molderer as well.

Speculation on what might have been in world history strikes me as idle, and speculation in personal history as painful. That is not what this journal is intended to do. They say that Henry the Eighth suffered from scurvy, and that scurvy victims are irritable to the extreme. If he had been made to eat his vegetables, would he have had the need to divorce Catherine of Aragon? Would we have had the Act of Supremacy, the Protestant Reformation, the Church of England? And would Christ have cared?

Nor did I dwell too long on why, that evening at the ranch, Weemo's mood changed, seemed suddenly to become intemperate. Weemo had his dark side. I don't subscribe to the bromide, so comforting to the dissatisfied, that simplicity breeds happiness. It's equally mistaken to think that people whose motives and chemistry are different, who are for example more physical and less intellectual, that those people are indeed simpler.

I realize that Weemo had a far more subtle warning system working for him that night than had I, deeper and more sensitive. He had been married to Claudia for years, and regardless of his behavior, he was her mate. Nature's best devices rarely use what we arrogantly think of as intelligence. During that holiday Claudia, Slatkin, and I took a hike over Pearl Pass. The ranger spotted an elk herd for us, and told us about their courting and mating. How in the fall the bull elk assemble their harems by bugling for cows. I was told to listen for a deep resonance, rising to a high pitch, then a series of low grunts. That trumpet brings in the cows, and every fall the young bulls bugle to lure away a harem from the old bulls, who bugle back. The bull doesn't seem to be influenced by the fact that he has several mates He doesn't like to lose any.

The chap who told us that also said that, despite all the noise, the bulls rarely fight.

The first August we spent in Aspen I recall with great warmth. After Claudia and I had our chat, I was infused with a certainty that I could do her some good in this trust matter. It posed something of a conflict for me, since if we won on the adoption issue, she would be more likely to stay with her husband to assure the inheritance. But the important thing was to be of service. She had determined to enter the choppy waters of negotiation and had chosen me as her cicerone.

Late in my visit that year, Claudia and I took Jeremy aside and explained our thinking about the adoption issue to him. We both viewed him as a worldly fellow, since he had obviously succeeded in a variety of business ventures. He listened carefully, asking an occasional question of me or her, always on point, and he said little. He commended her for taking action, and said that she was in good hands, for he could tell I had her interests very much at heart. Those were his exact words, and whether he meant them in the full sense I cannot tell, for he never so much as looked awry during our talk. Then he offered to help in any way he could, and mentioned that he knew several people in the legal communities should I ever want to discuss strategy or tactics with anyone. I felt quite reinforced.

Jeremy was a man whose opinion I valued. He seemed to understand the motives of all of us, and I have always admired people with that insight. It puts them at the ready and prepares them for decisions in life. I wonder how he came by it, whether he decided as a child to find explanations for the way people around him acted. In contrast, I prepared for life by reading the novels of Henry James.

More vividly than anything—the picnics, the hikes, the Mahler symphonies in the tent and Handel quartets on the mall— I recall that evening at the ranch. It was the last time the five of us would be together for a while. I see her by the firelight and on her bay horse and at the dance swinging, flushed, on the crook of my arm and Weemo's. I see her standing by Jeremy and laughing. I had always thought of her as of medium height. What is a woman's height? In heels or flats? Standing, seated, urging, flirting? Leaning forward to tell you a secret?

I see her green eyes in the light of the fire, her mouth that hinted of the rest of her. Slight, ajar in anticipation, a tongue darting to moisten the lips. I see her laughing, her mouth opening wide, the light reaching to her throat, sound coming out like a fountain. She had a laugh I will not forget. It wasn't lady-like. More like a man's, it was a way of taking her pleasure. If I envied Jeremy anything, it was his capacity to make her laugh.

I see them standing by the fire that brightened as the night came on. If you painted in oils, the glint of that fire would make you want to give up your eyes. I thought of them when I got back to New York, to the grey of our life in New York. I thought of how much I liked Slatkin. And then, on a November day looking out the window of my office at the windows of other offices, I realized what I hadn't been able to see in their presence. That in large part Jeremy was my friend because we both loved the same woman.

Chapter Fourteen

From the Journal

The recollection of the warm Colorado sun sustained me that year through an uncommonly harsh autumn. Evelyn and I fell back easily into our established patterns. She involved herself with a series of parties and with new draperies for our apartment, and I had my usual matters to deal with, tracings of the living and the dead. Congress was talking about reform of the estate tax laws. It is a periodic meditation on the balance of inheritance versus endeavor, and I was called upon to give my opinion through several professional groups on the wisdom of this year's deliberation.

More and more, I found that my attention to the practice of law was intermitted by hours of woolgathering. I fiddled with my article on flora in the Bible and I sat in the cement garage by my office listening to music. I had jotted down the names of much of what we'd heard that summer in Aspen, and with the help of an excellent music store on Liberty Street downtown, I was able to get recordings of many of the works.

I noticed, too, that the strain of melancholy in which I was indulging had its effect on Evelyn. I didn't doubt that it should. One evening in December, another chill and rainy evening, we were sitting in our living room. I had put on the Waldheim Sonata, a sombre piece I had picked, as I remember, because it so suited the weather.

"I can't remember when we've had so much rain," Evelyn said to me. She looked at rain running down the window as if expecting someone to cure her predicament.

"Yes," I agreed. "We've had a lot lately."

It is Evelyn's manner to characterize any disappointment as if it were totally unexpected and without precedent. She can never remember the stores at Christmastime being so crowded, there being so many crying children aboard our flight, or such prolonged spells of humidity in the New York summer. I had early learned not to contradict her by historical example, but merely to agree. It seemed to satisfy some need that Evelyn had to believe that every inconvenience in her life was of record proportions.

It was just then that Weemo called. He was in town to do some Christmas shopping, and wanted to say hello. I answered the phone, and after checking with Evelyn insisted he come over. Within ten minutes he was at our door.

He shuddered as he took off his coat and handed it and his umbrella to my delighted wife. I was equally pleased to see him. He was a cheerful fellow. He told us funny stories of shopping hazards, taxi drivers, the City's fabled rudeness which he seemed to bear with equanimity. It was easy to see this tall, conspicuously midwestern chap, with his summer tan unfaded—Lord knows how—winning over shopgirls and doormen. The fact is that he won us over as well, and as we grew enthused we surrendered our indulgence in the danker mood.

We all had several drinks, unusual for me late in the evening since I don't sleep well when I do. Evelyn asked after Claudia, and his reply was that she was fine. I could not tell whether the slight change in his position when he answered, for his head rose a fraction as if he was readying for a blow he could not elude, nor tell whether his change in posture was insignificant or whether he meant his reply to be ironic. Before I could pursue the question Evelyn had put, his face lit up.

"Oh," he said and he gripped his hands together. "Have you heard about Gordon?"

Of course we hadn't, and he told us that Gordon had paid a fortune to buy his neighbor's log cabin so that he could tear it down. But the City of Aspen had just declared it an historical building, and so preserved for all time. Gordon was furious and had sent a team of lawyers and architects to the hearings, but the People's Republic of Aspen, as Weemo called it with a twinkle, was unmoved. Now he was stuck owning a house he hated, and at a price that made resale a disaster.

Weemo was tickled by the story. He apparently held the same opinion of Claudia's brother as that shared by several towns-people, including, he would have us believe, the Pitkin County planning and zoning board. And the story was amusing. I wondered what effect the episode would have on Claudia's attempt to persuade Gordon to be lenient on the trust. If I had to guess, anger more likely stimulates cupidity than its opposite.

Shortly after my return to New York from holiday, I had made a call to Mr. Stillman to request a meeting. He was abrupt but not discourteous. He didn't see what a meeting would accomplish. I told him I wanted to describe to him Mrs. Abbott's position re-garding the language of the Parine Trust, and that a meeting seemed a civil and comprehensive way to do so. He agreed to dis-cuss it with Mr. Parine. I had waited on his response since then, several times calling to inquire and being treated as if I were selling newspaper subscriptions. Only this week, Stillman had answered. We tentatively set a date in mid-January. I needed to call Claudia for her schedule, but since Claudia had not included her husband in our deliberations thus far, I mentioned none of this business to Abbott that night.

We finished a pleasant visit with Weemo's urging that we reserve the same house for the same time in August this coming year. We assured him that we would and we told him we would be at Elbow Reef in February and would see them then. He stood and Evelyn retrieved his coat from the hall closet. He and I shook hands warmly, and apologizing for his condition he embraced Evelyn.

"Now I've probably gotten you as damp as me," he said and we laughed.

"Oh, I almost forgot." Here he reached into the breast pocket of his coat, a heavy English-made trenchcoat, double-breasted with an alpaca lining, just the thing, I thought, for this weather. He pulled out a package wrapped in robin's egg blue with a red ribbon. I recognized the colors as the mark of a large New York jewelry store.

"Merry Christmas," he said. To our protestations he insisted that this had been a special year for the Abbotts, meeting special people, and they wanted to commemorate it.

We wished him well and waited with him for the elevator we share with the apartment next door. After he left, we opened his present. He had brought us a tree decoration, cut from silver in the shape of a snowflake, with the year 1977 inscribed on one side and "To C. and E. from the Abbotts" in script on the other. We hang it on our tree to this day.

Weemo was a good-hearted fellow. I remember saying so to Evelyn, and her agreeing. It was very true. It was his redemption, if ever he should need any.

* * * * *

The day was brittle and cold, in the midst of New York's winter, and so bright that people squinted as they hurried along Fifty-seventh Street to get on their way. Cabs found patrons waiting for them as they dropped off a fare. People were willing to pay for the ride to warm themselves. It was a bonanza for the sidewalk vendors who sold knitted dickeys or earmuffs or woolen scarves, woolen scarves that began to unravel even before the five-dollar bill changed hands. Those with inventories of food or books or costume jewelry had no takers and stood clapping their arms against their bodies for warmth.

Slatkin had come for Claudia up at her hotel. At her invitation, he had flown to New York for the meeting with the lawyers. Tonight, the Merediths were joining them for dinner and then going to the theatre. Not quite Shubert Alley: listed in the magazines as Off-off Broadway. Her son had a small role in an experimental production in Tribeca, staged in a converted loft by the Hudson River. He played a man who lived in a garbage can, Claudia said to Jeremy when she'd called to tell him. Slatkin resisted the impulse to respond.

Now he'd called for her in ample time to get to the restaurant. He wanted to walk down Fifth, he said, to get something special. Was she game, or did she want a cab?

She agreed. She'd dressed for the weather, but she commented on his clothes. He wore a double breasted camel's hair overcoat, the only topcoat he owned, he said, since moving to the Coast. A silk scarf in a small blue foulard, dapper and too flimsy to keep out the wind. No hat. Light deerskin gloves, almost orange, with a dark stitch and fur lining. She scolded him good-naturedly about his dress as they scurried down past the Plaza Fountain.

"O.k.," he said. He walked back to a vendor, handed him some money, and returned wearing a kelly green ski cap with "Go Jets" written in script across its front.

"Better?" he asked.

"Much."

At the corner of Fifty-sixth he steered her into a bank.

"Only take a minute," he said.

He stood at a cashier's window, showing some cards, signing some documents, and as he returned, he put a white envelope in the inside pocket of his sport coat. She had noticed when he came to call for her that he wore a sport coat with an open shirt. He picked up her glance and replied to it.

"You have to look like Beverly Hills back here. Otherwise people are disappointed."

Again they walked into the wind, down the east side of Fifth. After a few blocks, he opened the polished glass door of Cartier's and ushered her in. "We need a present," he told her. "To celebrate."

"To celebrate what?"

"Your victory tomorrow with Gordon."

"But I haven't won."

"If you celebrate, you've won. That's a fundamental rule of warfare."

Claudia said he was being melodramatic. "This isn't warfare. It's simply an interpretation of some language." It was a mild reproof, but in fact she enjoyed the heightened importance Jeremy lent to the dispute.

Jeremy insisted his language was appropriate. "Don't be naive, Claudia. Your lawyer is, so you can't afford to be. Look. I want something you have and you don't want to give me. If I try to take it away, that's war."

A woman, perhaps sixty, eyed them carefully and asked if she could help. She wore a brown wool suit with black stockings. Her only jewelry was a string of amber beads, but her ostensibly modest dress did not diminish the clear feeling of condescension she intended to convey.

"You carry a bracelet. A gold link chain with a catch, so . . ." Jeremy described an arc with his finger.

"Of course. Right this way."

She seated them at a Sheraton desk fitted with a grey velvet pad in its burl top. Soon she returned and sat opposite them with a small case of black velvet. She opened the case. Inside were four bracelets exactly alike but for length.

"The very ones. We'll need one for me and one for the lady."

"Jeremy," Claudia protested. "Don't be silly. I can't let you buy me that."

"I'm trying to prove a point about money, Claudia. Please be quiet and watch. If you want to feed it to your fish afterward, that's fine."

The saleslady measured each left wrist. The linkage was heavy and perfectly fit, and the bracelet slid like a deck of cards being riffled. The clasp was made of two loops, formed in an omega shape, that interlocked. Jeremy reached inside his coat pocket and pulled out the envelope. He opened it so the woman would see the bills it contained.

"The bracelet is three thousand five hundred dollars," she said a little awkwardly. She was trying to spare his companion the details of the purchase.

"Exactly," Jeremy said. "We'll take these two," indicating the ones he and Claudia wore. He then removed the bills from the envelope, counted and stacked seven brand new $500 bills on the desk top.

The woman nervously fingered her string of beads. For the first time she looked away from Jeremy and at Claudia.

"I'm sorry. I must have misspoke," she said. "The bracelets are three thousand five hundred dollars each. And of course, there's tax."

"No," Jeremy said happily. "No, I understood. But I tell you what. I'd like two bracelets, and I'd like to give you this money for them. It's after Christmas, you won't sell them 'till next year, and you'll still make a handsome profit on them. Believe me."

"I'm sorry, sir. This is Cartier's. I can't do that." She began to stand. Jeremy remained seated.

"I tell you what. It's too late for me to go back to the bank. Here's what we'll do." His voice was warm, as if he were about to share some wonderful news.

"You keep the bracelets and the money. I don't need a receipt. You talk it over with the store manager. Here's where I'm staying." He wrote a hotel name and number on the back of a white gift card. "You talk to him and decide. Before you close today, either send me back a Cartier check for the money or deliver the bracelets." He unhooked his and Claudia's bracelets and let them slide to the pad. With that, he stood, pulled Claudia's chair back, and they walked out the door.

"Two more lessons," he said. "One, money is like a ground ball. Either you play it or it plays you." The wind gusted, and he pulled the Jets cap about his ears. "Two, it can be fun."

A cab rolled to a stop at the northeast corner of Fifth and Fifty-second. They both saw it and began to run. Jeremy reached it and put his hand on the door's handle steps ahead of an athletic young man sprinting north. They piled in the back seat, laughing. Jeremy gave the driver the name of a restaurant in the Village. There would be enough time in the taxi for Claudia to explain the circumstances of tomorrow's meeting to him.

* * * * *

When Claudia and Jeremy arrived at the restaurant, the Merediths were already seated. They ordered a light supper and ate with an eye to the clock. The play had a seven-thirty curtain, and the converted warehouse that held the theatre was a five-block walk. They talked of their lives since they had seen each other last, and of the shared times in Aspen. Charles encouraged Jeremy to consider joining them in the Caribbean that February, but Jeremy had business commitments. His activities kept him on the road, he told them. It was the only time Charles had heard him mention his work. Slatkin seemed to be free of that most common symptom of modern epidemic insecurity, that of being considered underused. If travel was vacation, he said, then he was constantly on holiday.

The dinner was pleasant, the food adequate. The group lacked the spark they had found so engaging that summer. Everyone sensed it, and they understood what Charles meant when he observed that he felt dull that evening. Evelyn agreed.

"Maybe it's the winter," she said.

"No," Charles said. "We need Weemo."

Yet walking to the theatre, his arm hooked with Evelyn's and moving quickly at the pace set by his friends, he realized there was another dimension to his malaise. He was constrained, conflicted by the circumstances. Paces ahead walked Claudia, without her husband but again beyond his reach. His place was with his wife. Claudia was being looked after, to, Charles realized, her obvious pleasure.

The play had been reviewed in the New York underground press. They read the blown-up notices on placards during intermission as they stood in the cramped lobby. Even the most sympathetic reviewers didn't praise the play. They complimented its heritage, called it part of the tradition of Beckett and Brecht, and congratulated the cast for taking it on. The performance was hard to enjoy. For three hours those who had survived a nuclear destruction of the earth shouted obscenities at those who hadn't. After the last curtain, the actors came down to the footlights in character and interrogated the audience. It was, Jeremy said, one thing to suspend your disbelief while the play was on, but he considered it an imposition to remain in suspension once it was over. The audience was asked to declare which side of the debate they wished to join.

"And you," a young woman whose face was daubbed with ashes asked Jeremy. "What would you prefer?"

"I would prefer an espresso and a small pastry," Jeremy said. He was hissed by the younger members in the audience but applauded by not a few others.

They waited for Harrison Parine in the lobby. He appeared with a soiled towel draped over his shoulder, and daubs of cold cream still on his forehead and cheeks. He was introduced to Evelyn and Jeremy, and roundly congratulated by all of them. "What did you think?" he asked them.

"Wonderful," Claudia said, and Evelyn agreed.

"Apocalyptic," Slatkin said.

Harrison seemed pleased. He declined their suggestion that he join them for a drink, thanked them for coming, and said his goodbyes. Charles noted how, unlike the other time he'd seen the boy, Harrison treated his mother with affection.

They determined to skip a nightcap. All but Evelyn were due at an early meeting at Stillman's office in the morning and they wanted to be fresh. Instead they walked to the nearest north-bound avenue and found a cab. The Merediths were going furthest uptown and would drop off Jeremy and

Claudia at their hotels. Charles got in the front seat and spoke through the half-open plastic divider.

"He seems happier," Charles said to Claudia.

"Yes, he does," she answered. ""He's thrilled to get this job. It's made him far less hostile."

"It's the business of youth to be hostile," Jeremy said. "It's an entry-level job. They only leave off when they get a promotion."

Charles wondered whether Slatkin was out on a limb. If Claudia had a weakness, it was her son. He was not disappointed.

"It's not like you to speak from ignorance, Jeremy. Even when you're joking. Harrison is trying to separate. He needs Weemo and me to stop giving him so much. Coffee makers, groceries, love, advice."

"He's merely growing up." Slatkin was unwilling to be chastised.

"Growing up is a complicated business," Claudia said. "He wants to fly on his own. And he's ready to fall. I just don't want him to fall too far or too hard."

"You make too much of it," Jeremy insisted. "Don't you agree, Charles?"

"I've been warned about speaking from ignorance. I pass."

"If what you say is true," Evelyn said to Claudia, "all you have to do is nothing. That ought to be easy."

"Yes," said Claudia, though not as if she believed it.

They were quiet during the rest of the ride. The lights going north were staggered and they sped to Fifty-ninth where the cab turned east. Slatkin left, then three blocks north, Claudia. The taxi left the Merediths at their co-op.

To his surprise, in bed that night, Charles found his wife especially amorous. Her moods always puzzled him. They blew over the hills like storms and he never knew what brought them on. Particularly this one. Surely, he thought later as she slept, it wasn't the dinner or that depressing play. He contemplated her as a lover. She has such openness, such lack of guile. She makes her body a sign of complete trust. That trust is, he supposed, what distinguishes sexual love. As long as he could remember, she had always been this way for him. Open, natural, feral. In that animus he found, from the start and even to this day, a personal communion. It was a level of commitment that he had never had from anyone. It did not occur to Charles that it was, as well, a level of commitment Evelyn never intended.

He began the slide to darkness. He thought of Claudia alone in her hotel room. Was she awake, and did she lie abed wondering about marital passion and marital distance? He often found comfort in contemplation that their thoughts might be parallel. Tonight, although his mood before sleep was passive, as he thought on Claudia he became unsettled.

He turned his mind to tomorrow's meeting with Stillman. As he did, he felt consciousness regain a notch or two. What would the day be like? He plotted out the meeting, who would play which roles. He had done a persuasive memorandum. When would he put it forward? Even if it went exactly as he hoped, he didn't expect Stillman and Gordon Parine to capitulate on the spot. There would be an agreement in theory, to be followed by papers for precision.

The process of rehearsal had a double pleasure for him. He knew the law, and there was an architectural satisfaction in rearranging the arguments. At its best, and not so often in Charles' experience that he'd become indifferent, the practice of law revealed a geometry, a hidden structure. Just as atomic theory described the structure in Nature. But here there was more. Here was a chance to do something for Claudia. If a gesture was needed, this would be an appropriate one. He was again awake and he smiled in the dark room at the private pun. Gesture, he knew, had the same root word as jester.

Chapter Fifteen

The law firm of which Herbert Stillman was a founding member had come into being as a result of a dispute at one of the country's oldest and most venerated firms. Several partners, then young men newly admitted to the venture, had concluded that the method of dividing the profits, based largely upon seniority and contribution to the reputation of the firm, that latter measure determined by the very members whom the determination invariably benefitted, was unduly monarchal. They were talented and aggressive young men, all as it happened in the litigation department.

They delivered an ultimatum to their seniors. Their bluff was called, but it turned out that they held significant cards. Having guessed they'd be turned down, they had already sequestered critical files at a Long Island warehouse and were ready to sign and to occupy a lease in midtown offices. Announcements and stationery had been printed, and the new firm opened for business Monday after the Friday of confrontation. Complaints with the greivance committee were filed by their former colleagues, since the clients whose files had been removed had had no say in their ultimate representation. But the young lawyers pointed to those complaints to argue that the old order did not understand the tools of modern warfare, and their argument persuaded several clients to change their allegiance. It was a brilliant strategy. Their former colleagues were astonished by the efficiency with which they had been duped. The best they could say, years later, was that the rules for the profession had changed.

So from its first day the firm and Mr. Stillman had enjoyed a reputation for aggressive representation. To the edge of ethical constraints and, until corrected, beyond. In another reversal of professional practice, they began generating their own publicity. They started by revealing their revenues and who their clients were. As the strategy of making gossip into news had worked for advertising agencies, it worked for law firms. And there arose around this new breed of lawyer a popular press that wrote about which firm was now the largest, who had taken whose clients, and who made the most money.

The very reputation of the firm disquieted Meredith. His practice afforded him the luxury, among others, of practicing law without discord. The planning side of his work—how the estate was to be passed, how it was to be overseen, how to reduce taxes and get the best value from the assets—that was a peculiarly intellectual function. Occasionally on the other side, the administration of what had been planned, contests would arise. But his firm would refer those unpleasant matters to a litigation firm, those matters would be plucked out of the practice like tomatoes too bruised to sit in their baskets.

Meredith's unease was in some measure due to his anticipation of Jeremy Slatkin's presence. Since their Aspen meeting, he had learned of Slatkin's considerable reputation in the New York and California business communities as an active investor in public corporations. Not exactly a raider, Jeremy had succeeded in taking significant positions in troubled companies. His method was to gain board representation on the strength of his investment and then change policy, through the force of persuasion rather than control. People criticized him, but more often than not his changes moved the stock. Slatkin had done it so often that news of his investment was enough in itself to cause a rise in the price of a company's shares.

He neither approved nor disapproved of Claudia's emerging reliance on Jeremy. Still, if it had been up to him, Meredith would have left him out of this conference. Charles judged that temperance would be an ally in inducing Gordon Parine's cooperation, and Slatkin's quick tongue put that in jeopardy. There was also Jeremy's romantic interest in Claudia, although in Charles' presence it was almost indiscernible. In any event, he'd been invited and he was there. Now, as they waited in an interior conference room on the fifty-second story of a midtown, Third Avenue building, Charles explained his plan of presentation to them both.

Slatkin offered encouragement and no resistance. "You call the shots, Charles."

After a ten-minute wait, during which Jeremy poured coffee from the decanter for Claudia and himself, Gordon Parine and his lawyer entered. They shook hands all around; Claudia and Gordon touched cheeks. Stillman apologized for the brief delay, calling it that, without explanation. Then he settled in the chair by the door.

"Well," he said, in a tone that implied the issue at hand was neither grave nor time-consuming, "what can we do for you today."

The conference room was stark. Its walls were painted in an institutional beige, and the only print was an elaborately framed but inferior reproduction of a Breughel. The ambience was almost flimsy, and as such it was noticeably altered by the presence of Herbert Stillman. He filled the room.

He was a heavy man, not five-ten but easily two-hundred and fifty pounds. He had black hair, though none at all from his forehead to his crown. He wore his hair to long sideburns, in the style of the sixties, and they, like a few long strands covering the rest of his baldness, emphasized what was not there. He had a sallow complexion and although it was early in the morning, his chin already showed a carbon shadow. Charles observed him closely. Stillman took care to drape his unappealing physique in elegant dress. He wore a tailored suit of dark blue flannel with a maroon chalk stripe, a shirt without pocket, white collar and blue body, tailored to his unusual dimension, and a black silk tie with a discreet pattern in its weave. All that elegance was upset by a habit, or more precisely a tic: as he listened, he would unpredictably stretch his head to one side, the right, exposing large folds of neck, as a labrador might before scratching.

It fell to Charles to explain their position. He did so without stopping. He went over the language of the trust, the history—as far as he had been able to divine—of its creation, the legislative and statutory background in Ohio, and the state of case law. When he got to this last topic, he reached into his briefcase and pulled out several copies of a short memorandum. He laid one in front of Stillman and gave one to Parine. Gordon took his and leafed through it. Stillman's copy lay on the table before him, untouched.

"There are three cases in Ohio which are instructive," Charles said. "In the most recent, it also happens to be from the highest court, the court determined that the adopted child was intended to be included within the language of general gift. That's *Pettingill*, where the language was 'issue' or 'grandchildren.'"

Stillman interrupted in a weary voice. "You should assume for this discussion, Mr. Meredith, that we're familiar with the cases. It will save time."

Charles looked up sharply at this rebuke. He nodded and went on.

"We're asking for your cooperation. We think it's clear what James Parine intended and it's clear what an Ohio court will do. We also suspect that Gordon, from his position as Claudia's only living sibling and given how close they've been over the years, we hope that Gordon would support a construction of the will in her favor even if the law weren't on her side."

Charles finished. Stillman turned his large, frog's eyes on him and waited.

"Is that what you came to say?"

"That is." Charles allowed a note of aversion at the attempted discourtesy to sound in his voice

"Well, then." Stillman made to get up.

"Are you going to favor us with a reply?" Charles asked.

"I don't know that a reply is needed," Stillman said archly. "You seem to know what James Parine intended when he made out this trust in 1927 and what the Ohio courts will do. You certainly don't need us."

"I should like to know whether you intend to oppose us."

"Oh, we do, Mr. Meredith. We do. We think that the law in Ohio is that if you use the word 'grandchildren' or 'issue,' you get one result. The adoptive children are included. But if you use the words 'heirs of the body,' you get another result. If you use that language, you mean to exclude adoptive children. Otherwise there's language available to you. All of that assumes you have a lawyer who knows the law, and James Parine certainly did.

"And so we don't think you and your client here have any right to revise the trust of James Parine. It's not a question of siblings or family or even what Gordon Parine wants or doesn't want. It's a clear case of leaving the intent of James Parine intact."

With that, Stillman nodded a brief goodbye and, gesturing to Gordon to follow him, left the room. Gordon shrugged enigmatically. One could have interpreted his move to mean that the matter was out of his hands or that he agreed with Stillman's succinct position. And Gordon too left the three of them as he'd found them. The copies of the memorandum Charles had passed around lay on the table.

*   *   *   *   *

It was too early for lunch, and too far for the trio to return downtown to Charles' office. They took a taxi to the club of Charles' university, tucked into the north side of Forty-fourth Street. There, in a private dining room on the second floor, they sat at a small, round table and discussed alternatives. A waiter brought cups and saucers and a samovar of coffee and placed them on the sideboard. Then he spread an ironed white cloth over the table and withdrew.

"The matter will clearly have to be litigated," Charles was saying. "They've made it clear they intend to be adverse. With your permission, Claudia, I feel we should retain this gentleman." He handed her the business card of a senior partner in a large Cincinnati firm. "The matter will take a local presence, and he comes highly recommended. Unless, of course, you favor someone else."

They sat in high-backed chairs, covered in a green leather, in the Federal style. Three bulbs burned overhead in a fixture meant to suggest gaslight. Framed simply and hung around the room, many of the glass panes cracked, were photographs of rowing crews from the first half of the century. Some of the men posed in their shells, others sat on a bench by the boathouse. Although the club admitted women, a decision it had reluctantly made several years after the college it represented adopted coeducation, the atmosphere was unyieldingly masculine. Claudia had commented when they came in that it was hardly a place that put her at ease. Her remark went unanswered.

Now she responded to Charles' suggestion of a Cincinnati lawyer to help. Yes, she said. She knew the man in question. Yes, she supported the assessment of him, and agreed that he should be hired. As she spoke her voice trembled.

"I'm sorry, but I'm terribly distraught. I can't believe this is happening." She was thinking of the long walks with her father, her hand grasped around a finger from his, while he explained how they had picked her from thousands of available babies. She was filled with rage and frustration that Gordon would have this final trump over her claim to the family, and she said so.

"That he would know all along and not tell me," she said to the ceiling. "That he would hear me out at Thanksgiving dinner at my table, in my house, and hear me out at stockholders' meetings, all the while thinking, her time will come. She'll have her come-uppance. She's not an heir of the body."

Slatkin and Meredith listened with sympathy. Both held the same thought, unaware of their error. Both thought her anger was directed at the years she had spent in her marriage, with an eye towards the clause of divestment in the case of divorce. If Stillman was right, that time would have been spent without purpose. They thought it cruel that she should have apprenticed so long for a guild to which, from birth, she was excluded.

Slatkin asked if he could suggest another approach. He turned to Claudia.

"I'd like you to send us whatever you have on the company. Parine Pen. Whatever you have in your files. You ought to be getting financial statements at least annually, but quarterly reports if you have them. From as far back as you can go. *B'Raishis*. In the beginning."

"From 1908?" she said.

"If you have them. But especially since Gordon took over. Also, I want you to find someone on the inside, preferably in the financial or accounting side, who doesn't like your brother. Someone he's fired, or someone he's put down or not promoted. That shouldn't be hard to do. He doesn't have a light touch."

"Just a minute, Jeremy," Charles put in. "Financial information that's available to every stockholder, yes. That's one thing. But I'm not sure we should be trying to find out matters that may be rumor, speculation, inside gossip. I'm not sure of the propriety of that."

"Leave Charles out of that part," Slatkin said without a pause. "Just send that stuff to me. But get it."

"What are we trying to do?" Claudia asked. "What happens to all this?"

"First let's see what it tells us," Jeremy answered. "If it doesn't say anything, there may be nothing to do."

They agreed to keep in close touch. Jeremy rose to leave, citing other New York business, and Claudia thanked him for his help. Charles felt equally indebted, but he was troubled by a sense of subordination that left him, alone now with Claudia, feeling more feeble than he would have wished. He had also noticed a curious fact, and did not know what to make of it. He saw it when he and Jeremy had shaken hands earlier. On Jeremy's wrist was a bracelet identical to the one Claudia was wearing, a gold woven thing with a clasp like a square knot. The coincidence struck Charles as odd.

Claudia did not dwell on the roles played that morning. It was not until later, on the flight to Cincinnati and afterwards, sitting at home waiting for the spring to break through the parched ground, that she would consider how differently they had reacted. The men concentrated on the method. And even there they had two ways. Charles seized on what had been done wrong, Jeremy on what needed to be done.

She cared little for whose approach was taken or what tactics came next. She wasn't particularly concerned about the stakes. Later at home as then when they'd sat over coffee, she was absorbed by her brother's readiness to argue that he was not her brother. That she belonged in the family conditionally, for restricted purposes, not for all. Could her father have known about that language, too? Her father, who watched over them, who for all his gentleness would have snapped at any threat and would have repelled any intruder. Could he have known, too? Is all sense of security an illusion?

She shared none of these thoughts with Charles. Instead she excused herself for not being helpful. She told him that she was so taken aback by Gordon's truculence and the arrogance of his lawyer that she couldn't think. And Charles comforted her. He was consoling but realistic. He explained why he felt that Jeremy's inquiry into the performance of the company was misguided. They knew, but Jeremy didn't, that under Gordon's aegis Parine Pen had recovered profitability. It may be that chance caused those two lines—profits and Gordon's term of office—to intersect, but in a court of law it wouldn't matter, Charles explained. The good fortune of the company would all but bar any legal remedy trying to attack Gordon's rule. Charles' words helped Claudia to understand that she should not expect a miracle from whatever Jeremy was up to. Better to know both your strengths and your weaknesses, Charles said in his chaplain's voice. She calmed down over a second cup of coffee from the samovar.

They agreed to talk as soon as Charles and the Cincinnati firm had prepared the complaint to be filed on her behalf. He would take the lead and instruct them on what he wanted done. She reminded him that they were to share another week together at Elbow Reef.

"It can't come soon enough," she said, leaning her body into his and kissing him lightly on the cheek. "I have had it with winter and the things of the world that are too much with us."

She had a flight reserved that afternoon from LaGuardia, and hadn't yet checked out. So she hurried off, leaving Charles to settle the bill amidst cups of cold coffee, dark oak bookcases, and photographs of men no longer at oar.

Chapter Sixteen

From the Journal

I*f I were asked to redesign the human species, now that it has been road-tested for one and a half million years, if you include the Pithecanthropus, I have several ideas. I would improve its speed and the way the muscles are deployed. By comparison, say, to the ocelot or the cockroach, it's underpowered. I would shrink the cranial cavity and move the eyes more to the side of its head. It also needs greater strength as a function of weight. All these would make it a more efficient hunter, closer to the felines, and would alleviate the need for it to rely quite so heavily on its brain. I would certainly do something about the construction of its knee, which has proved as unreliable as the electrical system in British Leyland's automobiles. And its back. Either design the damn thing to walk upright for sixty or seventy years or leave it on all fours. I don't care for the concept of our slowly falling over, like a pot of desiccated daisies.*

And then the difficult part: the psyche. I would be tempted, in the next model, to dispense with jealousy, love, hate, anger and ambition. For regardless of how good a hunter I designed, without that adjustment, within a couple of million years man would still be covering the planet with asphalt, cutting down forests to record his own words on paper, and trying to find the most potent distillation of gunpowder. It goes back to the tyranny of superlatives. On balance, though, I think I would resist the temptation, for if those adjustments were made, the human race would become as interesting to watch as a bowl of goldfish.

No, I would make only one change in the nature of the beast. I would dilute by several parts his degree of self-consciousness. That damnable vanity which compels him to draw causal rela-

tionionships between every event in the universe and himself, his fate and his digestion. If the python strangles the eagle, the Aztec kings take it as a sign to settle their city on that site. When the comet appears the seers predict famine. The birth of a two-headed cow is intended to tell the priests to forbid marriage.

Someone called self-consciousness the sixth and insatiable sense. I don't think egotism a function of intelligence, but if it is, I shall be happy to dilute intelligence as well, for that clearly is an overrated knack that has caused more mischief than it has spared. I would want merely to remove this conviction of man that he is the central fact in the universe. It is a conceit not indulged in by zebras, tortoises, or dragonflies. It isn't considered by them. And it makes for a great deal of unhappiness.

One would think that the single memory of my first year of boarding school was the death of my mother. It was not. I suppose that fact testifies to how far removed from her I was. I don't recall her dying so much as slipping away, evaporating. I must not have dwelled on her or her condition. It was years later that I realized her cure was indeed a large part of her illness.

My memories were instead of my own constant discomfort. Less than a day after my arrival on the St. Alban's campus, an exquisitely pastoral plain in the rocky hills of southern New Hampshire, I suffered my first mortification. It was to be one of many. I was seated in Latin class. I was thirteen years old. Latin—at least through the Gallic wars—was a requirement of every St. Alban's graduate. Indeed, two years of Greek had been until the year before my father enrolled me, and it was dropped only because the Greek master had died in a boating accident and the school was unable to replace him.

I had been several minutes in finding the classroom. When I arrived, the only unoccupied desks were in the first row. I made myself as inconspicuous as possible and slunk to my seat. But it was that circumstance of positioning that caused my embarrassment.

The desks in every middle school classroom were the same. They folded over a compartment where a student could store his books or leave his garbage, and the seats were bolted to the

*desks and to the floor. In the upper school, to simulate, I was
told, college classrooms, there were no desks but rather writing
seats, yellow oak and iron constructs with a broad paddle as
the right arm for a writing surface.*

*I sat quietly, studying the initials and numerals in the
wooden surface and grateful that my late entrance had not
stirred comment. Everyone else seemed to know each other. As
I found out later most of the class had started together in the
First Form, the seventh grade, the year before. Another influx
could be expected next year, when parents opted for boarding
schools over high schools. My father had explained this to me
twice, once on the train from New York and again in the hotel
dining room over breakfast. I don't know that I ever had a
conversation with my father that wasn't repeated. It was his
way.*

*And so I was led to understand that I could expect few new
boys to be entering with me. That would cause a particular
strain on my fitting in, make it even more important. New Boys
wore black socks to mark their status until the second term.
Unless Middlesex was beaten. If the football team won over
Middlesex, the black socks came off early.*

*I knew some of the lore of the place from my father and my
brother, twelve years my senior. Both had graduated in their
time, and St. Alban's was one of the few topics of conversation
I shared with them. Some of the lore, but not all. I sat at that
desk, frowning over the carvings as if they were on a cave wall,
lost in what loomed as the first day of hundreds of solitude and
self-pity. I was so absorbed in myself that I must not have heard
the hushed conversation behind me or its sudden conclusion.*

"What is your name, boy?"

*I looked up to find a portly, white-haired man not two feet
away. Grey eyes, which I observed through the bottom lens of
his thick bifocals, looked at me.*

"What is your name?" the man repeated.

*"Charles Meredith." I heard my thin, trembling voice and
was frightened by it.*

*"Charles Meredith, sir." The man's tone was kindly, instruc-
tive, but it failed to put me at ease.*

"You might try to remember, Meredith." He lowered his voice, though the class would have heard had he whispered. "At St. Alban's we stand when a master enters the room. It evidences respect, whether or not it is deserved."

I turned my head aslant and looked over my shoulder. The entire class was on its feet. Each boy wore the same flannel blazer, the same maroon and white striped tie, and on his face, the same sneer.

The episode might have passed except for the penchant of adolescent boys to water and nurture misery until it can be harvested. For the rest of the term, and even as an occasional inside joke in my brief upper school career, the cry, "Respect, Meredith," would greet me. It accompanied the snatching of my books for a game of keep-away, in which I ran from one thrower to the other trying to retrieve my property. It was crayoned on my sheets the day my bed was moved from the dormitory to the soccer field. Had I stayed to graduate from St. Alban's, I have no doubt it would have been inscribed under my yearbook photograph, where one's character is catalogued in epigrams.

Why were those short years at St. Alban's so difficult for me? From my childhood to then, I had undressed and slept in a room by myself. Summer camps weren't the fashion, and my summers were spent at our home in Litchfield County near the Aspetuck River. It may seem extreme in this world of prodigal nudity, but other than photographs in my father's books on Hellenistic Art, I had on the day I arrived at school never seen the bare human form, male or female. Now I was thrust in a common dormitory with eleven other boys. We were expected to swim without suits, twice a week, to shower communally in a vast slate room without stalls. And I lived with a hundred Second Formers whose every joke was scatalogical and whose every taunt seemed directed at my immature, flaccid body. Today when I read about blue ribbon grand juries formed to investigate execrable conditions at homes for the elderly or the retarded, I often wonder why they don't turn their attention to the nation's leading boarding schools.

Like its curriculum and its standard of deportment, the building plan of St. Alban's was modeled after the English school. On the highest elevation of the green and rolling campus sat the main building. Called the Old Hall, it was in fact not a hall but the perimeter of a square. Its center was a quadrangle, where daily, rain or shine, the student body assembled in ragged ranks for the walk into chapel. At every corner of the building were newer wings, each the result of its own capital fund drive. Looked at from the air, the building would have resembled a cubist pinwheel. One of these wings, an ell with a Georgian facade, contained the entryway, the headmaster's office, and the school administration. A second contained the commons, a third the upper school form rooms and laboratories. And the last, presented by the Class of 1927, the Memorial Chapel. Down the hill towards the river stood the dormitories, and beyond the playing fields, the gymnasium.

The serenity of my life followed the topography. I was on safe ground when I was in class at the main building, and the chapel was my sanctuary. I went downhill to living quarters and hit my nadir in the athletic plant. The school had a wide array of athletic opportunities, and in none of them did I show any aptitude.

St. Alban's required participation in athletics. In my first week I was diagnosed, correctly I have no doubt, as too fragile for football and too bronchial for cross-country. I was accordingly assigned to the residue, and was informed that I was the goalie for the soccer scrubs of the middle school. A blessedly peaceful spot when the ball was at the other end of the field, it turned into the very synapse of stress when the ball approached. I made futile attempts to wave the ball down but rarely succeeded. Occasionally it hit me full in the face. Either way, were it a goal that I had to retrieve from the nets or a block that bloodied my nose, its course reduced me to unmanly tears.

Classes were better. Neutral territory. I was adequate at studies, although the subjects were new and mysterious to me: Latin, French, algebra, and an interminable series of Dickens *novels, more, it seems now, than he possibly could have written. My father had urged me to find something I could excel in. Clearly it wasn't academics or athletics. When activities started, I determined to join not one but two.*

My father had emphasized to me that St. Alban's was important because the friends I would make there would be my friends at college, by which I understood him to mean his own college. Those friends in turn would determine what house I lived in, what clubs I would be invited to join, both as an undergraduate and later. Thus the very compass points of my life—if not the speed or final destination—were being determined then, in my thirteenth year. I didn't question how it was that I, not even the equal of Dickens' lowliest criminals, would never again be given a fresh start. And in my two years at St. Alban's, I never found those friends I would keep for the rest of my life.

I thought one or two of the comrades my father had foreseen might appear during the activities hour, and so I signed up for civics discussion and camera club. My zeal was rewarded, but not in the way I'd planned. Each group assumed I was in the other. Suddenly every Tuesday and Thursday afternoon I was blessed with an hour to myself. It was bliss. I spent my time wandering around the campus. There were glades beyond the practice fields, woods by the hockey ponds, little corners that no one but illicit smokers used. I spent my fondest hours there, watching tadpoles and blowing the seeds off dandelions.

St. Alban's had an unwritten rule that the school was to know where each boy was at all times. It was a companion piece to keeping the boys endlessly occupied, if not with schoolwork then with games, sports, clubs. The unspoken aim was a fundamental paedegogic end: to avoid the inevitable sexual exploration that the administration feared worse than a sentence that didn't properly parse. That rule was difficult for me, for I've always needed my solitude, and so when a way around it fell into my lap, I didn't complain.

My luck continued as the dual rosters carried me into the winter term without any accountability for my activities time. By then the weather had turned against me. The smokers wan-

dered down to the boiler room or on sunny days met in the groundskeeper's car. But I was far too young and not welcome. By luck I found a rear door to the Chapel that was left unlocked. If I lay flat in a pew, I could spend the time unobserved, sketching in a secret notebook, drawing flowers and the faces of beautiful, imaginary girls.

Again I had secured to myself two happy hours every week. A singular benefit of a St. Alban's education is how it lowers expectations to a point where a meagre supply of life's crumbs can provide sustenance.

My indulgence was not to last. On a January afternoon, reclining while drawing the face of an idealized girl with Rita Hayworth lips and flouncy hair cut in a style then called a page boy, I was startled by a loud "Aha!" at the end of my pew. Looking over my shoes, I saw the fierce frown of Uncle Frank. Uncle Frank headed the music department. He led the glee club and the band, but my exposure to him was in Chapel. For hymns and for the weekly sing, when the words to songs like "Mandalay" and "The British Grenadiers" were flashed on a screen from yellowing reflector slides. Uncle Frank would patrol the aisles of the Chapel and if he spotted a boy, usually a lower former, singing with insufficient gusto or not participating at all, he would stand the poor wretch in the aisle and force him to sing aloud. Uncle Frank had a thin face, a booming tenor voice, and shaggy grey eyebrows that he would furrow like, I imagined, God Almighty. The upper schoolers seemed to like him, though the only reason I could divine was that he embarrassed a few to the merriment of the many. I lived in fear of the day I would be singled out.

He seized my notebook and riffled its pages. Then he asked for my name and form. I replied in terror. It was clear my game was up.

"And where are you supposed to be during activities, Meredith Second?"

"It's unclear, sir. Camera thinks I'm to be at civics and civics wants me at camera."

"Vice versa," he shouted in its Latin pronunciation. "Meaning?" and he turned his black eyes on me.

We had just studied in Latin class a page of terms common in English. I had read it two nights ago.

"Vice versa," I recited. "A turning change, a turn-about."

"Precisely. The ablative singular of 'vicis', a change, and the participle form of 'vertere', to turn. And tell me, Meredith Second, where would you like to be?"

I had no answer. No one since I'd come to this school had asked my preference over anything so trivial as dessert.

"You would prefer," he announced grandly, "to be here. In Chapel. And you shall. Do you know, Meredith Second, what a beadle is?"

"It's a little bug, sir."

"Yes it is, yes it is." My answer seemd to please him. "And you shall be my little bug."

I was mystified, but I soon found I had duties I could easily perform. It was my charge to straighten the hymn books, to place the Bible marker at the proper reading for the headmaster, and to retrieve from Uncle Frank's office the slip with the hymn numbers and arrange their display in the two wooden racks that flanked the chancel. Once done, I was free to resume my position in the pews and to daydream of girls with heart-shaped lips and hair flopping over one eye.

That was my single accomplishment at St. Alban's. It led to my moment of recognition during a Chapel sing. Uncle Frank was roaming the aisles during the round, "Great Tom is Cast." The Second Form had its own part, which I was following assiduously, although the Third Form ahead of us bellowed their part so loud that most of our fellows were being led astray. Uncle Frank stopped at my pew and heard the kidnapping that was occurring, and raising his pointer, used to slap the screen for timing and in mock attack on non-singers, he pointed at me and bellowed, "No, you chowderheads, listen. Listen to Meredith Second." I remember the pride I felt, and I now see vividly how spare my expectations had become in six short months.

Not my father's. When I told him that June of my appointment he frowned. Beadle to Uncle Frank was not what he had in mind.

"You must make the acquaintence of the important members of your class, Charles," he told me. "Even if you can't play football, you can be friends of the football players. Those are the men with whom you'll spend the rest of your life."

His insistence that my range for finding comrades was shrinking, combined with my unremitting certainty that most of the football players were simpletons, filled me with a sinking despair. Was I really to spend the rest of my life with them?

That fall, however, I did have a chance to fulfill my father's wishes. One of the duties of the beadle was to lock and unlock the Chapel. It could only be done with the key. And when several Sixth Formers realized I held that key, I became their friend overnight. I let them use the Chapel once, to meet secretly with a case of Narragansett beer, to celebrate a great football victory, and my resolve was broken evermore. The best I could do after that was to insist that a look-out be kept. Naturally, the look-out most often was I.

The covert parties began only with drinking. Beer, then blackberry brandy. Then someone started mixing Seven and Sevens, boilermakers, and for a special celebration, I think it was Washington's Birthday, French Seventy-fives. I appealed to Malcolm Eckerman, the ringleader, for moderation, certain that the expanding cabaret would cause notice and get us all dismissed. Malcolm listened, considered my wish, and granted it. I thought it was because of the strength of my argument. Instead, Malcolm had discovered a higher and better use for the sanctuary. He had just arranged his first date with Sally Jardeau, daughter of the football coach and bearer of a torrid reputation, one that had trickled down even to the ears of a Third Former. Malcolm agreed that the drinking parties were over, that from now on he would be the only one to use the Chapel. He assured me he'd be especially quiet. But I would have to keep a sharp watch.

It was a spring afternoon. Activities period. I sat in a middle pew, where the Fourth Form ordinarily sat, reading Silas Marner. I had lowered the windows with the long ash pole to let in the new warmth, and a breeze blew through the Chapel. I kept my eyes on the page, trying not to peek behind the altar where Malcolm and Sally, mostly covered by the garnet and gold altar cloth donated by the Class of '32, wrestled, giggled and grunted.

There was a bang at the door. I stalled as long as I could, looked to see Malcolm make a heroic leap to the open window and out in what doubtless would have been a school record for the Western roll, and unlocked the door. Uncle Frank looked hard at me.

"What's going on?" he said.

Light-complected, I could feel my skin color. Before I could deny anything, I turned to see what had dropped Uncle Frank's jaw. I glimpsed the plump and unmistakeably bare haunches of Sally Jardeau cross the chancel and run down the backstairs to the rear door.

By keeping my mouth shut I didn't intend anything noble. I wasn't taking the fall for Eckerman. I recall thinking that I was in for it one way or the other, and that it was better to suffer the inevitable consequences alone than drag him into it. During the hearing before the headmaster I did not mention his name, and pleaded no defense but my own apology. It was sincere, since I had disappointed the man who had designated me beadle and had been my sole friend. The headmaster cited my clothed state and my spotless record, an unintended pun, I feel sure, in suspending me from St. Alban's for a year. It was a lenient punishment, he felt. My record, of course, was not so much spotless as invisible.

Still, I felt relieved. The gratitude of Eckerman would live on and stand me well when I returned, and hearkening to my father's instruction, I assumed he would be a friend for life.

My father was of a different mind. He too felt that the punishment was lenient, and he superceded it by removing me from St. Alban's altogether. It would be a fitting punishment for dishonesty, he said, to be forced to finish one's preparatory career at any of the several schools which attract rejects of this sort, children of divorce and children of the military. A place none of whose graduates, he added, went on to the right colleges. Which of those schools he left up to me. He had washed his hands of my upbringing.

I took no lesson from these episodes. I was too young, or too hurt, or too self-centered. I can't determine which. I do know I enrolled myself in one of those very schools and my father paid the tuition but never visited. Including the day of my graduation. The story of my expulsion had reached the school before me and had grown muscle and virility even when I had not. I found I was popular from the day I arrived, and as a consequence I was able to abandon the search for my life's companions and spend the time instead on studies. I finished academically at the top of my class, attended my father's college, to his surprise and mild disappointment, and took my law degree, as he had done, at the same university. And so made it my own.

Chapter Seventeen

From the Journal

Three brief weeks after our fruitless trip to see Mr. Stillman, Evelyn and I were packing to go to Elbow Reef. She could not remember, she said, signs of spring coming so early. I heard the oaken note of sincerity in her voice. This time she wasn't cataloguing the vicissitudes of her life. I think she was glad for the turn in the weather.

The fact was we were both looking forward to our vacation, for the climate since September had been harsh. Our Christmas plans that year included a week spent at the family home in Connecticut. It was an experiment, done at my urging. We had always stayed in town. I had envisioned a pastoral few days, doubtless patterned on some sentimental movie that had played Radio City over the holidays when I was a boy. The facts were a disappointment. Evelyn doesn't care for solitude, and the lovely inns we had remembered were in fact sandwich shops or fried clam restaurants. The house was drafty, and a family of phoebes had nested in the flue, so our evenings by the fire had to await the chimney sweep. And of course the chimney sweep was on vacation in Fort Lauderdale.

I spent the time reading and walking in the woods, but my decision to flee the City had deprived Evelyn of the most active part of the social season. She passed hours morosely fiddling with the television set, trying to draw in something other than the weather report from Atlanta. It was a mistake to think we could play the roles of Bing Crosby and Rosemary Clooney.

This year we looked forward to the Caribbean trip even more than usual. Getting into the warmth was only a part of it. The *close of my firm's financial year, a period of evaluation and debate, had been nettlesome. Our accounting each year seemed to be more elaborate, our meetings on distributions more strained, reflecting growing dissatisfaction. It is a fact that the firm's fortunes were declining at the very time younger lawyers, particularly those who looked to their earnings from the practice as their sole means of support, wanted a bigger share of the pie. There was that unpleasantness to put behind me.*

But mostly, I knew I would have another week with Claudia, a week of timelessness and reflection. I had been all too keenly aware of her attraction to Jeremy at Aspen and again in New York, and knew that this week he would not be in the competition. I could expect, in the words of the tournaments I avoided, a bye into the next round.

Fueling my ardor was the belief that Claudia shared it, at least in some measure. She had told me that she and Weemo had tried to make reservations for the exact dates we were to be there—the first two weeks in February. But reservations at the Elbow Reef then followed a pattern of entail that was almost feudal. Everyone who came booked the identical time for the following year as they checked in. It was as early as the Club allowed, and the practice was looked upon by the heavily East Coast crowd as both a necessary allegiance and a way of getting a leg up on the rest of the world. What is more satisfying to the true New Yorker than a reservation that excludes the rest of the universe, regardless of the event?

And so, just as last year, the Abbotts were confirmed for a visit that began and ended a week before ours. But seven overlapping days, I thought as I packed several long-sleeved cotton shirts for the beach, seven overlapping days with nothing to do but walk the shoreline, spot birds, take our morning swim. I thought of it as a pool of fresh water at the edge of a desert I had crossed.

Our dinner at Elbow Reef the first evening confirmed our expectations. The four of us were in high spirits. Weemo had reserved the very table we had occupied last year. He had ordered tropical corsages for the ladies and even had leis— which he had had to teach the kitchen staff to make—for all of us. His instruction must have been flawed, for the flower necklaces dissolved as dinner went on, to the peals of our laughter. The Abbotts were quite at ease with each other. Weemo told of Claudia's perserverance on the golf course. She had gone around with him every day, occasionally hitting at the ball. "Curious thing about Claudia," he told us. "She doesn't play every hole. Some she just picks up the ball and meets me at the next tee. Now, I know players who do that and when you ask them what they've shot they say, put me down as a par. But Claudia, she says, Oh, a nine. She's the only golfer whose score gets worse when she cheats."

Claudia teased Weemo in return, saying she had tried to get him to come bird-watching with her, but he wouldn't reciprocate.

"Birds never do anything worth watching," he explained to us. "Or when they do, it's nothing you can discuss over dinner."

They had made plans for us almost every day of the week and asked for our concurrence. One day we were all to take a day sail on the club's yacht. We were down for the dinner dance mid-week, and Weemo had entered Evelyn and himself in the mixed doubles tennis tournament. Last year they'd won in an exciting third set that Claudia and I had watched. The same opponents were back this year, he told us. He'd gone ahead and ordered a special champagne for their last night, what Weemo called the awards dinner. The wine was being shipped in from the mainland. They had planned a full schedule.

I remarked to Evelyn as we retired that evening that the Abbotts would run us ragged if we let them. It was said without criticism, an observation really, since Weemo seemed to enjoy activity where I came to the beach for leisure. It must have touched a spot in Evelyn, for she responded that at least it wouldn't be dull. No, I agreed truthfully. It wouldn't be dull.

Did she find life with me tedious? She and I differed in appetite. I'd been taught that gratification was faintly lubricious, that self-discipline was preferred. As a child, when the dessert tray was passed, I had to choose between halving an eclair or losing my parents' approval. I think that was why, *later, I suspected a young woman who wanted to exercise her cravings with me. It seemed like the other half of the eclair.*

Does that make life tedious? Or was Evelyn worn down by the predictability of it all? Surely I have always been orderly, even predictable. In the long run, I think steadfastness an important trait. It lets people know where they stand, what to expect, and I think it would be easy to live with. I didn't pose the question.

So began our second visit at Elbow Reef with the Abbotts. I had hoped to recreate our first, to find that pattern of sun, sand, and intimacy that had so marked me the first time. Breakfasts on the screened porch, perhaps a swim in the pool, walks on the beach. But it is a curious thing. Patterns establish themselves in nature and are infrangible. The seasons, the circle of courting, mating, parturition and death, they give definition and fibre to time.

But in human conduct it is quite different. You can't set patterns. You can't count on things not to change. Quite the contrary.

* * * * *

On their first full day at Elbow Reef, the Merediths rose early. They had breakfast served at their cabin, on a tray with legs and casters that served as a table as well. They sat on the screened porch and ate a large meal of mango, broiled fish, fresh banana muffins and coffee. Then they dressed for their separate plans and went to meet their companions.

Evelyn had a ten o'clock tee time with Weemo, and she dressed in a lime green shirt with crossed clubs at the pocket and white walking shorts. "We'll probably play two rounds," she told Charles. "Don't count on us for lunch."

Charles found a light Madras shirt and white ducks and put them on over his bathing suit. He wore the tan poplin cap he'd had last year, really for ten years, sunglasses and woven leather huaraches. When he reached the beach, he was delighted to find Claudia waiting for him, the chairs set exactly so, his in the shade under the striped umbrella, hers at its side in the sun.

He settled back in the canvas sling, reached into his beach bag, and removed a tube of sun lotion, field glasses, and a large book. "Civil war epic," he said, holding it up. "Covers six families for three generations. Written especially for Elbow Reef, I think."

Below her glasses, her mouth turned to a smile. He noticed she wore a new bathing suit, white with red piping. Other than that, she looked the same. She rested both arms on the wooden supports of the beach chair, and looked up with closed eyes at the sun.

"Charles," she said. "How have you been?"

He was surprised at her solicitude.

"Fine. I've been fine. And you?"

"I'm improving," she said. Did she mean because he had only then arrived? "It's just that, when we were in New York, I never got to ask you about you. We talked only about me. We were busy with all that nonsense."

"Claudia," he said paternally. "Almost twenty percent of Parine Pen is hardly nonsense. It deserves being busy with."

"Isn't it ironic you would say that. You see, I've begun to think just the opposite." They sat for several minutes without speaking. Charles watched the waves break on the reef a hundred yards from shore. Once or twice he put the field glasses to his eyes but there was nothing to see.

"You got the papers?" she asked him.

"No, I've received nothing. What papers?"

"They came here special delivery yesterday. From the lawyer." She put her hand into a large raffia bag and withdrew a manilla envelope. "The letter shows a copy to you."

"It must have been late to my office. Actually I didn't go in yesterday, what with the flight, so perhaps it's there now." She began to place it back in her purse.

"What is it?" he asked.

"The complaint. Is that the right term? The law suit they're going to file asking the court to interpret the trust."

"May I see it?"

Claudia turned her head to him and lifted the sunglasses from her eyes. "Charles, you've already gone out of your way for me. I'm not going to ruin your vacation by asking you to read legal papers that can wait your return next week."

"Two weeks," he said. "I'd like to. It won't take me but a minute."

She looked at him with a maternal skepticism, as if he had asked for ice cream but promised not to eat it. She handed him the envelope.

Again they sat in silence. After a moment, Charles opened the flap of the envelope, withdrew the pages, and began to read. In a quarter hour he had finished. He put the papers on his lap.

"Well," she said.

"It's very good," Charles said. "It covers the necessary ground and lays out the case but doesn't appear greedy. It simply asks the court to decide whether old language could possibly have an outmoded meaning. I have one or two thoughts. . . ." He looked down and unconsciously put his right hand to his shirt pocket. Claudia reached into her bag and gave him the pen she'd found there. He spent another half hour writing in the margin of the pleadings, printing in a precise hand.

"With these changes," he said at last, "I think it's ready to file. Assuming you still want to go forward."

"Yes," she said. "I suppose we're at the bridge. I must cross it or jump."

Charles printed a message on the back page of the mailing. He signed his name and handed it to Claudia.

"You should sign too."

Claudia read aloud the words he had written. "'Please consider these suggestions, and with such changes as you deem appropriate, proceed to file the case.'" Then she signed her name under Charles'.

"Thank you," she said, touching his hand. "One other thing, will you? Ask them to tell Jeremy. I promised I'd let him know what we're doing and he's been working hard on this."

"Of course." Charles added a postscript under the signatures. "Working hard doing what?"

"I don't really know. I sent him boxes of material. I had drawers full of old files in the attic and I sent them all to him. And he's made two trips to Cincinnati."

"Since January?"

Claudia nodded. "Yes. He told me to keep it all under my hat, but I know he wouldn't mind my telling you. He keeps saying that you're the quarterback when it comes to the lawsuit."

"What's he been doing?"

"I don't know. Seeing people. I got him the names of three men who used to work at the company and he's been to talk with them all. One moved to Milwaukee and Jeremy made a special trip to look him up. I really don't know what he's about."

The conduct struck Charles as odd, and he told himself that it bore contemplating and, eventually, a call to Jeremy. He intended to contemplate as he sat, but Claudia rose of a moment with a shake of impatience.

"A swim?" he asked.

She ignored his question. Perhaps she hadn't heard.

"Did I tell you I've been doing some reading about falcons? Do you know the males are tiercels and only the females are called falcons. That they can get up to 200 miles an hour when they dive for a kill. The dives are called 'stoops.'"

Charles was puzzled. "No," he said. "No. I didn't know."

"They hunt by striking their prey from above. They just crash into them. Then they grab it before it falls to the ground and take it back to the nest to eat."

"Do you feel like a swim?" Charles asked her again.

"Oh, I don't know. Suddenly I feel . . . " she shrugged in a girlish way while she looked for the word, . . ."restless. Then, her voice rising, "I know." She stretched to look to the horizon where several boats plied. "Let's go for a sail. I'd like to learn how to use that thing." She pointed down the shoreline where four or five tiny craft lay beached. Then, glancing to see whether he was coming, Claudia turned and walked towards the boat shack. Charles rose and followed. By the time he arrived, she had found Gideon, the Club's boat boy.

Gideon told them how to use the Sunfish, more a surfboard than a craft. Its single mast, rudder and centerboard were its only permutations. He drew lines in the sand to show wind, sail and rudder. Charles found it difficult to concentrate. He had never had much success with coaching. In his years he'd been taught: to ride, to shoot trap with a twenty-gauge, or to toss up a tennis ball so it might be served. None of it took. It was all perplexing, the ease with which they described it and the impossibility of doing as they said. He

sensed coaches knew this, and could always discern the disbelief in their voices.

"Very easy, really very easy, ma'am," Gideon said, erasing
the pictures with his foot. "Light breeze today. Remember
what I tell you, you'll have no problem."

"Come on, then," she said to Charles. "Let's give it a try."

Charles slid off his trousers but kept on his shirt against
the sun. They pushed and tugged the hull over the sand and
into the shallow wash of a wave. The boat went out as the
water retreated and they had to run to keep up with it.
Charles realized he still wore his glasses. While Claudia
shoved the board through the easy surf, he removed the
glasses, tucked them into his shirt pocket and buttoned the
flap. He caught up to her beyond the breakers.

She was sitting with her feet in the shallow cockpit. "Come
aboard," she yelled. "You handle the tiller."

He struggled to get his body on to the deck. He was sure
he heard the crunch of his eyeglass frame as he scraped
himself up, Claudia laughing all the while as if he were doing
it for her amusement.

The wind was blowing gently in to shore. They floundered
for a while just beyond the breakers, unable to make the
little boat gain any momentum. Charles realized they were
drifting back to where the waves would catch them.

"It's not working," he said. "We probably ought to swim
back. The waves are going to catch us."

"Not that way," Claudia was saying. "You've got it back-
wards."

He looked down. She was right. He had meant to push the
rudder so the boat would turn aslant of the wind. But he
hadn't realized the tiller was levered, and he'd been pushing
it the wrong way. They were becalmed. The first wave lifted
them up, moved them back a few feet, and rushed into the
beach without them. The next one would get them for sure,
he felt.

"Come, Claudia. Let's swim for it."

The sea swelled in front of the bow. Charles was about to
jump when he felt the boat propelled by a push. The bow
knifed into the crest of the wave and settled in the trough
on the far side. He looked back. Gideon's head bobbed up in
the water just behind him. Gideon grabbed the stern and
gave another push. They were beyond the breakers.

170]

"Here, man. This not in the right place. What do I say about this rudder?" Gideon reached from the water and aligned the tiller properly. "Now you got it. Remember what I say," Gideon scolded him. He had explained it so well to the lady. Hadn't Charles listened? Everyone called him a boat boy but he was close to Charles' age.

Wind filled the tiny sail and the boat began to lap upwind in a hesitant tack. Gideon turned and swam back. They were moving now.

After several tries they managed to get the craft to come about without a complete stop. Claudia suggested they change places. Gideon had given them elaborate instructions on what to do if they capsized, how easy the boat was to right, but Charles didn't remember a word of it. Balancing carefully, they traded so that she sat at the stern and Charles sat by the centerboard, manning the sheet. The new post had its own anxiety, for he knew what would happen, with Claudia as inept as he but having an adventurous streak, pushing the tiller first this way then that. He was sure that her sudden movements would cause the boom to swing about without warning. He gripped the rope with one hand and the gunnels with the other. They sailed across the mouth of the bay, and then out, past the reef that guarded the cove. Claudia understood the concept of tacking, and after a few tries, managed to sail close to the wind and out to sea. The water turned from yellow green to blue to a deep blue that had no end to it. The shoreline was now visible only on the swell of the sea, and even then appeared to Charles blurred and foreign.

The bay of Elbow Reef was almost a perfect half-moon, guarded by the reef. White sands had collected in the arc, then a jutting mid-point of rocks which led into the reef itself. But beyond the reef, the ocean floor fell off severely. It was fathoms deep and the water looked cold.

"You seem worried," she said to him at last.

"No," he disclaimed. "I'm not worried. It's just that without my glasses people always think I'm frowning."

"Would you like to go in?" she asked.

"Yes," he said. "I think so." She turned the craft so its bow pointed at the boathouse.

Running downwind had none of the sensation of movement that Charles had felt going out. The boat plodded through the waters, and he felt little strain. He wondered why he'd been so nervous. When they reached a point upwind of the breaking surf, she asked if he wanted to swim in from there. Only then did he realize she intended to sail back out without him.

"Sure," he said. "Are you coming in?"

"I think I'll stay out a while," she said. "I'm just getting the hang of this."

Charles turned on his spine so that his feet were in the water and let himself slide off the deck. His white shirt billowed with air. He called to her back.

"I'll see you on the beach then. Be careful."

Claudia moved instinctively to balance the boat as he disembarked.. She found the point of comfort to handle both tiller and sail, picked up the sheet, and laid it across her thighs. She waved to him, then pulled in the sheet to fill the sail and brought the boat upwind. It caught the breeze and moved away.

He swam the short distance easily. Quite a little outing, he thought. When he checked his pocket, he was pleased to find that he hadn't damaged his glasses. The popping sound he had heard was a button snapping off his shirt front. His glasses were intact.

Chapter Eighteen

In the next days, the foursome found themselves spending time together. On two successive mornings they went around the golf course as a group. Charles and Claudia made a particular effort to keep score and follow the rules, hitting at the ball until, eventually, it fell to its hole. Only on occasion did either of them kick it or sweep it along, and it was not until the end of their tour that Claudia simply abandoned her ball, propped conspicuously on the fairway fifty yards off the tee. Her indifference didn't bother Weemo or Evelyn. On these mornings she and Charles quit the course after nine holes. Evelyn and Weemo insisted that they would finish, and produced their completed scorecards for analysis at dinner that night.

They made other accomodations to be together. Evelyn and Weemo agreed to join in on a hike. The two couples drove up island and walked along an uninhabited beach that Charles recognized as the site of his and Claudia's picnic of last year. It was charged with memories for him, and he would not have selected it for the group. Claudia had.

The day of their hike was warm and cloudless. They found shells, conch and cowrie, nothing exotic, but they were pleased since the beaches at Elbow Reef had long since been picked clean by its members. The sun heated the sand so that to walk became uncomfortable in bare feet. They wandered by the water's edge, in the dark, moist sand. Evelyn suggested a swim, and Weemo explained that no one had brought suits. "Oh, come on," Evelyn said. "We're all friends."

The men became embarrassed at the suggestion. Evelyn teased them and called them prudes, and Claudia laughed along with her, but to their relief the subject was dropped.

They spent the morning on the beach. The sun made them thirsty and irritable, and so on the drive back, they stopped in a scruffy town, no more than a church and a tavern at a crossroads, and took lunch at the bar. It was a wooden building, a single room divided by a rude plank partition. The two couples seated themselves at a table in the center, and the owner brought over a soiled red cloth and spread it for them. The other tables were bare. Sunlight leaked in where the boards were ill fitted. By the far wall several slats were missing and you could see into the street. A single Kelvinator refrigerator stood wheezing in the corner. It held the beer and all the food.

Several patrons sat on stools by a high counter. Now behind it, the owner took the orders from Weemo and Charles and made their sandwiches in front of them. He was a Carib with reddish hair and freckles across his nose, and he treated them well, without deference or resentment. By the patrons they were mostly ignored. There were eight or ten others in the bar, grizzled men, all drinking the local beer from bottles. Some glanced at them furtively through lugubrious eyes, and they realized that beyond the boundaries of the resort, white people were a curiosity.

They were served chicken sandwiches on a coarse bread with slices of yellowish tomatoes. On each plate was a bag of potato chips. They had a second round of the local beer. It was cold and tart.

They were drowsy from the heat and the beer and the buzzing surf. Charles drove back. On the way they passed a man relieving himself by the road. Charles intended to ignore him, but Evelyn pointed him out. Weemo had been dozing in the rear seat and stirred.

"What did I miss?" he asked.

"Nothing," said Claudia.

"A man peeing," said Evelyn.

"Oh damn," Weemo said. "Do you suppose we can go back?" and they laughed.

Charles was annoyed. "He puts his own comfort ahead of ours," he said.

"Charles, for Christ's sake," said Evelyn. "He doesn't even know us."

When they returned to Elbow Reef, Weemo and Evelyn changed for tennis. Charles took a shower. Then he went to the library to deposit his annual donation of books and enter them into the Club's filing system. Claudia met him there and helped. She read the titles and authors aloud while he inked in the proper notations on filing cards.

"My contribution to a better world," he said when they had finished. They sat in wicker chairs, the color of ivory, and looked across the dining patio at the rolling surf.

"It's different this year," she said, responding to his thoughts, not his words.

"I can tell. What do you suppose it is?"

She stared out the window. The reflected light of the sun gave her profile the look of a magazine photograph.

"I'm different," she said. "I've become aware of all the tugs on me."

"Self-awareness," Charles said absently. "They say if the honey bee knew anything about aerodynamics, he couldn't fly."

"It's as if I'm supported by everything except myself. Not financially, you understand. I mean, I've lived my life for my son, my husband, the Parine Pen Company, even my inheritance. I think especially the stock, and now I may not even get it. I don't know whether I'm supported by these . . ." again she searched for a word, impatiently, ". . . by these things or sapped by them." There was vexation in her voice.

"We all have things like them," Charles said. "They're our bodies of influence." She looked to him to explain.

"Bodies of influence. The earth's orbit is affected by the large bodies nearest it, Mars and Venus, but mostly it's determined by the sun. If the density of the sun were to change, the path the earth follows would change too. People are like that."

Claudia thought only a moment. "No they're not, Charles. We're not planets. Sometimes we act like that, but all we have to do is act differently." They walked out from the dark, shuttered library into the sun and looked across the sand at the brightness.

"I think I'll go for a sail," Claudia said.

Charles walked to his cottage, intending to take a nap. But he did not sleep. Evelyn was still off at tennis. The bungalow was hot and close. During the day the club manager shut down the electricity needed to drive the ceiling fan, to conserve the storage batteries, and so Meredith lay on his bed in a faint sweat.

At four he showered a second time, and, taking up a sketch pad and charcoal, walked to the clubhouse. He meant to draw the patio, with its woven rattan furniture and beach umbrellas against the long laterals of the sea. But at the bar there was a fellow who had introduced himself earlier. Name of Halaby. Ever eager to chat, to find out what you did for a living and where you were from. There was something about Halaby Charles didn't like. He seemed typical of the kind of member the Club was admitting lately. Must be under some financial strain, Charles thought, if it's taking in people who want to know what you do for a living. Charles greeted him with a brief nod and walked past the bar to the rock point.

On the horizon he saw the dot of a pink sail, a sail he imagined to be Claudia's. It disappeared and came back into view on the hills of the sea. He watched it slide back and forth across the sky without any apparent destination. He could find nothing that caught his fancy to draw, so he went back to the cottage and read. He was now well into the novel he had brought.

It was not Claudia's sail. She had taken her Sunfish around the point, where she couldn't be seen from the Club's beaches. She handled the boat well in the light chop, playing with the sheet to make the craft heel with the wind. She'd pull the sail tight and the hull would angle into the waves. You can see how close you could cut it, she realized. See how close the sail would come to the water without actually capsizing.

Interesting what happens when you travel alone, she thought. You do what you want. She found fewer and fewer things she liked where another person was helpful. Sex, she thought with a smile. Although even that could be argued the other way. A cast of two was neither necessary nor suffi- cient. It needed something more. Without a certain amount of story line, of stage craft, it could all be a bit silly. How does the act, the plumbing of man and woman, affect us? If the physiology were different, we wouldn't carry around the same baggage. Pursuit and conquest, tumescence and sur- render, who's up and who's down. Positioning. It was all murky, connotative, undefined. No, she decided, and her thoughts pleased her. Sailing was empirical. Sailing was simpler.

*　*　*　*　*

The day after their hike they had chartered the Club's
yacht, the *Naught Availeth,* for a sail. As it turned out, the boat
was not the Club's at all, but belonged to the Demmings, a
quirky English couple who served as its captain and crew.
They had bought it several years earlier from a large London
insurance company. Change in management, Captain Demming explained as if he'd been involved in the decision. Divestment of nonessential assets.

The Demmings were in their fifties, both grey and remark-
ably fit. He was browned from the sun, but she stayed out of
it, she told them. "And I'd advise you to do likewise," she
said. It had long been the Demmings' dream, Mrs. Demming
went on in a practiced voice, to own a boat and sail the Caribbean. Day charters barely allowed them to meet their
monthly payments to the bank, but they were hoping to de-
velop a regular clientele. And, she said, it was better than a
row house in Luton, working at a lunch counter, which she
had, and running a kennel and cattery, which the captain
had. For twenty odd years, raising ungrateful children and
not even liking animals, a queer way to make your living, if
you asked her.

Originally they chartered out of Charlotte Amalie on St.
Thomas, but for the last three years they had anchored off
Elbow Reef to make the boat available for its guests and those
of a similar resort on a neighboring island. A very good
clientele, Mrs. Demming assured them, using the French pro-
nounciation. "Very much the class of people you meet at the
Elbow Reef Club." There were good things about it and bad.
She met interesting people, although she had to admit they
were mostly Americans. And it kept them busy, she said. Busy
and in debt.

All this before they sailed. While the others stood cornered
on the pier listening to Mrs. Demming, Weemo lent a hand
with the loading of the wines, the personal baggage, the
scuba gear. At last they were ready. The boat motored out of
the bay and past the reef. Once at sea, Captain Demming cut
the engines and, with Weemo's enthusiastic help on a halyard
that could as easily have been driven by its electric winch,
hoisted the sail. The boat bore away on the land breeze, lay

[177

for a moment becalmed in the intervening seam, then caught the trade wind and climbed into pace.

The *Naught Availeth* was a fifty-two foot sloop. She had raced three times in the Bermuda's Cup, but was built for luxury cruising. She slept six in three private staterooms, and could take a crew of four besides. Although, as Demming said proudly, he could sail her as easily alone.

The Abbotts and the Merediths had chartered her just for the day. Evelyn led Claudia and Charles on a snoop below decks. She bounced gaily on the beds. Claudia was charmed by the tiny brass fireplaces in the corner of each room, by the library shelves by each bed, their books secured by elastic cords. The boat had a beautiful wood finish, hand rubbed and spar-varnished so it shone like glass. There wasn't a piece of fibreglass on board, Demming told them. Touches of teal blue paint on mouldings brought out the brightwork.

They were under full sail by eight o'clock. The sun had burnt the purples and reds of the dawn out of the sky. At Mrs. Demming's urging they assembled at a table behind the wheelhouse for coffee. She served them in heavily weighted cups, pouring dark coffee brewed in the European manner. And she passed platters of cinnamon cakes, lemon squares and almond flavored scones. Then she took the wheel while her husband lectured the guests on the boat's geneology and construction.

"Now then," and he paused professorially. "A bottle of Caribbean rum to anyone who can tell me where her name came from."

The group was silent. He took a breath to go on when Claudia spoke.

"'Say not the struggle naught availeth.'"

"Very good," Demming said. Weemo patted his wife's knee. "Very good indeed. Arthur Hugh Clough. Can you give us more, Mrs. Abbott?"

"No. I'm afraid you've just exhausted my knowledge of Arthur Hugh Clough."

Demming looked over their heads and recited the entire poem, four quattrains, ending dramatically,

"'In front the sun climbs slow, how slowly,
But westward, look, the land is bright.'"

In the style of a grammar school declamation contest, Demming stretched his arm and pointed, and Charles looked. Westward lay only the sea.

He went on to describe their day's prospects, his life in suburban London, and his philosophy of finding the Lord in everything he did. It was no doubt a speech he gave to every tour, and it hopped from seamanship to geography to hygiene to eschatology. Where they might anchor, what not to throw down the head, the toilet to them, and how it had come to him and his wife to see God's face in the charts of the Lesser Antilles. The two couples were captive as impressed seamen. Evelyn was restless and stirred as if to wander off once or twice, but Demming's ministerial manner kept her seated. When he was through, he invited them to wander about the boat, to try their hand at the wheel, and to enjoy themselves.

With the wind abeam they sailed at a constant clip. Demming rigged both jibs and, once done, sat by the wheel as each guest took a turn. He showed them how to watch the luff of the sail, to keep it filled and how to come off or into the wind as needed. Charles took his stand at the helm, then went to the foredeck to read. Weemo went over the charts with the captain, took pictures of everyone, helped Claudia and Evelyn with their turns and even opened cans for Mrs. Demming. Midway through the morning a school of dolphin joined the boat, swimming not ten feet off the bow. Charles spotted them first, and, excited, he called his wife and friends to watch.

"They like the wake of the boat," Demming explained. "They get a lift from it, like a motorcar racer staying in the drag of the lead car."

The dolphin looped and dove as they swam. Everyone, even the seasoned and dour Demming, smiled to see them. There was a catwalk on the bowsprit and Claudia stretched out on it to watch, holding on to the iron stays that held the rigging for the jibs. Charles watched her with a shiver of fright, for the beam on which she lay was slender and oval, and her perch looked precarious over the seas rushing below. Only Demming noticed his concern.

"No need to worry, sir," he said privately. "There's only water below her and we can stop the craft in two two's if she slips in."

Charles was reassured, although he had no idea how long a distance Demming meant.

Claudia lay on the slender walkway watching and thinking of the dolphin in the Yeats' poem. Why should an old man not be mad? Was Charles mad, watching for birds and seeking order in a world where he himself could hardly wiggle free of the order he had imposed? The poem talked of nymphs and satyrs copulating in the foam and of a girl who once knew all of Dante. The sun was hot on her back and the plunging of the boat made it easy for her to imagine what it was to be one of the dolphins as they rose and plunged through the sapphire water.

By midmorning the boat had completed its long reach. Straight as an arrow on the trade winds, Demming had said. Like taking the underground. He brought the boat head to the wind and set anchor in a quiet bay formed by three or four uninhabited islands, shreds of land elevated only a foot or two above the water.

"You may want to swim here," he announced. "There's good snorkeling and diving, and you might explore the islands."

The women went below to change into bathing suits. Both Weemo and Charles had worn theirs under their trousers. Weemo fetched the air tanks and regulators and set them out on the foredecks. He had brought gear for everyone.

"What do you think, Charles? Want to give it a try?"

"No thanks. I've never had any lessons. Don't you need to be certified?"

Weemo assured him it was safe, that they'd be in shallow water and he could teach whatever you needed to know. Charles declined.

Instead, he took a snorkel, mask and fins from the pile of gear. Then he lowered himself down the ladder that Mrs. Demming had set for them on the leeward side of the boat, and, clearing the tube, floated face down in the warm water. All he could hear was the rasp of his own breathing. They had anchored in about thirty feet of water, and he swam within sight of the boat, watching the coral heads move under him like a film. In time, he saw his companions make their awkward submergence. Bubbles rose from them as they sank. They descended until they seemed to be crawling along the sea floor. They passed directly under him, Evelyn rotated, turned towards the surface and waved. The three followed the ocean bottom out to sea. It was a curious sensation. Charles felt more alone than if he had not seen them at all.

He stayed in the water for a long time. He looked down, down at the massive brain coral, at the sea-fans and sea-feathers, at the barnacles with scarlet plumes, at fish painted like clowns, like zebras, fish shaped like coins and cucumbers and butterflies. It was a bursting bag of life and color and, to Charles, who wanted to know the names of everything he saw, of frustration. Once he swam to the close island and rested on its sand beach. When he returned to the boat, Claudia was on the rear deck, unstrapping her tanks.

"That was quite remarkable," she said to him. "You ought to give it a try. I've never done that before."

"Did you drown the others?"

Claudia squeezed the water from her hair. "They're still down there. Weemo told me a newcomer would use up air twice as fast. I certainly did. They wanted to finish the dive." She was breathless as she spoke, not from the dive but from her excitement.

They dried themselves off, spread the beach towels out on the hardwood deck and lay down, side by side. The Demmings busied themselves with fixings for lunch. It was pleasant to lie on the wood, listening to the lap of the water against the hull and the substantial clink of china and silver being set on the brass and mahogany table.

The sun warmed their skin. "I had a cable from Jeremy," Claudia said.

"Oh?"

"We sent him those materials, you recall. I think he was just responding."

"What did he say?"

"Something like, 'Fire when ready.' My sense was that he thought the papers looked fine. And he asked that you arrange another meeting with Gordon."

"I wonder why."

"He didn't say," Claudia told him. She turned on her side towards him. "I suppose we could call him from Elbow Reef to find out."

"It will wait," Charles said. "We'll get the suit on file, then I'll call him when I'm back in New York."

Charles realized this might be their only time to make a decision. "We're ready to go, then," he said, although it came out more as a question than a statement. When she didn't reply, he asked her, "Are you still prepared to take on your brother?"

"Yes," she answered. "Let's go forward before I lose heart."

Charles nodded. It was his strong feeling that she had everything to gain and nothing to lose. He had told her as much, in those words, regretting not the sentiment but only how melodramatic it sounded. Unless she acted Gordon had made it clear that he would demand the trustee follow the old Ohio law and preclude her from the distribution. The way the shares divided among the cousins, coupled with Gordon's holdings, Claudia Parine's stock represented control of the Parine Pen Company.

"I'll call Cincinnati when I get in tonight," he said. "The suit can be filed while you're tanning on the beach."

They lay on their backs and the sun dried them completely. Butter was popping in the skillet and soon something was frying in it. Claudia let out a soft sigh.

"You sound happy," Charles said.

"I'm on the verge, Charles. I'm on the verge. That dive, this whole week. It's been a new sensation for me."

Evelyn and Weemo climbed up the ladder. The Demmings rushed to help with their weight belts and tanks.

They were served a memorable lunch. Mrs. Demming's modest description of an apprenticeship at a lunch counter understated her skills as a chef. When they told her this, she glowed and said it was always her ambition to cook for people who cared about food. She served individual mushroom pies, steaming sherry through a light crust. Then she made a ceviche with fresh barracuda, and for the main course served grouper in a red sauce that from the coriander and green olives she guessed was Algerian. For each of the courses, the Demmings had selected a particular wine.

The settings showed Mrs. Demming's eye as well. The crockery was a handsome stoneware, ecru with a trim in teal the color of the boat's detail. Each course came with a fresh glass of Irish crystal that mixed the light of the sun into the wine. They drank the wine and asked for a second bottle of the burgundy with the fish. Captain Demming, whose care for his guests was avuncular, suggested they rest before attempting the water again. They sat around, giddy in the sun, while the places were cleared. Mrs. Demming served fruit and cheese and an iced coffee made black and very sweet.

Charles had retrieved his field glasses and was watching a group of birds circle the far island.

"What ho," cried Weemo. "Anyone we know?"

"Terns and gulls. All common ones like those. . . ." Charles pointed with the glasses.

Claudia fell to a light sleep. Weemo and Evelyn found a cribbage board in a stateroom and brought it to the dining table on the rear deck. Weemo began teaching her the game.

Suddenly Charles gave a shout.

"What is it?" Weemo asked, coming to his side.

"There," Charles said. "Beyond the grasses. Damn. It's down now."

"What was it?" The commotion awakened Claudia and she stirred from her air mattress.

"A Black-headed Gull," Charles said. "I think it was. Hard to say."

"Oh for Christ's sake, Charles." Evelyn turned and went back to her hand of cards.

"Is that good?" asked Weemo.

"They're quite rare. I've never seen one in all my years coming here. It would be a new bird for my life list."

Weemo squinted at the horizon. He borrowed the glasses and had a look himself.

"There you go, Charles," he cried. "The ones over the channel. They're black-headed."

Charles took the glasses and swung them to where Weemo pointed. "No," he said. "They're Bonaparte Gulls. They look just like the Black-headed. The ones we want have a red beak."

"That's it?" Evelyn asked, now looking at Weemo's hand. "That's it? It looks just like those except it has a red beak?"

"That's the way you can distinguish them. That's the easiest point of identification."

"Why the fuss, then?" Evelyn asked but no one answered. "If that's how they look."

Weemo stood by Charles' side for several moments. He was trying to keep the birds separate, those he had studied and those still worth a look, but he had consumed easily a bottle of wine and the birds wheeled in the sky. Charles too stood watch.

Evelyn called to Weemo to come back to the game. When he didn't return, she called his name. Then she took the pegs out of the board and rearranged them. She substituted cards in Weemo's hand. Still the men stood by the railing, watching and pointing.

"Look," she shouted. "Quick. There it goes."

She waved to the windward side of the boat. The men spun around and crossed to the far railing.

"Did you see it?" Weemo asked. "Did you see the one?"

"Does it have a black head and a red bill?" she asked.

"That's it," cried Weemo. "That's it. Good girl."

"Could be," Charles said hopefuly. Captain Demming appeared from the galley and handed Weemo and Claudia each a pair of nautical binoculars, enormous Royal Navy issue with a rubberized coating to prevent light glinting off. Now all three scanned the sky that Evelyn had pointed to.

"No mistaking it," Evelyn said. "Black heads like the ones over there, but with a red beak."

They watched eagerly for almost a full minute.

"Damn," said Weemo earnestly. "I don't see it. I can't even find a bird." The remark, its intensity, was too much for Evelyn. She burst into a giggle.

"She's fooling," said Claudia. "She's teasing. She didn't see anything."

They resumed their places. Claudia lay back down on the mattress and slept. Charles watched for a while longer but eventually went below to get out of the sun. Weemo played a few hands with Evelyn. He was a little dizzy now. He'd been in the sun since eight, and the only liquid he'd had was a Moselle and two excellent white burgundies. He put down his hand and looked sharply at her.

"Why would you do that?" he asked her. "What kind of a joke is that?"

"Come off it, Weemo," she replied. "Don't be so serious. It was only a prank."

"I don't understand it. Charles really cares about his life list. You know that."

He rose from the table, went over to the stairs that led below decks, and called to Captain Demming.

"Shall we weigh anchor? We probably ought to be getting under way."

Demming came up. That would be fine with him. Whatever the ladies and gentlemen wanted to do. Weemo asked to help. Demming took him forward. Together they towed the boat by its anchor chain until the bow stood directly over the mooring. Then Weemo pulled on the chain until the sea anchor flopped on board. He was sure his posture looked like the illustration in a book he'd had as a child. A Boy's Book of the Seven Seas. He didn't remember the stories, but he had loved the drawings. In one, a golden-haired youth, stripped to the waist and wearing a seaman's tam with a pom-pom, hauled a dripping anchor from the sea. Weemo stowed the chain as Demming had shown him and made it secure. That was Demming's term, too. Weemo liked nautical terms. He might want to have a boat like this. Maybe he would after Claudia came into her trusts. Only six years to go.

Demming sailed under motor on the way back. Much of the trip was upwind, and rather than go through a series of tacks, he kept the sails down and the twin screws chugging. His guests didn't seem to mind. They were sleeping off the wine.

Back at the Elbow Reef, the foursome split up without discussion. Charles and Weemo each took a light supper in their cabins delivered by room service. Claudia went for a walk around the point and skipped the meal entirely. Evelyn slept until dusk, and then went down to watch the weekly movie in the game room. It was Singing in the Rain. She enjoyed it every time she saw it.

Chapter Nineteen

From the Journal

How could I not have seen what was coming in those last days at Elbow Reef? The question is not rhetorical. One is taught in psychotherapy that no question is, especially the ones we ask ourselves. And this particular question has an answer. I was looking the wrong way, just as I was off the port side of the ship for that gull. A gull that didn't exist. I was watching the intimacy I had had with Claudia crumble like a hole a child digs by the sea's edge. He digs until he hits water, until he can dig no deeper, because the water and sand become one. Then he puts his feet in and waits. The first waves don't reach him. It may last for a single wave or ten, for ten minutes or an hour. But when the water spills into the hole it closes up. His feet have disappeared under the sand and he pulls them out. The hole is gone.

I had done much of the legal work that went into the case we filed in Cincinnati. And while I am not one for courtroom work, I do understand the process. I am told I also have a certain ability to write persuasively, and so I took charge of the briefing of the arguments. There is a satisfaction in researching the law for a brief. You can draw from the whole of history and then try to change it. Not in a big way, I admit, but in determining where the next cobble will be placed. Reasoning, a construct of reasoning. That can be a satisfying enterprise, and I threw myself into it with an energy I can't recall giving to any project since.

I thought to present this case as a conflict between history and logic, and hoped that the court would side with logic. That *is not so facile as it sounds. Common law puts a high value on predictability, especially when dealing with property, and predictability favors history. Lawyers and judges revere what happened before. I went on a rare retreat with my law firm where the moderator started by asking my partners to set down their goals for themselves. They wanted to know how other firms had answered the question.*

In the case of the Parine trust one had to take history head on. The law had established a mannerism, a mode of expression. The words, "heirs of the body." They meant something specific at a time when blood lines were channels through which property was distributed. Indeed one could limit property to pass according to sex and rank, so that the eldest son took an entire estate, and only his male heirs would qualify for subsequent inheritance. Claudia's lawyers would argue to the Surrogate's Court of Hamilton County, Ohio that the language of the past should not be stretched to wreak an inequitable solution on the present.

Those were the subjects that occupied my thoughts, as Claudia slipped away from me and the hearing on our petition approached. Not Evelyn's increasing petulance or Weemo's charity towards me. Instead, what were the case's chances? And how would its outcome affect me? I had urged Claudia to take on this fight. If she won, she could resolve the question of divorce independently, an adverb that more and more easily suited her. Equally important, if she won, she would recognize the signal part I had played in that victory.

There was certainly the chance that she might lose. It could turn out that Stillman was the legal genius he pretended, or it could be that the Ohio court had no interest in coming into the Twentieth Century. The most likely risk was that the Parine Pen lawyers would produce testimony that would hurt us. Even if they were neutral, they might have evidence, unknown to us, of old Parine's intent to exclude adopted children. It was not likely that they were neutral. We had to assume that they feared the loss of their principal client and that they'd figure out a way to help the case of their client's president.

All possible courses. If Claudia lost, my advice would have been flawed. The responsibility that came with this role made me uncomfortable. I had become used to the luxury of giving advice where its effect was indeterminate, where the advice isn't proved bad or good until the recipient was long buried and his will admitted to probate. Unless you believe that the afterlife includes courts with jurisdiction over legal malpractice, that luxury allows one's life to be led in peace.

I called Jeremy Slatkin from the ancient phone in the Elbow Reef lobby and asked whether he had anything for us before the complaint was filed. I had assumed that he was trying to find support among employees or the Parine family for Claudia's position that her grandfather regarded her with equal affection and therefore as an equal object of his benevolence. I was wrong there, too. But I never asked. Jeremy told me, when I spoke with him that last day, that he thought the pleadings were fine, that I should go ahead and get the case on file, and that he'd tell me more about his inquiries when we next saw each other. If only I would arrange another meeting with Gordon Parine and his arrogant lawyer. I told him I would and we compared calendars.

I had just hung up from that call when I struck up my fated conversation with Halaby. I note it in this private journal, but not to prove my intuition. Merely for its singularity. Intuition is not my strong suit. I rarely grasp the significance of an event until long after it has passed. I believe our fate surrounds us and would instruct us if only we knew how to recognize it. There is the old Vedic fable of the man who walks to the end of his country. And there he looks down and sees Fire grinning at him. He journies out every day, and every day he sees Fire, whom he knows to be the end of life, grinning at him. Finally in desperation he leaps into Fire's arms, and gives up his life. As he does so he asks Fire why he has haunted him. And Fire says, I was not haunting you, Master. I am simply there to mark the bounds of the earth.

I had talked with Halaby before on only one brief, tedious occasion. At the Elbow Reef's bar while I waited for Evelyn before dinner. He had quizzed me until he found common acquaintances. When we finished comparing our views on them, he relented and let me be, although I could tell that he was judging my financial and social background by theirs. After that, he looked for me and I avoided him. Again at the bar, once in the library, and once when he came to sit by me at the beach and Claudia thankfully appeared to claim the second chair.

Had I managed to avoid him on that last day—what? Would my life have been different? The candid answer is no. Unless I rewrite my life as a novel, its circumstances would be the same. My perception of it, my comfort in the reciprocity that I believed held together a loveless marriage, they would have been spared. Do perceptions matter? I think only actions. They say Napoleon had a sleepless night before Waterloo and it made all the difference. If Judas had not betrayed his Lord, would we all be heathens?

*   *   *   *   *

Halaby sat with one leg stretched out before him and the other bent with its heel on the first rung of the bar stool. On the bar in front of him was an old-fashioned glass, whiskey filled close to the brim. He had been there for an hour. Most people at Elbow Reef ordered the rum or gin drinks of the tropics, but Halaby drank Kentucky whiskey. He sat watching his drink as if it might flee. Then he rotated the glass slowly on its cork coaster. He wore madras, knee-length shorts, the blues and lavenders bled into each other, and high white socks that covered his calves. For the evening meal the men at Elbow Reef by house rule donned coats and ties, and in allegiance to the rule Halaby wore a linen, cream-colored sports coat with a silk knit tie in pale maize. He sat frozen, as if he had been posed. He might have been in a Bellows oil. Then he noticed Charles walk into the room and sit at a far table. There was no one else in the lounge except for the black barman, whose conversation he had exhausted.

"Meredith," he cried, too loud for the room. Charles pursed his lips and nodded.

"I'll join you." Halaby was walking over as he spoke.

"Shame on you," Halaby said with good nature in his voice. He pointed to the yellow sheets which Charles was folding and putting inside his coat pocket. "I heard you on the telephone just now. Shame on you, doing business on vacation."

"I beg your pardon," Charles said. He had just hung up from his call with Slatkin, and, as was his habit, had taken notes. Was the man really boasting that he had eavesdropped?

"Well," said Halaby offhandedly, to excuse his admission. "Can't help it. That phone's out in the open. If you want to have secrets you can't talk on a public telephone."

Charles determined not to correct the manners of the man. Halaby went on about the Club's deficiencies. The help was getting more and more sullen. Had Charles noticed? And there used to be a better class of people among the members. Halaby had detected an element. Had Charles noticed that? Then he asked Charles if he and his wife would like to join the Halabys for dinner.

"Thanks," Charles said. "We have a date. We're dining with another couple."

Halaby paid no attention. "I never take this seating," he was saying. Charles found himself hearing every fourth or fifth word. Where were Evelyn and the Abbotts? He glanced at his watch. It was he who was early.

Halaby noticed he was losing his companion's attention. "Tell you what," he said in a voice turned hoarse and excited. He leaned forward and Charles could smell the whiskey on his breath. "Tell you what. I've seen something that'd make you sit up and take notice."

"Oh?" Charles said, looking around. Couldn't he avoid the next tale from this odious man, a tale that he knew would be too lurid for his tastes?

"This is supposed to be some fancy club. I mean, that's what my wife said when we got in. She said we'd be the envy of everyone in Syracuse. I mean, they've never heard of it. But they've never heard of this, either. I swear."

"What is that?" Charles asked absently. He wasn't sure that Halaby hadn't made his point and he'd missed it.

"I sleep late every day. That's my idea of a vacation. I sleep 'till noon and have breakfast on my back porch. Everyone else is gone by then. I look up the hill, Honeymooner's Hill, from my porch. And you are not going to believe what I've seen. You know those cabins they don't use? Supposed to be remodelling going on, I'm told. Well, remodelling is not what is going on, I can tell you."

Halaby took a gulp of his drink. He wore a faint moustache of perspiration on his lip, and he licked at it with the meaty triangle of his tongue.

"No," said Charles. "I would guess in season they need all their extra hands for the resort. I would guess remodelling stops."

"Maybe. But the cabins don't stop. Let me tell you. There's a guy here who uses those cabins every afternoon. He's meeting someone else's wife up there and they're screwing their heads off."

"Oh," said Charles, more interested than he would have thought. "And you see all this?"

"I see them coming out. They give the maid some dough, a twenty I'd guess, every day. She watches the place and brings them stuff. You know, lunch and a pitcher of iced tea."

"How do you know they're not simply housed in that cabin?"

"'Cause they're only there in the afternoons. And another thing. They always carry their excuses."

Halaby looked him dead in the eye. His face was animated and he breathed through his mouth. Charles could hear the breathing.

"Carry their excuses?"

"They bring their golf bags, sometimes tennis rackets. I mean, they're supposed to be somewhere else, but they're not. They're up in the cabin, doin' what comes naturally."

Charles had no response to this. He contemplated it, he considered his involvement in it, but he discounted the story as an exaggeration. Charles never accepted unpleasantness at face value and he assumed that all men who told stories of the flesh exaggerated them. At that moment Halaby grasped his forearm as he held the drink in front of him. He could feel the dankness of Halaby's hand through the sleeve of his blazer.

"Hold on," Halaby said. "Here he comes now, but not with the woman. No, but damn it. He's with a different one. You better look out, Meredith. He's visiting with your wife."

Before Halaby said those last words Charles had the flicker of a thought that he might be talking about a man Charles knew. But that the man was now entering with Evelyn meant of course it could not be. It could not be Weemo and Evelyn. He hadn't really thought it could.

And then he turned. He saw the Abbotts enter the lounge. Claudia wore a floor-length chiffon dress the color of her eyes. And Weemo had dressed in a white dinner jacket for the last night of their vacation. They looked elegant. She had linked her arm in his. They looked as if they were night-clubbing in a black and white movie. This evening was to have been awards night, as Weemo had said, but he and Evelyn had unexpectedly been knocked out of the tournament.

"Are you sure?" he said to Halaby. "Is that the man?"

"Absolutely sure. Better watch out for your wife. That man's a real masher."

They waved at Charles and began to walk towards him. Charles rose, and without saying a word to Halaby crossed the room to greet them. The trio sat down at a far table. The Abbotts ordered drinks. Charles demurred, for he hadn't finished his first. As he sat there he thought through what had happened. He understood the reasons for the man's mistake. Halaby had seen Charles and Claudia together all week. At lunch, on the beach, even coming in from a sail. He had assumed that Claudia was Mrs. Meredith. And that could leave only one candidate for the role of Weemo's afternoon paramour.

"Oh, Charles," Claudia was saying. "That dreadful little man got you at last. He's been waving to me everywhere but in the lady's room." Charles watched her speak.

"He's from upstate New York," she went on. "And he used to own the franchise rights for fried chicken or spaghetti or lasagna, some food, I can't remember which. For a state, a large, rectangular one, and he never has to work again. He'll tell you whatever you want to know, if you'll wait."

Weemo remarked on the man as well, although he said he hadn't noticed him before. Evelyn joined them within minutes. She had needed a seamstress to fix something. "Isn't the service here getting worse?" she asked. "I don't remember when the service was ever this bad. I think the Elbow Reef is falling on hard times."

"Charles," Weemo said with genuine concern. "Is something funny. Why are you smiling?"

"Am I?" asked Charles. "No, nothing's funny. I wasn't aware that I was smiling."

The two couples went in for dinner. The Club served the champagne that Weemo had specially ordered, although they drank only one bottle of it. "The rest," Weemo said, "you'll just have to drink after we've left. You can take it out on a midnight cruise and drink it from Evelyn's shoe."

A five-man band played dance tunes. Charles excused himself. He didn't feel like dancing. The Club had cleared a small space in the middle of the dining hall. Weemo danced with both ladies. He danced and sang his own lyrics to *Deep Purple.* Even the line with the title in it. Charles paid him no mind.

"Those aren't the words," Evelyn said, laughing. "I don't know where you get the words from, Weemo, but those are all wrong."

Chapter Twenty

From the Journal

In a world of emotions laid out like cookies baking on a sheet, where popular psychologists urge us to identify our deepest feelings and reveal their ingredients, my ambivalence towards Evelyn's conduct may seem odd. It did not to me at the time. Nor, however, was it explicable. I suppose I was quite the fool not to realize that their affair was going on, for how long I do not know today. I have never asked. I remember sitting through dinner that night wondering whether I should make a scene, whether I should confront Weemo as a cuckolded husband might in a short-run play, but I never did. I could only think as we ate our way through the Club's seafood buffet —and I am sure this reveals both some weakness in me and a Puritan fastidiousness—that those very hands which were pouring an excellent champagne in everyone's glass, my glass, had probably that very afternoon been plying their way around Evelyn's body. It was that juxtaposition of the familiar and the erotic, it was its presentation at our dinner table, that I could not forgive Weemo.

Did I hate her for it? I don't know. Writing about it today, I understand what happened. But when that understanding came to me and whether it replaced rage, I truly cannot remember. Our memories are flawed, and they no more replicate for us the taste of anger or hurt than the color of a sun that has set. I knew from the first that Evelyn was attracted to him. It was evident. He has an easy manner with everyone, and Evelyn greatly prizes affability. She also would enjoy his yen—which he pursued with an earnestness I saw him apply to little else, but then I had limited exposure—to put people at ease. Those are two pleasures she cannot find in me. From the beginning I understood she enjoyed his company, and during our acquaintance it was always she, and not I, who was the force that interlocked us for these holidays.

She had made her interest in him known early on. When she became, in the language of a gentler past, his lover, I could only guess, and I chose not to. It couldn't make any difference, and there were more important questions to examine.

Since the day Evelyn and I were married, friends have speculated on whether we would stay together. That's more than a guess. Once or twice some of my bolder companions would bring it up, tentatively, and I was easily able to scotch the subject by letting them know of my distaste for it. I don't doubt that Evelyn's friends have done the same, and knowing how she likes check-out counter fiction, I suspect she has been more candid than I in responding. She savors gossip, especially about herself. But I have always thought that those who inquire demonstrate either a disrespect for history or an ignorance of character. Our coupling, like the most mean and the most miserable, was not without its passion. And now that I have passed sixty and understand how passion can be sated, if not cured, life with her is not without its comfort. To reduce our loyalty to each other to its rudest equation, Evelyn does not like to be alone, and I do not like to see her unhappy.

If it takes all kinds to make a world, a bromide invented, I am convinced, by humankind to masquerade its inadequacies, then it is one of Nature's lucky quirks that the weaknesses of one are symbiotic with the strengths of another. It's like the old joke of the perfect marriage between the sadist and the masochist. There are few men who would indulge Evelyn's flighty intellect, her theatrics, her coquettishness. Her ability to fill her life and the lives of those around her with trifles. But I don't delude myself. A similar few women would put up with my brooding, my penchant for contemplation over action, and my doubtless unsought solicitude. It is, as they say, a perfect match.

I determined to say nothing to Evelyn about Halaby's revelation until I'd thought it through. The Abbotts left Elbow Reef

*after that most uncomfortable dinner, and I endured the em-
braces of Weemo and Claudia who reminded us that the arrangements had been set for Aspen in August. They had
secured the same house for us. Claudia said that she would
wait to hear from me about a New York trip, as soon as Jeremy
and I had our schedules straight. And Weemo. Although I
cursed him at the time, I realize he held the best of motives.
Weemo shook my hand and, before he bent to get in the airport
taxi, placed his hand on the nape of my neck in genuine affection.*

*Several days later we returned to New York. Once back in
our apartment, I allowed professional obligations to steer me
around for a week or so. Evelyn sensed that I was disconsolate
and asked me once or twice about it but then, as is our manner
with each other, let it drop. I telephoned an imperious Stillman
to arrange for another meeting in early April. His response to
my request I should have anticipated.*

*"The matter will be resolved in court, Mr. Meredith. You've
filed papers and we'll respond, to represent the wishes of James
Parine."*

*"I understand that, Mr. Stillman. But I am asked to set up a
second meeting with you and your client. Surely for a matter
where this much is at stake, you would agree that further exploration can't hurt."*

*"I agree to nothing. But if my client is willing, we'll attend.
You have no objection, since we are suiting your convenience
by coming in the first place, to holding the meeting at these
offices, I assume. Tell me, what's the nature of this further
exploration."*

*"I think that should await the meeting itself." Stillman
seemed satisfied with that, and of course I had nothing more
for him.*

*For the rest of the week, I had an unusually dramatic sched-
ule. An estate the firm had been handling had a valuable
collection of Georgian silver and vermeil, and it came to auction that week. I attended all three days, conferring with the
auctioneer and the auction house doyenne who was in charge
of Eighteenth Century antiques. The results were gratifying.*

For reasons we didn't understand, Japanese and Near East buyers had become interested in the market, and we realized almost twice what we'd hoped from the sale.

I returned home on Friday earlier than usual. The last lots had been sold that day, and rather than travel downtown to my office, I walked the few blocks from the auction gallery to our apartment. It was warm for February, and the constant melancholy I had been carrying since we left Elbow Reef had been neutralized. Whether by the balmy skies, my own meditations on inevitability, or simply by the fact that melancholy, like love itself, needs an impetus to keep its momentum, I cannot say.

Evelyn was just back from a class at the New School on German expressionist painters. The year before it had been biorhythms and beta waves and the year before that, dietary changes to increase your intuitive powers. She was dressed in a suit that I especially liked, peacock blue, with a black military braid. The color set off her complexion. I laughed to myself as she stood thumbing through the course materials and talking about her instructor's views about how to depict the super ego on canvas. Were these materials, the handsome art book and text, another golf bag, to be toted around and left in the entry hall of a new lover's apartment?

"What I mind about your affair with Weemo," I began without preface or thought, "what I really mind was its proximity." The statement hit me as delphic even as it came out. What in hell did it mean? "We are so different in how we view our behaviour. I don't expect you to be like me. But I expect you to give me room for my own self-regard. When you have an affair with Weemo Abbott you trample on that."

She looked at me and her mouth trembled. Those lachrymal eyes, those eyes that so often counterfeitted tears, now filled with them. I confess I was moved and gratified.

"What do you intend to do?" Evelyn asked. I had no answer for her but found myself giving one.

"I'm going to Connecticut for a few days. I want to think about this."

I packed a small grip, called the office to tell them I might not be in next week, and drove to the family house in Litchfield

County. It sits on a lake, and most of the houses are summer places though, with the interest in Nordic skiing, there are often people at the homes and at the one or two resorts on the lake all winter. The unseasonably mild spell had melted the snow, and now, as I drove up the gravel drive, I realized that there was no one around. The solitude and quiet of the house made me think I had made a mistake, and I contemplated driving in to Danbury and staying at a motel. Instead, I built a fire in the parlor, poured myself a large Scotch and soda, and went around switching on lights and turning up thermostats.

By the time I had made my rounds and a second drink I was feeling much better. Ages ago I had put in a store of tinned goods in the pantry behind the kitchen for just such an unplanned visit, and I rummaged through the cans of stew, soups, sardines and hash planning a meal. I opened some smoked oysters and ate them with soda crackers and a third drink, while a pot of vegetable soup came to a boil on the stove.

Only a trained monk can contemplate in the time he sets aside for it. To the rest of us, thought comes like hail in the summer and insight like snow. I found myself regretting my decision to throw out the television set in the country house, as I sat spinning the radio dial in an unsuccessful search for music without amplified guitars. Hey, said one disc jockey to me, if it's too loud, you're too old.

I ate the soup as the fire burned down. Perhaps I would read through the evening. I took down a volume of Sherlock Holmes from the shelves, but I was unable to concentrate through a paragraph, even on stories I knew well. Three drinks are beyond my capacity.

I walked out on the porch and listened. There was nothing, no sound. Too late in the day for road noises, too early in the year for crickets. I heard a wooden squeak and realized it was the ancient board of the porch under my own weight. The silence had a vitality, its own single breath, not in or out but a single breath without break. I spoke my own name and listened. Far off a car's engine murmured and died away. I could see my breath condensing in the air, but it made no sound. Across the lake I saw the light of another house. I stared at it, and as if preternaturally I heard the thin voice of something from inside it. The siren of an ambulance from a television set or the cry of a child or a violin's cadenza. I couldn't tell, and it didn't matter. Satisfied, the silence broken, I went back inside.

I came away with no insights from that weekend, and few enough recollections. For some reason I remember getting into bed that first night. I chose to sleep in a single bed in the room that had been mine as a child. When it had been last made I don't know, but its flannel sheets were fresh and cool. Like a glass of water left standing. On its top rested a quilt of precise pattern, forest green diamonds hosting bunches of yellow, orange, and purple asters. The quilt had been in the house for ages. I pulled it back and, folding it into quarters, placed it carefully on a chair in the corner.

At the head were two pillows. The one underneath was over-sized, with a coarse filling. The other was of fine down fitted into a percale case. The bed had been made with almost military tautness, and the top sheet was pulled over the grey wool blanket a satisfying six inches. Like a man's cuff showing just the right amount of linen. The bed struck me as a prospect of great stability. To come in the dark upon this perfectly made bed, cool sheets on a frosting February night with the promise of one's own body heat to warm the space, to spend the time suspended with one's own thoughts, cozy, alone.

For the rest of the weekend I occupied my time. We had had a cord of wood delivered that needed splitting, and I took the double-bitted axe to that task. I've always enjoyed chopping wood. The trick is to chop through it, to hit for the stump and not the log. It took hours and I ached from the exercise, but by sundown on Saturday I had separate piles of pine, apple and oak, all but the apple —too small in diameter to split—quartered and stacked on the side porch.

On Sunday morning I went into town for breakfast, and read the New York Times over a meal I assumed Paul Bunyan would have cooked for himself. The day was clear, the light was bright and blue enough to make a sound. Afterwards, towards noon, I walked from our house to the marshy creek that feeds into the north end of the lake. There at the water's edge I could see the inaudible commotion of a hatch of insects. The warmth of the past weeks had brought them out prematurely. It was a hundred mayflies, hatching off the surface. The order Ephemeroptera, ephemeral, short-lived. I knew about them from my sketching. The summer I was twelve I collected water insects and drew them. Mayflies had been my favorites, delicate forms with gauzy wings, each a perfectly rounded deltoid, a satisfying shape to draw.

A little cloud of them carried off downstream. Light shone through the bare trees, the maple and birch, dappling the ground with shadow. Pattern over pattern. The husk of some seed blew in the breeze, lifting off to follow the path of the mayflies now out of view.

I returned to our New York apartment that night. Evelyn was watching television and when I came through the door she rose to turn it off. She asked me to sit beside her. She told me she had called Weemo and ended their relationship. She would never see him again if I wished. And she told me this would never happen again. I was sitting on the large sofa that was covered in a precise hound's tooth check, and I realized how silly I'd been. I'd had a view of marriage that Evelyn had never shared. We both honored it not merely out of conscience but out of mutual benefit. But Evelyn no longer needed me to find her way in the world, and so my loyalty was misplaced. The very sense of loyalty that had prevented me from coming forth to Claudia had now disappeared, but I feared so had Claudia.

Evelyn asked to be forgiven, and I forgave her. Am I too passive? Am I too ready to accept the proposition that we follow our own nature much as do ragweed and rhododendron, as do walruses and spiders? I had come to no conclusion during my brief retreat. It seemed pointless to be angry at Evelyn for being the way she was. I understood her interest in someone not her spouse. Indeed I shared it, and I secretly envied the way in which she had pursued it to a tangible resolution. It is a way I wish I could be.

Evelyn was surprised at my reaction. She does not see the apposition between her point of view and mine. She leads with her passions, I with my explanations. Cause and effect. It's all a matter of training, I suppose.

Nor did she understand, later, after Jeremy, Claudia and I had had our confrontation with Stillman, why I would want to keep our plans to be at Aspen with the Abbotts that summer. The fact is, I liked Weemo. That fondness now blended with a curiosity, probably mean-spirited but virile, to see how he and Evelyn would deal with each other in light of my being included in their cabal. That it was mean-spirited I should not doubt, for at the first opportunity, I shared my knowledge with Claudia.

And I confess that in the blend as well was my hope, unsupported by action or word, that somehow Claudia might yet be ignited by my feelings towards her.

Chapter Twenty-one

Evelyn Abbott used the week-end that her husband was away to sit down and reason. As it happened, deduction, or as much as she needed, took far less than the entire week-end. By the time she retired Friday evening at her usual hour she had analyzed her alternatives and had come up with a decision. That left the rest of her time free. On Saturday morning she shopped for shoes and met a friend for lunch at a sushi bar. They went together to a gallery on Fifth and Ninety-fourth for an exhibition, mostly nudes and land-scapes, shot by women photographers.

Sunday was a brunch party she and Charles had been in-vited to and had declined. Charles didn't like the people. She called to tell them she was available and they were happy to have her. It lasted until early afternoon. She left with a nice young man she had met there and they went to a movie together. He ran a firm that assembled electronic parts in New Jersey. He was good company, and while she had noth-ing in mind she wondered if he weren't gay.

In the evening, an hour before Charles returned, she called Weemo and told him they had been discovered. She told him they would have to cool off, and he said certainly, that he understood. His response was sympathetic, a bit too ready, she thought, but then again he was always prepared to concede if you really wanted something. She cared for Weemo and thought he cared for her.

But she had decided to let Charles make the next move. She recognized his predicament: that he yearned for Clau-dia, while at the same time he was inhibited from announcing himself by uncertainty and a sense of honor. It was, she be-lieved, not through strength but weakness. Some oath of alle-giance, something to do with a boarding school mentality that he carried around. She had long since perceived that Claudia was about to make some changes. Charles might be unconscious of it, but with her good nose for the musky aromas of passion and movement Evelyn knew what was going on. She had observed Claudia's conduct with Slatkin and her husband and knew Claudia was entering a season of migration.

She didn't think Charles would leave her. It wasn't like him. But if he did, she needed to be prepared. That meant examining her alternatives. The answer to the question Are you happy, Evelyn believed, is, Compared to what. Weemo was an alternative, and one at hand. It was too early to do anything, she decided Friday night, parking her mind on the decision as if it were an all-day spot by the curb outside her apartment building. No need to commit. Wait and see.

* * * * *

Charles greeted Claudia at the firm's reception desk. She wore a deep-necked linen jacket, mauve he would call it, paired with a straight linen skirt of the same color. The jacket fastened with four oversize brass buttons. At her throat was the single strand of pearls. It was clear that the clothes had been selected to achieve a result, and to Meredith's eye, unpracticed in the encoded language of fashion, she looked less structured, almost foreign.

"Do you like it?" she asked after they brushed cheeks.

"Was I staring?" he asked.

"Was I complaining?" she said with a flickering smile. "Do you like it? It's Italian, very expensive and new. I don't usually dress this way, and I'm insecure about it."

"You look wonderful," he said.

He led her to his office, and regretted as he did so not having reserved one of the client conference rooms. The accomodations of his firm were adequate and the conference rooms almost pleasant; but the lawyers' offices, even those of senior partners such as Charles, were constricted by the high rents of the financial district.

In the smallish room, crowded with files and books, he swung about the two upholstered side chairs so they faced each other. She didn't seat herself immediately, but instead walked about and looked at the bookcases. They were filled with the accumulation of a quarter-century of the practice of probate law. There were form books, tax treatises, manuals for Surrogate Court practice. Then she noticed the paintings. They were the only personal items in the room. Four watercolors hung on the wall behind his desk, unsigned, handsomely matted and framed. Two were of birds, gulls on the wing and a small bird in a pine forest. A third showed a white frame house by a lake, in a setting that was clearly New England. And the last was a seascape. Two beach chairs lounged by the water's edge. One was empty. In the other chair was a woman, faceless because of the distance but, from the color of the bathing suit and the auburn hair, unmistakeable.

"These are quite good, Charles," she said.

"It passes the winter. I make all those sketches, you see. I must do something with them."

She looked at him intently, awaiting his words. He turned to the stack of documents on his desk.

"About tomorrow," he said. "I really don't know what to expect. Jeremy is still overseas. It was he who wanted this meeting. He called the office an hour ago and told my secretary he'd missed his plane so he won't be joining us today. He was to have explained what all this is about." Charles indicated a thick stack of photocopy paper. "Now it seems he'll get in just in time for our meeting with Stillman. I'm in the dark," he said with exasperation. "I thought perhaps you could tell me. . . . "

"No," Claudia said. "I don't know any more than you do. Gordon telephoned last night to pump me about the meeting. But I put him off. I told him I didn't know anything. I'm sure he thought I was posturing." They looked at each other, perplexed. Charles picked up the stack from his desk.

"Jeremy's sent me these papers," he said. "Copies of his notes. But I can't make heads or tails out of them. A lot of numbers, and his undecipherable handwriting. It clearly is financial analysis, historical stuff about Parine Pen. But more than that. . . . "

She met his shrug with one of her own.

"Tell me about our lawsuit," she said.

There he was on firmer ground. He was in charge of the case. "Nothing new to report. You've seen their response to our petition. Now we simply go to hearing and let the court decide."

"What do you think? They filed that long paper from the company's lawyers. How will that affect us?"

Meredith had read their responsive papers with a tinge of anxiety. As he had feared, the firm that had drafted the trust for James Parine did indeed still represent Parine Pen. Charles could not tell from the affadavit they had signed whether the facts were against them and Claudia's case was weak, or whether the company's law firm had gone out of their way to support the position of Gordon Parine. In either event the affadavit was harmful to Claudia's side. The firm had come up with no direct evidence on James Parine's affection or antipathy towards his grandchildren. But, demonstrating an ingenuity Charles admired despite his allegiance, they had prepared an analysis of wills and trusts drafted by their firm during the same era as the Parine trust. It showed that other documents had used language not so restrictive as "heirs of the body," that many wills and trusts of the time were drafted more expansively, using words that showed an intent to include adopted children with natural children. The unstated conclusion was that if James Parine had meant to include Claudia, their firm knew how to do it. They called it a frequency study. If it was allowed into evidence, it would damage Claudia's position. Charles explained its effect to Claudia. She sat impassively, rolling her pearls between thumb and forefinger.

"Are we lost, then? Should we abandon the case?"

Meredith regarded her carefully. She was an extraordinary mixture of intensity and insouciance, and he realized how unconsciously she moved from one to the other. Surely she must see the economic consequence of this suit. Yet she acted as though, were he to tell her to walk away from it, she would abandon the case. To her it seemed no more than a handfull of wildflowers she had picked to link into a necklace, flowers that might wilt before she could finish her chain.

"Claudia, your portion of the James Parine Trust, the Parine B Trust, amounts to just over nineteen percent of the voting stock of Parine Pen. Parine Pen today has a book value of eighty million dollars. For years its book value was probably the upper limit of its fair market value. In the last few years it has made money. A lot of money. Even with a conservative market capitalization, Parine might be worth as much as twice that. So. You are involved in a fight for an asset worth sixteen to thirty-five million dollars. It may cost you two or three hundred thousand dollars to prosecute this case. I never espouse litigation, you understand. I'm not in favor of it. But given the relationship between the cost and what's at stake. . . ." Meredith trailed off and raised his palms as if handing her a conclusion the size of a small melon.

She breathed in deeply and exhaled through her mouth. "Of course you're right. We must go forward. It's just that, I have enough. I have what my parents left and those Parine shares Daddy gave me outright. That's plenty to live on. But I suppose you're right. And there's Harrison to think of."

Again she looked at him and waited. And again he assumed that his feelings, feelings he had not articulated to himself, would not articulate to himself until years later, could be read on his face. He thought to speak them, too. Instead, he raised something quite different.

"Claudia. I have knowledge I feel I must share. I don't know how to tell you without hurting you."

"About Weemo and Evelyn," she said.

"Yes." He was astonished.

"Oh," she said easily. "I appreciate it. But I've known for ages. And Weemo felt he had to tell me after Evelyn called him."

"And you didn't care?"

"This isn't Weemo's first fling. I cared, but no more than I've cared before."

"And you kept coming on these holidays? Knowing?"

She reached over and patted his hand. "Of course. Otherwise how would I get see my wonderful friend?" she asked with a smile. "If I regularly came to visit him in his office, there would have been gossip."

They talked little more about it. Charles provided no insights. He was caught so unawares by her candor, caught in territory of the heart he found so unfamiliar, that he could only speak in commonplaces. He had anticipated that he would be consoling her about her wayward husband and agreeing that Weemo was not worth standing by. Instead he found it was he who needed the consolation, to help assuage the remorse he now felt. And even though he had not given voice to the remorse, Claudia consoled him.

She looked down at his hand. Hers rested on it. "Your watch," she said. "It's running slow."

It was true. He had several watches, but the one he wore today, a gold chronometer that had been his grandfather's, was running ten minutes off. He glanced at it and realized as well that its tan leather band had become dark from sweat stains. He must not have noticed it before.

"We'll talk more tomorrow," she said and patted his forearm. "After the meeting."

This time she kissed his cheek, and pressed both his hands with her own. He escorted her through the reception area to the elevators.

*   *   *   *   *

From the Journal

What was a train of thought called before the invention of the train? Surely not the stream of consciousness, for a stream is uninterrupted and it flows to a destination controlled by its geography. An avalanche of thought? Thought that falls from a cliff? I must ask the next philologist I meet.

My concentration on the lawsuit was intense, a product of an interest in the subject and the conviction that a legal victory would plead my case to Claudia. I was happy preparing for the hearings. I was on a continuous track. It presented a chance to establish new law, albeit in a minor corner of a minor field. Still, those chances don't often come to a lawyer in a large, commercial firm, unless he practices with a disregard of his firm's economics. I have the necessary disregard, but not the indifference to my partners. More, the source of my joy was a belief that my work signified in Claudia's life.

I was wrong. It was Slatkin's work, and not mine, that turned out important. It's folly to think that each of us can prove himself in his own way. In that observation my father was right. Each of us proves himself by his deeds. Jeremy had the wonderful gift of doing, of moving things along. Profluence. What I'd believed to be a minor achievement—the creation of a well constructed brief on Claudia's behalf—was fusty scholarship, work that, as it turned out, changed nothing.

I am beginning to think this journal will not explain my acts to me. What if I were to rewrite it, in novel form? I could adopt the third person omniscient, speak for every character.

That would be more than a lark. It would be an easy way to make the result what I want. It would be a magician's trick. For of course there is no such thing as third person. Every point of view is subjective.

If ever there was a time for me to come forward to Claudia it was that afternoon before our final meeting with Stillman. I see it now as opportunity almost to the point of dramaturgy. Yet again a different subject preempted our conversation and the chance slipped away. Not her financial affairs, though I thought my comments to her were direct and necessary, and firmed up her resolve to go ahead with our plan. And I was convinced that the success of our plan would pave the way for us to consider our own futures.

No, instead we found ourselves discussing the incontinence of Weemo and Evelyn. And she was so sympathetic, so knowing. My surprise at her reaction, my consternation, took away my composure. How is it that she could be so prescient and I so naive?

She asked me my reaction and I said an unkind thing. I made some reference to a natural order, an affinity for one's own kind. I did not intend to condescend, but my words or my expression communicated the inference and of course she grasped it at once. She scolded me for it.

"Charles," she said in that most intimate voice of hers. "You really are a snob, you know. A gentle, sweet snob and the dearest man I know, but a snob nonetheless. How else could you view their carrying on as a class trait?"

Chapter Twenty-two

They arrived at the midtown offices of Stillman's law firm promptly at eleven o'clock the next morning, and gave their names to a thin, handsome woman at the reception desk. The offices had been designed to suggest elegance and military efficiency. Her post was less a desk than a control station. It was the perimeter of a large oval with a cherrywood base and a black marble top. She and two other women, equally well turned out, sat within and worked its elaborate electronics, routing telephone calls, dispensing messages, calling names in perfect diction over a microphone with the hushed modulation of a tennis umpire.

The woman invited them to seat themselves in the area behind her. They walked around the station and were relieved to find Jeremy staring out the corner windows of the room. The view was spectacular. It faced south and west from Fifty-third Street and included most of the famous midtown spires and towers. The day was clear and they could see all the way downtown.

Jeremy had heard them announce themselves at the front desk and he waited until he knew, from their reflection in the glass, that they were just behind him. "Every time I see that building," he said without turning and pointed to the Empire State, "I think of King Kong. Poor bastard."

"King Kong," Charles echoed. "What is the moral of that story?"

Jeremy turned and hugged Claudia. Then to Charles' pleasure and embarrassment, he embraced him. "The moral of that story is, If you think it's so tough in the African jungle, you haven't been downtown."

They sat on leather and chrome Bertoia chairs around a coffee table. "You have a New York outfit on today," Claudia remarked. Jeremy was dressed, like Charles, in a dark suit, pattern tie, white shirt. Jeremy's clothes had a more severe, more tailored cut. He also wore French cuffs with plain oval links in gold, bearing his monogram. "When in Sodom," he said with a slow and winning smile.

A blue-haired woman approached, identified herself as Mr. Stillman's secretary, and asked that they follow her. Charles had hoped for a few minutes' privacy so they could quiz Jeremy on the morning's strategy. He got only a brief, importunate whisper from Slatkin while the woman stood by an interior door, waiting to escort them to the offices beyond.

"Look, I'm sorry I haven't had a chance to explain. When I start talking all I ask is that you back me up. This may be a little gritty for your taste, Claudia. He's your brother, not mine, and if you like you can back off later. But unless we hang together this morning, a lot of leg work will go down the drain." Puzzled, they assured him of their support and followed their guide down a long hallway. She showed them to a conference room, a tiny room just large enough for the five of them, where Stillman and Parine were waiting.

They seated themselves around the small round table. To the side, a mock Empire telephone commode held, besides the usual equipment, a kitchen warmer. Two full pots were steaming on it. The room promised to be uncomfortable. And, Charles thought, it was doubtless chosen for that reason. Stillman indicated the pots of coffee and tea with a brief gesture, and Claudia, in an attempt to introduce a moment's civility before they began business, offered to get everyone a cup. Parine said no, Stillman declined with a shake of the head, and Charles and Jeremy accepted.

Stillman turned his mournful, owlish face to Charles and uttered his first words.

"You've asked for this meeting, Mr. Meredith. Will you now tell us why?"

Charles made no pretense of his role. "Mr. Slatkin asked that I set it up. Let me turn it over to him."

Jeremy placed a battered briefcase on the table. It looked like something he had had since sixth grade, cracked black leather, the cheap kind that showed through its aging. He unsnapped its latch and unfastened one of the two buckles. The other was missing its thong.

"As you know, gentlemen, Mrs. Abbott has filed a complaint in the Hamilton County Probate Court."

"And we have entered an appearance," Stillman interrupted, "on behalf of interested parties and heirs of James Parine."

"May I continue?" Jeremy's tone was friendly. He might have been about to tell a funny story he'd heard.

"That case is set for argument in several months," Jeremy said. "In September. You lawyers know more about that than I do. I suppose it's merely a question of the court's hearing whatever testimony each side intends to introduce."

"I must stop you again, Mr. Slatkin." Stillman paused between his sentences. Then he leaned over his folded hands and looked up to catch Jeremy's eye. He intended that Jeremy speak only to him. "That suit is at issue and we are not prepared to discuss it with you. We'll have our say in court."

"I'm not here to discuss that suit either. If I can go on . . ." Stillman waved his hand like a conductor bored with an amateur orchestra.

"Now you represent Mr. Parine, Mr. Stillman, with your Ohio counsel, and technically what I'm going to say concerns not Mr. Parine but rather the company that employs him. Parine Pen. And since its counsel isn't here, you may want me to repeat this for their benefit or," and now Jeremy paused with a parody of the other's hauteur, "even take notes." He reached into his briefcase and produced a yellow pad. He also pulled out a thick memorandum, bound in clear plastic. On its first page it bore the name of one of the nation's leading public auditing firm.

"I have no concern with Parine Pen," Stillman said.

"That's a pity," said Jeremy. "They may be generating a lot of legal fees in the near future. You might get yourself concerned with it. It's a very interesting company." Jeremy opened the auditor's memorandum. He had not yet mentioned it.

"Very interesting. For example, it created a European joint venture to manufacture ink. A joint venture that has been costly over the past three years. Three million dollars in losses. Of course you're aware of that, Mr. Parine?"

"Yes, I am. One of our few loss subsidiaries."

"One of the very few. You had to sell off the bottling plant and the loading docks and the warehouses outside Bremen last year. The company took a beating there, too. Sold it for less than book."

"I don't see what this has to do with my client," Stillman said.

"I think he does, Mr. Stillman. I think he's remembering that he owns a piece of the buyer of those plants."

"Listen here, Slatkin. That deal was approved by the board. Everyone knew what was going on." Gordon Parine's voice narrowed with animosity.

"And most of them got a chance to own some stock in the buyer, too, didn't they?"

"What business is this of yours, Slatkin? How do you deal yourself in?" Parine had both hands on the table in front of him, palms down. He and his lawyer had been taken by surprise, and although disquieted, he realized he ought to get as much information as he could.

"Deal myself in. What a curious expression, Gordon. Just what a court might say about a major stockholder who uses losses in his company to channel assets to himself.

"And how I come in is simple. You may remember that, despite the way you act, you do have other stockholders. Your sister is one of them. The trust for her benefit is another. And I," here Slatkin pulled back from the table and stretched his arms as if he might be first awakening, "I am a third, having bought one hundred shares from your cousin in Scottsdale, Arizona. For an outrageous price."

"Mr. Slatkin," Stillman's voice turned conversational. "Your reputation precedes you. You are mistaken if you think you can take a small position in this, a private company, and use it to shake down management. These people won't scare."

"I think you have your directions confused, Mr. Stillman. You mean shake-up, don't you? A shake-down sounds illegal and I'm sure you wouldn't be about to slander me." Stillman lowered his eyelids a trace. Slatkin went on.

"I hope these people won't scare. Scared people run. I simply want them to stand and explain. The Bremen deal. The fact that an outfit which is doing pen assembly for our company in Guadalajara has a high-paid consultant on its staff named Gordon Parine. The fact that last year Parine Pen spent five million dollars on a fabulous house on Red Mountain that's been visited by only one employee of the company. And it turns out he lives there. Nice view, though. And, I hadn't thought of it, but this year the company'll have to pay an inflated price for a log cabin which our president didn't like to look at."

Gordon Parine was a fan of books on negotiating strategy. He had read a dozen authorities on what to do in a squeeze. But he forgot all the advice now. His lips thinned and went white as he stretched them against his teeth. "For your information, Slatkin, the board has approved all of these transactions. And for your further information, in the past year, Parine Pen has had the third highest profits in its history."

"Ah," Jeremy said. "I didn't realize. I didn't know that confraternity and profitability were valid defenses to theft."

At the word the room filled with angry voices, Stillman and Parine's demanding and hostile. Charles responded with explanations, but to be heard his voice was also raised. Jeremy sat back and leafed through the accountant's report. There was an argument about what had been said. There was shouted talk about apologies, and the lawyers disputed whether defamation in the course of a lawsuit was grounds for a separate suit. Jeremy turned to Claudia and asked her softly what she and Charles had planned for lunch.

"Nothing," she said.

"I think the meeting is over. Shall we go?"

He touched Charles lightly on the arm and with a nodding of his head and upraised brows indicated they were leaving. Claudia stood and Charles pulled her chair back for her. She looked to her brother and his lawyer in their chairs and said with a smile,

"Please, gentlemen. Don't get up." And she led the way out.

In the reception room the blue-haired woman cheerfully found their coats. She commended them for dressing for the calendar and not being misled by the false warmth of the past days. "We'll have cold through April," she said. "There's a lot of winter left. That's the way people come down with spring colds."

She was helping Claudia into the far sleeve of a camel's hair topcoat when Stillman came out, looking from face to face. He found Charles and charged him, approached as close as he could without touching.

"You can't do this, Meredith. You can't let your client come in here and defame Mr. Parine. I'm going to take this up with the greivance committee. You haven't heard the end of this."

To his surprise, Charles was unruffled by the attack, even delivered as it was inches from his face.

"I'm sure you're right, Mr. Stillman. I haven't heard the end. But if you call the greivance committee, be sure to get your facts right. My client said nothing today. I don't represent Mr. Slatkin. He's . . ." and Charles looked to the two of them, "he's a friend of the family."

* * * * *

Mr. Stillman's secretary had been right. The day was blowy and chill and a steady wind came in from the water. The air smelled like rain. Rain and cement.

They went into the restaurant under the office building they had just left. It was twenty to twelve, early for lunch, and they were seated without a wait. The place was a New York landmark. It had been an old saloon whose owners had refused to sell out to the developers, and so, to the warning cries that they too hadn't heard the last of it, stayed while around and above them a new skycraper was constructed. The developers meant to shut them in and deny them any future value for their land. Instead, they made the bar—which even now served only passable food at outrageous prices—famous.

Claudia ordered a chef's salad and the men hamburgers, beer. Something called for a celebration and beer seemed fitting.

"Now you see what I mean about King Kong," Jeremy said after they'd settled in. "Can you imagine what he felt like, alone in this town with everyone gunning for him? And him not represented. No agent, no attorney, no CPA."

"I'm confused," Claudia said. "I'm not sure I see the point of what just happened." She sipped at the foam of her beer.

"Don't misunderstand. I'm just delighted to catch Gordon with his greedy hand in the cookie jar. But explain to me how this will help our case? The judge who decides the adoption question won't care whether Gordon's behaving himself or not."

Even while she talked, Jeremy was agitated. He wanted to find the waiter, and he was caught between answering Claudia and risking that his hamburger would be overcooked.

"All a matter of leverage, my lovely," he said. "It is the glass holding the beer, the table holding the glass, the floor supporting the table. All a matter, in polite terms, of who is under whom." With that he rose and walked the few steps to intercept their waiter and tell him what he had remembered.

Charles finished the explanation. "Your brother and his lawyer are sitting back there," he told her, "wondering if we are going forward with a stockholder's suit. Wondering how the two are tied together, and how to cost themselves the least amount of damage."

Jeremy returned. He had been calm during the meeting but in the restaurant it was hard for him to sit still.

"Now tell me," Claudia said after she'd thought about Charles' remarks. "How did you come up with all those facts?"

"Facts," Slatkin said with a vaudeville look of surprise. "Who said anything about facts? You want facts, buy the Brittanica."

They laughed, Claudia's full voice turning heads at the bar a room away.

"You can't mean it's not true. Otherwise, why would they be so upset?"

Jeremy took a drink of his beer and smacked his lips. "What's true, what's not true," he said. "Ask Roskolnikov. The Aspen thing is for sure. I picked that one off the Pitkin County records. The house was bought in the company's name. But the lead on that and the Mexican assembly plant I got from someone Gordon fired from the controller's office. Seems the fellow came out of the closet in Cincinnati's gay rights parade. Gordon saw him on the front page of the Sunday paper and canned him."

The waiter brought their plates. For a time they ate without talking. Jeremy attacked his food as if he'd been deprived.

"And Bremen?" Charles asked after a moment. "The sale of the plants at a loss?"

"A lucky guess. That auditor's report we commissioned came up with damn little. The fact is, Parine Pen is a well run company. But for a well run company to pump up the inventories of a subsidiary and then sell it for less than book didn't make sense. That was a Hail Mary."

"Hail Mary," said Claudia. "Is that a mergers term?"

"Football, my dear. Eat your greens." Jeremy pointed with his knife. "Also occasionally used, I am told by reliable sources, in church."

"What happens now?" Claudia asked. Charles let Jeremy answer. He thought he knew, but today was Jeremy's show.

"We wait. Maybe nothing. Hearing on the adoption issue is set for mid-September. Maybe they withdraw, maybe they come at us with spikes on. Maybe they call to make a deal." Jeremy signalled the waiter, who stood by the table and wrote out the bill. "Who'd ever have thought?" he said, wiping the corners of his mouth with a red and white checked napkin. "Twelve ninety-five for a hamburger. My grandfather should have kept that newsstand on Nostrand Avenue. Great upside. Sold too early. Never sell too early. That's my advice. To hell with Bernard Baruch. Otherwise, you're out of the market, life is still going on, and you miss out."

They laughed. Jeremy was at his most outrageous and his clowning fit their moods perfectly. As they walked through the restaurant to follow their separate days, they found themselves agreeing to another full schedule for Aspen in August. Charles had not decided whether he would in fact return, but now in the company of these excellent friends he determined they would go. He would put the past behind him and he and Evelyn would go.

They stood on Third Avenue arguing about who would take the first cab.

"Jeremy, I meant to mention something to you." Charles had looked up the answer to be sure. "That suit you told me about. The one Robert Schumann brought against Clara's father. He won. I looked it up. It took four years, but he eventually won."

Slatkin smiled. "So he did. And they had eight children and a passel of études. But Schumann ended up jumping in the Rhine and dying in a looney bin. Not a good example, Charles. My advice still holds."

Over Claudia's protests about false chivalry, they assigned the first cab to her. Charles took a second downtown, and Slatkin, head bent against a dirty and increasingly cold wind, started west across Fifty-third on foot.

Chapter Twenty-three

Charles' apprehension about how the four, or more accurately five, since Slatkin, who had been spending summers at Aspen for years was now welded to the group, how the five of them would get on was misplaced. Their public activities were unchanged: Jeremy, Claudia and Charles went to concerts, rehearsals, and master classes and took long and, to Charles' relief, gradual walks in the alpine meadows. As Evelyn had promised, the private interludes between her and Weemo stopped. That newly found leisure put upon them an increased athletic strain, and they bicycled and played tennis even more vigorously than before.

Their acceptance of each other, of the adjustment in relationships between each other, was seamless. One could not discern by watching them as they picnicked, shopped, dined, or listened on blankets spread outside the tent to a Gershwin concert, that they shared a knowledge of an old affair. It had slipped into the past, as if the past were a file cabinet and each day in their memories were simply a brown envelope in that drawer, retrievable, and to the eye indistinguishable.

Although he had little precedent to do so, Charles accepted Evelyn at her word that the romance was over. Claudia had become enured to Weemo's philanderings, and had more than once continued a casual friendship with their object. And if truth be told, she and Charles were both absorbed in their own circumstances and the ferrago of choices that seemed to open from them. Of the four, Evelyn had given the matter the least amount of thought, but in keeping with her nature had come to the most direct conclusion. That was to bide her time. The decision would cause her no discomfort, would cast her in no unfamiliar roles. She found it easy to act now as if nothing had happened, just as she had acted as if nothing was happening before.

It was only Weemo's behaviour that modulated, moved by a few degrees. He became more solicitous, even if only by the lightest shading, of Charles, more eager to hear his views and to understand his tastes. Twice Weemo accompanied the three music lovers to a concert because Charles was particularly fond of Brahms, or because Charles had urged that we should try to understand a modern composer if we were to understand our times. Afterwards, it was Weemo who spoke up. He had tried, he told them, but it sounded like pots and pans to him and he had no idea what the damned piece was about. So he supposed he didn't understand our times either. His ingenuousness made them all confess, happily, that they hadn't liked the music either and maybe it wasn't necessary for wisdom. Weemo liked the Brahms, though. It was one of the symphonies, and he liked it greatly, he told Charles in gratitude.

Accompanying them whenever invited, and always invited, was Jeremy. He was a man of merry spirits and everyone save Evelyn sought him out. She suspected that no bachelor adheres to two married couples unless there is an advantage to be had. On that cynical premise, she had decided that he was after something, and it could not be she. She had heard enough about his tangential involvement in Claudia's family business to cause her to suspect that he sought his advantage there.

As the five of them came and went, they would run into Gordon Parine. In summer evenings while the music festival is in session, young musicians who have come for instruction gather in clusters on the town streets and play for loose change, and Gordon and his wife would be there, strolling in the cool night. Once, all five were walking through the aspen groves that surround the music tent. It was dusk. In the sky, in the path of an early moon that was not quite full, a young man soared in a hang glider. He looked like a drawing in da Vinci's sketchbook. When he banked away from the tent, the wings of his craft reflected the light of the moon into their eyes. They stopped on the gravel walk to watch. Charles wondered why that light, reflected from its own reflector, why it seemed so much more personal than the moon itself. In the midst of his thought, a thought that excited him much the way the music of the evening had, someone bumped into him from the rear. Gordon Parine started to apologize, but when he realized whom he had run down, he grunted and hurried past.

Other than these encounters there were no developments on the Cincinnati lawsuit. The only time Jeremy had discussed the matter with Charles and Claudia he had said it was too early to know whether they should pursue a stockholder's suit. He would have to talk with the other stockholders, for one thing. Did they side with Gordon or with Claudia? "If we get Claudia her stock in the Cincinnati court, we'll have enough shares to make a suit worthwhile," he said. "If we lose, we'd need the other shareholders to join us if we're to have any leverage at all." It was one of Jeremy's few affectations that for certain words, including leverage, he used a British pronunciation.

"Then again, in order to win our case on the adoption issue, we may just have to give up our rights to sue as stockholders." On balance, he told them, we should wait. Patience.

The word set Claudia off. "Patience is a habit I'm trying to break," she said." On your advice, Jeremy, I'll hold off for a while. But I no longer think it's a virtue."

Charles computed the time before the stock in trust would be Claudia's. Assuming they won the suit, an assumption he made by force of will, it would be distributed in less than five and a half years. That did not seem to him an untoward wait.

So they waited, but no word came from Parine or his lawyers. Jeremy had predicted that they wouldn't hear until immediately before the court date. "That's the way someone like Stillman works," he said. "Maximum pressure. Charles will have to do all the legal work and we'll have to be ready for him. Otherwise we'll never settle from strength."

Charles and Claudia confided to each other that Jeremy's hope of forcing a settlement was too optimistic. His strategy wasn't very thorough, they said. She called it transparent, he called it unsubstantiated. They told each other that the hearing would occur and that they had best prepare themselves for a protracted fight. Neither of them liked the prospect. In her parents' house, Claudia had been taught always to discuss, never to argue. The danger in caring too much about a subject was that one might defend it too strongly and ruin a pleasant atmosphere.

Of the two, Charles was the more anxious, and Claudia found herself repeating these conversations to assure him. At the very least, disagreements were a private act, to be done behind doors. And to argue over money, they both felt, was upsetting.

"Demeaning," Claudia said.

"Is it that you want to give the impression you don't care?" Charles asked her.

"It's not that. I don't give a damn about the impression. I don't want to care."

* * * * *

All they need do now was pass the time. And where better? The peaks, the wealth, the music. Aspen was the perfect place for the Merediths and the Abbotts to spend their days until the hearing. There was every diversion. Every sense could be tickled. A balloon ride or a glider plane over the mountains. The new beaujolais. Restaurants serving the prettiest sauces and the tiniest vegetables. The stores in summer were stuffed with inventory: clocks of onyx and lapis lazuli, rucksacks, Leicas, sable coats, crampons, turquoise belt buckles, racing bikes of space age metal. All in a setting where you needn't feel that you were indulging yourself. You were outdoors, on the edge of a frontier, in the midst of a wilderness. You were simply better equipped.

But even the perfect place, the wilds tamed and merchandised, cannot prevent harm that is self-inflicted.

Maroon Lake sits at the foot of two granite summits, each over fourteen thousand feet. The rock of the mountains is unusual. It is in geologic terms schistose and in climbing terms rotten. The beauty and complexity of the formation continue to draw climbers, and over the years these peaks have claimed several deaths, including Molderer's the year before. The rock structure is crystalline, and the minerals in it have formed parallel formations that don't adhere to each other. Technical climbers warn that the rock will run. It is this very impermanence that makes the face of these mountains breathtaking. They rise sudden and majestic over a shallow, glassy lake just large enough to provide on calm days a perfect reflection of the mountains framed by sky.

For all these reasons it is a popular picnic spot. In the summer, because of the heavy demand, the Forest Service closes the access road and runs buses to the campgrounds. One can cycle the fourteen-mile grade, steadily uphill, and coast back, or ride the bus. Or, as the Abbotts, the Merediths and Jeremy Slatkin did, one can arrange to be driven up and, having luxuriated in the lee of these peaks with an ample lunch, steer one's bike down the road on an effortless and exhilarating run.

Since it was a bicycle outing, Weemo was put in charge of the arrangements. He hired an outfitter to truck up the two mountain bikes from his house and three others that they rented. The five friends piled into the outfitter's van, leaving their cars in the parking lot at the bottom of Maroon Creek. They carried blankets and field glasses and extra sweaters and two bottles of red wine and a cooler that chilled three bottles of white and a pewter cocktail shaker filled with Bloody Bulls. Claudia had gone to town to shop and had packed a large picnic hamper. From it the thick aroma of warming Stilton filled the van. Their appetites awakened on the drive, and Weemo poured a drink from the shaker for everyone including the driver.

When they unpacked they found that the outfitter had included one racing bike with the rentals. Weemo was annoyed. He hectored the driver—he'd specifically asked for mountain bikes—but the young man apologized and said that was all they had left in the store.

"Forgive my ignorance," Jeremy said. "What is the difference? They all seem to have two wheels less than they need for stability."

"Just that," said Weemo. "Stability. The mountain bike is easier to ride. Wider tires, brakes right at the grip." The young man apologized again, but there was nothing to be done.

"No problem," Weemo said. "I'll use the racing bike." He and the driver checked the pressure in the tires and filled them, while the other four found a good site for the blankets.

They lay in a meadow where earlier wildflowers had bloomed and now were going to seed. Columbine and purple lupine bloomed late, and the ground, warm from the August sun, was covered with the deep green of high country moss. The sun shone on them directly overhead. Weemo took off his shirt.

They drank off the Bloody Bulls while Jeremy and Claudia unpacked the hamper. They ate a salad of sweet onions and artichokes with a Dijon dressing, and then thin slices of Bavarian ham on a crusty bread. There were potato salad and olives and for dessert the cheese and strawberries and ripe green gage plums. The Abbotts had supplied the white wine, intending it as the only supply, but when Jeremy showed up with the red they brought it along as well.

"Do you think there will come a time when people believe California wine is wine?" asked Weemo.

"Wouldn't that be a tragedy?" Jeremy said playfully. "People will assume that astroturf is grass, California chardonnays are wines, and VCR's are life."

"I think this wine is wonderful, Weemo," Charles said. He knew Claudia had picked it out. "I think you're just trying to be amusing."

"Don't take him seriously," Claudia said. "Weemo doesn't mean to be taken seriously."

The conversation had nowhere to go. Claudia had tried to explain Weemo, but her audience was skewed. Charles had intended his remark as protection of Claudia and equally as a rebuke to Weemo. Weemo chose to treat it as an insult, probably because of the amount he had had to drink, and Evelyn knew Weemo meant both to amuse and to provoke. Each of them had a vested position in the topic, save Jeremy, who didn't inquire into their motives for lack of interest. Charles topped the wine glasses again as crackers for the cheese were passed around.

Someone called to them. They leaned and twisted lazily to see. In the parking lot, where every twenty minutes or so the bus let out its cargo of tourists, was an older couple. They were in their sixties. The man was fooling with an elaborate camera set upon a tripod.

"Look over here," the woman called. She was not more than five feet tall, portly and dressed in jeans and a sweatshirt. Beyond caring. "Look over here," she called again, needlessly, for now all five were doing as she asked.

"What do you suppose . . . ?" Claudia began to say.

"They're taking our picture," Evelyn answered. "They want our picture."

"Do we know them?" asked Charles. They straightened up and smiled while the man peered through the lens. He was too far away for them to hear the shutter click, but soon he waved to show he was through. In minutes, he and his wife were walking along the path to where the fivesome had spread their elaborate lunch.

"Thanks," said the man. "That makes for a great shot. With the mountains and everything." He wore an ancient tan windbreaker over a white T shirt, and in one hand he carried the tripod, with the camera still appended. Behind him came his wife, in a yellow, long-sleeved jersey several sizes too small for her, with "Rocky Mountain High" printed across a panorama of snow-covered peaks. The shirt stretched over her rolling flesh.

"Would you like us to send you a copy?"

Charles' reaction to their question was so slight as to move only the smallest muscles on the flare of his nostrils. He was wondering whether the man's offer was a commercial one, one that Charles understood but found, in this most natural setting, unduly familiar. Perhaps the man was simply motivated by the comraderie, the delight of finding other human souls with whom to share the vista. Neither explanation suited his sense of decorum, and his distaste for an interruption of his private moments with friends must have shown in the corners of his nose, for the man said immediately,

"Oh, no charge. Just give us an address and we'll send you a print."

"No, thank you," Charles answered. He presumed the question had been directed at him.

"Don't be such a stick in the mud," said Evelyn. She turned to the man. "That would be wonderful. We really don't have any pictures of the group."

Evelyn fished around in her purse while Claudia, who had raised up out of a sense of propriety, offered them a snack from the plates and trays in their midst. They declined.

"Gotta watch what I eat," the man said.

Evelyn wrote down their New York address, they exchanged goodbyes, and the couple walked down the path towards the lake.

"How could you give them our address?" said Charles without emotion. "You don't know who they are."

"Charles, what an old tree you are," Evelyn said lightly. "They're two people from Dubuque who have followed us to

Colorado to take our picture to get our address so they could hurry back to New York and rob our apartment. Sometimes, dear, I worry about your powers of reasoning."

"I think we ought to be flattered," said Claudia. "Now we're part of the scenic wonders."

"Don't you see," said Jeremy. "They've come all the way to Aspen and they want pictures of the rich. We're rich, and they want some pictures of us in our habitat. Eating our native foods. Paté, strawberries, medoc. It's like a snapshot of the bears in Yellowstone."

They finished the wine and ate most of the fruit and cheese. It was a long afternoon and the sun crossed the cerulean sky and sent the shadows of the great twin peaks across the lake in front of them.

They piled their blankets, dishes, hamper, glassware and silver together for the fellow in the van, who would pick them up and deliver them to the Abbott house. Then, as the summer heat floated outward from the valley into the thin air, they assembled for the bike ride down.

"I haven't been on one of these since I was twelve," Jeremy said. "Do they still work the same?"

"Exactly the same," Weemo answered. "Just watch your speed going down. It's a steady decine."

"But a coast, isn't it?" Charles had been assured that no effort was needed for the ride.

"A coast," said Weemo. "An absolute coast."

They boarded the bikes and started down the long, undulating road. At first they stayed in a pack, admiring the countryside as it sped by, commenting on how quickly you accelerated if you weren't careful. But soon, both because he wanted to lead the pack and because his bike was the fastest, Weemo edged away. For the fun of it, he leaned over the handlebars in the racer's position to find the most aerodynamic silhouette. He knew how to brake himself into control merely by raising his body against the rushing air. It *was* fun, feeling the wind go by you then catching it in your chest as if you yourself were the parachute. And he went faster and faster down the hill. Faster until he wanted to slow down and then, perhaps because he had been using a bike with hand brakes at his fingertips all summer, where these were further out, and as likely because he had consumed his portion of the wine, he couldn't find the brakes. Not thinking clearly, he began to backpedal. Nothing happened. The brake levers were inches from his fingers, but he kept his eyes on the road as it sped by. He had pulled so far away from his friends that they didn't hear the whirring of his pedalling, or the sound of the bike skidding on the cattle guard or spilling, Weemo flying over the handlebars as if he were in a cartoon and coming to land, thirty feet beyond his bike, on his face in the pea gravel that bordered the pavement.

They caught up with him only minutes later. He was already in mild shock. Charles flagged the shuttle bus as it came down the road. They helped him on board and took him off to the hospital, by good fortune built at the bottom of that very hill. While they went off Claudia attended to Evelyn, who at the sight of her former lover, flaps of skin hanging from his face, had become ill by the side of the road.

* * * * *

The injuries were serious in a cosmetic sense, the doctor told them that night as they stood in the main receiving hall. It sounded like a paradox. They would mar Weemo's face until he could have restorative surgery. The surgery itself was uncomplicated and indeed if Mrs. Abbott wished there were two or three people right in Aspen who were very good at it In the meantime, though, the right side of Weemo's face would look as if he'd been made up for a horror movie.

Other than that, there was nothing medically serious. The pieces of flesh he had lost would reform. If not, they could be reconstructed. No loss of sight or hearing, no broken bones. He had landed on his cheek and right forearm, and he'd skinned his elbow.

"It was painful and an injury like that can have a dark effect on the psyche. But any psychological effect is usually temporary, and he was damned lucky he didn't break his neck," the doctor said. "You can lay it off to his physical condition and his state of relaxation. His blood alcohol could have been bottled and sold."

When the group went to visit Weemo in his room they were pleased at his spirits. His eyes were bright and his manner chipper. All but a lower quadrant of his face was covered by bandage. After their visit Evelyn told the doctor that he must be wrong about the expected psychological reaction, because Weemo wasn't depressed. Just the opposite.

"After the bandages come off," the doctor said. "That's when he'll need support."

"But then he can have plastic surgery," Evelyn reminded him.

"Not until some of the healing takes place. Not for several months. And those months can be difficult ones. He'll be disfigured and that's a hard change for many people."

The doctor's remarks were chastening. They understood that their summer had ended. It had been cut short, they realized as they found their cars and arranged for who would drop off and who would be dropped. Evelyn was particularly quiet. Jeremy had driven the Abbotts' car and they had taken Claudia home. When the Merediths stopped at the mountain home of the Abbotts to let out Claudia, Evelyn got out and took Claudia's hand.

"Don't worry," Evelyn said in a voice of genuine concern. "That doctor doesn't know Weemo. He's psychologically indestructible."

Claudia nodded indulgently but did not give the reassurance, the assent that Evelyn was seeking. Evelyn embraced her and tried again.

"This won't bother Weemo. He'll be good as new soon, and what difference for a few months."

Claudia nodded her head but said nothing. She turned and walked to the side door of her house. The others waited to watch her let herself in, then drove back down the hill to town.

Chapter Twenty-four

From the Journal

M*y reaction to Weemo's accident surprised me. I was caught up in an admixture of emotions. I'm not expert in disinguishing among them. Some blended so well as to defy separation or analysis, and others maintained an alien texture, like coffee grounds in coffee. When I first came upon him, stunned and bloody on the shoulder of the road, I was filled with pathos and revulsion. I have never been one to delight at another's pain. I don't fool myself: it is not because of some sanctimonious humanity. Rather my upbringing taught me that around the next bend the same or a worse fate awaits me. Weemo was pitiable enough, his hindquarters hoisted up in the air as if he had stuck to the ground where he hit. Slatkin and I rolled him over and lay him flat on his back. On Jeremy's instruction I watched for the outfitter's bus while Jeremy took on the clinical task—one I would not have been keen on—of wetting down a kerchief in the neighboring stream to stem the bleeding.*

By the time the shuttle came by, Weemo had receded into a trance. Someone had balled up a sweater and propped it beneath his head, and every so often he moaned softly. Evelyn and Claudia sat on the ground, on either side of him, each holding a hand. Claudia pressed the cloth Jeremy had prepared, now red with his blood, to the right side of Weemo's face.

The bike shop fellow took forever to arrive. During the wait, several well-intended trekkers and bikers stopped by to see if they could help. One fellow, outfitted with a thousand-dollar bicycle, racing pants and a sleeveless top, stopped to lecture us. He said that Weemo had no one but himself to blame. There

*was a sign warning of the cattle guard, the local bicycle club
had put it up, and he should have been wearing a helmet. I
was tempted to tell the fellow off, but Jeremy treated him politely
and thanked him.*

*It was then that I began to experience a different feeling. A
feeling of satisfaction. Not only had Weemo been upended, but
he'd been upended at one of his several games. The fellow's
phrase, No one but himself to blame, fulfilled me. In an odd
way it was an answer, as if I had been wrestling with an
obscure tax problem, a problem with a single and specific solution, and as a function of study or recall or random day-
dreaming, I had hit upon it.*

*Once again, I was unable to read Claudia's thoughts. At the
time we were all concerned for Weemo and horrified at the
messy appearance of his injury. The ear bleeds as if it were an
opening of some secret body source, and the amount of blood
Weemo spilled on the side of the road was a shock for those of
us unused to tearing into each other except by metaphor. Claudia too was upset by it and more than any of us felt Weemo's
pain with him. That night as we waited in the hospital we
talked about how one's face was so vulnerable, so open. The
comments did not escape Claudia. I could tell by the way she
agreed that she knew how hard this would be for her husband.
For Weemo especially, his face was his pennant. To be treated
with respect and not to be dragged through the mud. But
whether this particular stain evoked in her only sympathetic
emotions, I could not say.*

*We went about our summering. Claudia was concerned but
she kept up appearances, while Evelyn reacted visibly to the
fall. During Weemo's convalescence, she became docile and
agreeable to suggestion. The three of us took charge of her
activities, and she was content to follow us along for the most
esoteric music, for lectures on world economics and opera buffa.
She came on walks to examine beaver lodges in the high mountain streams. She was happy to have the companionship. Oddly
enough she seemed uncomfortable about our outings only when
we made our regular visits, and we always did in a pack, to
see Weemo in his hospital room.*

After he'd emerged from the anaesthetic, administered to pick out the stones from his face and sew up his lip and eyelid, we called on him twice a day. Midmorning we marched in, armed with presents and good spirits, and entertained him for an hour or two. And then at dusk, usually after a concert and before dinner, we dropped in for a brief stay. Weemo was not a reader, and by our second visit we had loaded him up with more books, he insisted, than he had read in his entire life. After that, Jeremy hit on the idea of taking him toys and games. We scoured the pricey boutiques in town for wind-up toys. According to the packaging they were suitable for a young child, but they delighted patient and visitors alike. By the end of his first week, we had assembled a chorus of bears that beat drums, nodding horses, trains that chugged and clanged, and enough whistles, tambourines, and ocarinas to start an orchestra.

And the box games. We passed up the electronic stuff. They were for a different generation. Instead we brought old favorites. Chutes and Ladders, Parcheesi, Go to the Head of the Class, and Risk. We would spend much of our visit reading instructions and rolling dice, until the nurse came with meals or medications and ushered us out.

All the while Weemo sat in bed with most of his face bandaged, talking out of the side of his mouth and looking as if he belonged in a bad science fiction movie. The days were quite jolly, and I wondered if my mood had not been improved by the coincidence that, in one stroke, had brought my wife to a new dependency, made her lover an invalid, and seemed to bemuse his own wife into thinking that at last fate was collecting some promissory notes.

On the day of his discharge, Weemo determined to see a plastic surgeon in town. It was advisory, since he would probably have the work done back in Cincinnati. One wag told me Aspen has as many plastic surgeons per capita as it has Lamborghinis, and because Weemo was eager to know the prognosis, he had made an appointment straight from the hospital for an early view. I remember that Claudia went to retrieve him from the hospital. Most of the bandages were coming off that day. Weemo had asked us to meet him at the doctor's office, for support, and he even scheduled his visit to coincide with our usual visiting hour—right before cocktails—so his friends could come along and not interrupt their cultural schedule.

Seeing him that evening heightened my reaction, but did not help me understand it any better. He had been disfigured by the fall, and though eventually, so I was told, a few simple procedures corrected his looks, the sight of him half-satyr, half-Halloween mask was chilling. I cannot deny I enjoyed a sense of private glee that the man who had made love to my wife at some of the most exclusive resorts in the world had been so marked, and marked by his own intemperance. That may reveal me as petty or hateful, but I felt it clearly, just as now it gratifies me to write it down.

*   *   *   *   *

The doctor's office was housed in a small Victorian cottage near the center of town. From the casement window in the front parlor you could look up and see Ajax Mountain, and on the second story deck you could sit, winter or summer, and bake in the sun of the southern sky. Of course the doctor warned against it, but himself sported one of the best tans in town. Then again, as he told his patients, they shouldn't use him as an example. He could get his small skin cancers removed for next to nothing. It was a professional courtesy.

Charles, Jeremy and Evelyn arrived well in advance of the hour. Claudia was to check Weemo out of the hospital and drive him to this appointment. The three entered the sitting room, furnished to create the illusion of a prosperous past. To the nurse—who greeted them as if they were intruders—they identified themselves as friends of Mr. Abbott, the five o'clock appointment, and stood uncomfortably looking at the bric-a-brac spread on the shelves and tables for their entertainment.

The room had been effectively appointed to indicate a haphazard taste. A table full of photographs of skiing and backpacking and shooting upland bird, portraying the doctor's family one assumed, and momentos of his hobbies. Magazines of sailing and gardening. A man of broad interests. A bull's-eye mirror in an oak frame against one wall that reflected the entire room. On the other long wall were floor-to-ceiling bookcases filled with literature and studies in fine art. A Chinoiserie print, hung in a frame the bamboo shape of which was repeated in a stencil on the wall. Three perfectly matched apple logs flamed in the fireplace.

Claudia led Weemo into the room. Despite herself, Evelyn gasped. But the loud and hearty greetings of the men drowned out that sharp sucking of breath. Weemo's scars started with a slight line on the bridge of his nose. It led to the cheekbone under his right eye, which was a deep purple and black color, the color of a Caribe's skin. The right side of his mouth was askew: much of the lower lip had been scraped off, leaving only a thin, pink crayon line. His right eyelid drooped, a low hood that slanted across the orb and would not lift, lending his face a touch of irremedial melancholy. If you had seen only this side of his face, you would not have known him for Weemo Abbott.

He shook hands with Jeremy and Charles, though he had seen them only that morning at the hospital. He held Charles' hand a moment longer than needed and gave a nervous, ambiguous shrug. Then he said hello to Evelyn and, even with an eye almost lidded shut, read the revulsion on her face. Inadvertently, he touched his fingertips to his right cheek. It was a gesture he would repeat long after the corrective surgery.

Of them all, Claudia was most at ease. Her manner was maternal. She watched over Weemo as he removed his coat, she hung it up for him, she took him by the arm and led him towards the Dutch doors at the end of the room to speak to the nurse. Claudia gave their names. The nurse made no sign of recognition.

"You will let us know when the doctor can see us," Claudia said with firmness to the bowed head under the starched white cap, and turned back to the sitting room without waiting for an answer.

They became aware that they were standing. It was from discomfort. Except for Claudia they were anxious about Weemo's injury and made uncomfortable by his appearance. The result was a mix of affection and aversion that made them nervous. Claudia sat first, saying she assumed they'd be there for a while. She chose a chair of green and black brocade, a Queen Anne wing chair with brass studs and carving on its legs. It forced her to sit formally, and she chose it for that reason.

Charles, as if to support her, to balance her choice, went to the opposite side of the room and sat on a green velvet davenport facing her. There was room for two on the sofa, but he sat in a manner to preclude sharing it.

"I suppose doctors always keep you waiting," Evelyn said irritably. Then she flopped down into a large easy chair with wide, padded arms. Weemo followed her over and sat on one of the arms. No one thought it odd.

Only Slatkin remained standing. He walked over to the bookcase and inspected the titles. Soon he had taken down a volume, a jacketless, cloth-bound book, its spine faded to grey. He opened it and looked inside the front cover.

"Please, Jeremy," said Evelyn. "Please don't say, You can tell so much about a man by the books he keeps. I hope you weren't going to say that."

Slatkin looked at her with humor in his eyes, but he declined to respond. He flipped the pages and turned again to the frontpiece.

"Listen to this" he said. "It's on the book plate."

"'These books are my children
And I'm the spider mother
If one runs away
Please send me another.'"

"Burma shave," said Evelyn. She was turning the pages of a catalogue from a New York department store.

Weemo laughed at Evelyn's remark, a short, shallow sound.

"What?" said Charles. "What does that mean?"

Evelyn turned a sharp look on her husband. "Burma shave. Like the billboards. You know, Charles. Don't be tiresome."

"I just wondered," Charles said. "I don't see how you could remember those signs, that's all. They were from the thirties. Long before you were born."

"Later too," said Weemo. "I can remember them, too."

"It was a joke, Charles. For God's sake." Evelyn said the words without looking at him.

Slatkin had been holding the book in one hand, and with a deft movement he closed it so that it gave off a report, a small pop in the close room. Everyone looked up at him. He slipped the book back onto the shelf. It was one of a set.

"Odd," he said, as if the intervening words had not been uttered. "Choosing that for your bookplate. It seems so . . . ."

He looked around to his friends, inviting the others to finish the sentence for him. It was in that spirit or perhaps out of a sense of the growing tension, that Claudia helped him out. "So childish."

"Yes," Slatkin said and smiled. "So childlike. Odd, what people will stick in their books."

The nurse came through the door and announced Mr. Abbott. Weemo and Claudia went in, their arms hooked together and he leaning down to her for strength.

The three did not talk more during the entire visit. Charles realized that it was one of the Abbotts that gave the group its glue, its common element, but he wasn't sure which one it was. He was about to make this observation to Slatkin when, no more than fifteen minutes after they'd gone in, Weemo and Claudia reemerged.

They clustered around the patient while Claudia found his waxed cotton golf jacket and sun hat and helped him put them on. No one questioned what had gone on in the doctor's office, and Weemo volunteered nothing. Finally Claudia announced it to them.

"One or two simple procedures, the doctor says. He should be fine. We'll have to wait until after Christmas but then he'll be good as new." Jeremy and Charles congratulated him on the news, and though Weemo thanked them, he seemed to be somewhere else. He clung to Claudia's arm, the anxiety of his dependence written into his posture, and they walked out the door and down the steps of the wooden porch.

Claudia had parked her jeep on an angle across the street from the doctor's house. Leaning against it with folded arms was her brother Gordon. When he saw them, he headed straight for Slatkin, passing Claudia and Weemo on the way with only a nod.

"Can I have a word with you?" he asked Jeremy.

They moved off as two confidantes might, walking a pace apart and leaning their heads towards each other to hear softly spoken words. Charles and Evelyn waved to the Abbotts' car as it drove off and waited where they were. Minutes later, Jeremy returned. Gordon had disappeared down the street.

"He saw our cars," Jeremy explained. "Knew we were around and wanted to speak to us. He'd rather track us down than pick up a telephone. Odd man."

"About Weemo?" Evelyn asked.

"He didn't seem to know about the accident. If he did he never asked. No," here Jeremy looked up at Charles. "He wanted to talk about the law suit."

"And?" Charles asked.

"And he thinks we ought to reconsider. That's the way he started. We ought to reconsider. But then he said, they'll quit if we'll quit. He said he doesn't want four years of litigation. Nothing to be gained. He's offered to drop his contention on adoption and let Claudia take her full share of the trust if we'll waive all rights on the stockholder claims. And agree that the actions the board has taken were proper."

"He's throwing in the towel," Charles said.

"He's throwing in the towel." Jeremy repeated flatly.

Evelyn listened to some of what they said, then wandered down the street to look in the windows of the nearby shops. Her interest in these casual acquaintances was waning with the heat of the summer, and she wondered why it was that they had seemed so intertwined with each other only a few months ago. Maybe it was good for Charles' business to get involved with people. She didn't know much about where lawyers' clients came from. Charles never discussed it. When they entertained it was people she picked. Maybe he was changing. He had mentioned that the firm hadn't been doing well. Maybe he was courting new clients and this was what it was to be like. Business talk bored her.

"You must call Claudia and tell her," Charles said. "She'll be delighted. And once Weemo is feeling up to it, we'll have to celebrate."

"Yes," Jeremy said. He looked overhead at the fingernail shape of a lambent moon in the sky. It was the sky of a perfect August dusk, cloudless, lighter to the west where only Venus shone low and bright, and dark, already night, to the east down the long valley.

"You don't seem pleased," Charles said. "You should enjoy your victories."

"You as well," Jeremy said. "You've worked hard on this trust issue."

Charles realized that he wasn't pleased either. He had an empty feeling. But unlike Slatkin, he hadn't thought to ask himself why.

"You can imagine what will happen," Jeremy said. It was as if he had read Charles' mind. "Now she has everything but the money. To get it she merely has to stay married to him for a few more years. Not much longer than it's been since you first met her. And now, with Weemo's accident, she's back in a comfortable role. Familiar. It'll help the time pass. Watch. She'll see him through the recovery from the fall, then through the operations, then through the recovery from the operations. Pretty soon she will have stayed the course.

"And that's why we're not celebrating, my friend."

Slatkin put his hand on Charles' upper arm and squeezed forcefully. It was an old world gesture, the way father might pinch the flesh of his son to signify the pain or truth or importance of his words. It moved Charles greatly, the impact of what Jeremy was saying, his insight into all of them, the curious and not unpleasant feeling of receiving paternal attention.

Their summer was ending. The last light of the day slipped behind the mountains and nothing could stay it.

They caught up with Evelyn and talked a moment more. Charles suggested that Jeremy dine with them. Evelyn shivered, an involuntary gesture that could have merely been a reaction to the onset of the evening's cool air. Slatkin declined the invitation without giving a reason. The Merediths found their car, parked a block from the doctor's office, and drove off.

Chapter Twenty-five

From the Journal

It was Evelyn's initiative that had formed our little colony back at Elbow Reef that first winter, and it was the absence of that initiative that now dismantled it. Walking in the Connecticut woods I have come upon the carefully constructed nest of a wood thrush blown down in a wind. It is a laboriously finished bowl, cemented together with the care and spit of the parent birds. But leave it untended and open to the weather for a month and the cement washes away, and when you return all that you find is a pile of twigs and leaves and string.

Evelyn simply stopped being interested. That is her way. I don't mean she was rude. In the last days of our Aspen stay we had an occasional dinner with Jeremy and the Abbotts. But it had all changed. Before our lives and theirs had impelled and steered each other's. Now we were casual acquaintences. Evelyn sat around during the day leafing through magazines or dropping into shops whose goods she'd long since browsed over. It was a vacation that lasted a week too long. There are worse things. If I'd feared she would find it difficult to stay away from Weemo despite her vows, I would have been wrong.

Claudia took the news of her brother's proffered truce with complete calm. Jeremy and I drove up Red Mountain the following morning, having phoned to ask her for some time. She received us on the flagstone patio and poured tea into glasses filled with ice and fresh mint. She and Weemo had been sitting at an ironwork table under a square canvas umbrella, playing a board game. When we came, Weemo excused himself and went inside.

"He has to stay out of the sun," Claudia explained. "Of course, it's not good for any of us."

She had on a tan poplin skirt with a silk blouse the color of a Caribbean lagoon. The sleeves were rolled to the elbow, a characteristic touch of hers. She wore no jewelry save plain gold earings the shape and size of collar studs. Whether she had dressed for her husband or for either of her visitors or for none of us, I could not tell. I suppose we could all think what we liked.

Jeremy told her of his conversation with Gordon. He went slowly, repeating in far greater detail than he had for me the words Gordon had spoken. His voice was soft and considerate. He might have been telling her of the death of some person they'd known long ago. I do not know what effect he intended the story to have on her, but whatever it was he must have been disappointed, for she took the news impassively, not as if she expected it but rather as if it related to the inheritance of a distant cousin. I had to remind myself that we were talking about a negotiation which would insulate her from attack, an attack with an unpredictable but definite chance of success, on her and her son's right to an inheritance of some twenty million dollars.

"What is left to do?" she asked, turning her gaze from Jeremy to me.

I had thought about the question. "If Gordon is to be believed, we should get him bound fast. I'll speak to my office today and have them draw up the papers. There'll be a release for you to sign. The trustee and Jeremy, also. And then in the lawsuit, they should withdraw their present pleadings and, if we can rely on their word, file an auxilliary brief supporting our position."

"I don't intend to rely on their word," Jeremy said. "Get them on paper."

We agreed that the safest course would be to draft the writing and present it to Gordon and his lawyers as quickly as possible. I felt I needed to place the news in perspective. It was a victory, but one couldn't tell from looking at the two of them. I volunteered my opinion that this was an extraordinary development.

That Jeremy had brought in a highly providential settlement. Claudia would be releasing a claim that we hadn't known she had in exchange for her brother's support that, in Ohio, an adopted child should be treated the same as a natural one. It was only fair to Jeremy to credit him with the result.

Claudia listened carefully. "I understand you to say, Charles," she took my hand, "that I should thank Jeremy for striking this bargain. For holding them up and getting them to agree. And I am. I'm grateful to both of you. You've done so much work on my behalf and you've been so effective. But you've given me far more important things, and I'm thankful for them too."

Praise from the woman one loves can never be excessive, and I confess I sat there in the warm August sun while she held my hand, hoping she had more to say. Over her shoulder the toy town of Aspen lay in its carved rows. I would have sat there until the snow flew, while Claudia Abbott told my fortune or taught me multiplication tables or forgave my sins. Again Time tricks us: in my mind's eye when I view that scene, Time has abandoned us. So has Slatkin. We sit, frozen, facing each other. But my mind's eye has watched the hand and not the coin. That sense of my recollection, that the scene will not end, is an indulgence, a fantasy.

Real emotions, Stendahl wrote, have no memory, and so I can record only my feeble description of what happened. I've long admired the great nature essayists. Darwin, Linnaeus, Thoreau. They note fact. But I've tired of facts. Facts recorded on these pages would be out of place. I am not after some scientific thesis that can be postulated, tested against new circumstances, proved or disproved. I need some distillation of fact to fuel my journey if it is to reach its destination.

Claudia told us to go ahead, to write up the papers we had described and of course she would sign. She asked how Gordon seemed, and neither of us answered. I hadn't seen him long enough to observe. Jeremy, who talked with him, didn't care to. Or perhaps he didn't want to incite Claudia by giving his views on her brother.

Claudia must have thought we were holding back rather than expressing our reprobation, for she chided us. She said she could understand what Gordon had done, that he'd seen an opportunity to seize control of his life by owning that stock and we shouldn't judge him too harshly for having acted as he had.

Our meeting had come to an end. She asked Jeremy and me to help her move the game board into the house. We noted the positions of pieces, picked up cards and tokens and play money and carried everything inside to recreate their game on a library table in the living room. They intended to come back to it, she told us, after Weemo's nap. She invited us to stay for lunch, but I thought she wanted to attend to her husband. We declined and she did not pursue it.

I couldn't wait to share my observation with Jeremy. "You were absolutely right," I said as we drove down the hill.

"Was I," he said, without an interrogatory rise to his voice. "In what way?"

"What you predicted about Claudia. You knew Gordon's capitulation would mean that she would stay. Stay with Weemo. Look at her, Jeremy. She's become a virtual grey lady to the man. She's prepared to nurse him back to health and to see the marriage through, at least to the vesting date."

"Do you think so?"

"Do I think so? Yes, I damn well do. But it was you who discerned it originally."

"Yes," Jeremy said vaguely. "Perhaps I did."

I dropped him off in town. He needed some razor blades and the New York Times, and his house was in the West End, near ours, a short walk. So I let him out by a drug store and I never saw him after that. I don't quite remember how we got out of Aspen without a farewell dinner, but when we went to say goodbye to the Abbotts, they told us Jeremy was on a hike, in the back country on a two-day trek. We asked that they carry our wishes to him and they promised to.

We corresponded. I sent him copies of the revised brief Mr. Stillman filed and he had to sign releases for the stockholders' actions he had threatened. In that way we kept in touch. When the case was over, I mailed him a copy of the decision in the

Cincinnati case. The court held that in light of the circum-
stances of the adoption, and of the equal and demonstrated
affection of James Parine for his grandchildren, the context of
this trust required that the words "heirs of the body" be read to
include all descendants, natural and adopted. The court said
that it had relied heavily on the fact that all living heirs af-
fected by the case were in favor.

Shortly after that decision, perhaps two weeks, I was aston-
ished by the voice of the receptionist at our law firm announcing
that Mrs. Abbott was there to see me. That last day in my office
was the briefest of our meetings, and I realized how brief a
period one needs to announce changes in one's life. It is the
coming to them that is time-consuming. At least for some of us.
It was a whirl-wind visit. Claudia was there before I could
prepare for her and gone before I could reflect on her presence.
But of course by then my preparation, my reflection were like
snow flurries to an avalanche. To no effect, not even noticeable
in the rumble of what was going on.

*　*　*　*　*

"I came to pay the bill."

"What?" Charles was delighted to see her but he was put
off by this abrupt opening. In his practice, he did not concern himself with billing or collecting money. Indeed, in the
style of another era, his firm strove to give the impression
that its lawyers engaged in their profession indifferent to
whether or not they received fees. Affectations can be expensive, and the result of theirs was that they sometimes were
not paid. Still, to discuss financial arrangements with a client,
and with this one in particular, discomfitted Charles.

"To settle my account. I want to make sure your firm bills
me for all the work you put in."

"I will assure that they do, Claudia. Now, sit down and tell
me how you are. And Weemo. How is Weemo?"

Claudia sat at his bidding and let the jacket of her loose
suit fall open. She wore a jacket and skirt of plum, and a
scarf blouse the color of cream. On her wrist was the bracelet
Charles had noticed that day when Jeremy had worn its twin.

"He's very well. He's to have his first operation after Christmas. And then a small one the next month. And then, the doctor says, he should be through."

"That's grand. That's really grand."

"And so will I."

Charles took her meaning to be that her term of nursing would soon be over. She had come to impart one message in particular, and she realized from his unchanged expression that he hadn't understood what it was.

"I'm leaving, Charles. I haven't told Weemo yet. I want to wait until after he's fully recovered."

"You're leaving? Divorcing?"

"Yes," she said. "I thought I should tell you in person."

"But we've won the case. The trust. . . . "

"I know," she said softly. She intended her voice to be calm, for she wanted him to know this was a considered decision. "I've talked to Harrison about it. He supports me. He never hesitated. He's so much freer than I."

"Well," Charles said. "I wish you'd told me, Claudia. I'd like to think this through."

Again she reached out, in the confines of Charles' crowded office as they sat on the guest chairs side by side, she reached across and touched the back of his hand. It signalled that she wanted to say more.

"And I'm going to live in California. With Jeremy."

"Are you marrying?"

"No. He's mentioned it, even says he wants to try. But I think no."

"Then," Charles said hesitantly. In his office his first reaction was as a lawyer. "Then you needn't divorce. The right to the trust corpus defeases only if you divorce or get a legal separation. You could merely. . . ."

He let his words trail off.

"I understand," Claudia answered. Of course she did, he realized. "It wouldn't be fair to Weemo. I don't want the money, you see. I would like to be on my own. Uncommitted. At least for a while. If I can do this, dear Charles, I think I will have achieved a miracle. Uncommitted, unmarried. Just me. For the first time ever. It will put some meaning in my life."

"Meaning?" he said with a charged voice. "Surely you aren't looking for that."

"Perhaps not," Claudia said gently. Her eyes looked to the ceiling. "Perhaps what it will put back into my life is merely fun."

Charles smiled. "That's nothing to sneeze at. That would be enough."

They sat for a moment in silence. Her fingers still rested on the back of his hand and when he spoke again he turned his hand to hold hers.

"We spend so much time looking for text, don't we?" he said at last. "Poring over parchment with inscrutable figures on it, assured somehow that if we could only discover the cryptography we could read the message. And yet I suspect those aren't symbols at all, only marks. That maybe a seagull walked across the page or the author is a madman scratching down lines at random."

Claudia rose and buttoned her jacket. For a moment she looked as if she might smile, or speak some words she'd prepared. But she didn't. Instead she grasped him by the backs of his arms and pulled him toward her, pressing her cheek against his, the top of her head knocking his glasses askew. And then she left.

Chapter Twenty-six

From the Journal

Why, I have asked myself, did I not do more? Was it reserve, or as I prefer to think, did I lack the imagination to match the deed to the thought? What I did was, I now see, oblique. But at the time it seemed the logical way.

In any event, I was not the victor. My acts were not the equal of my passion. I was alone in that trait, one that my father would have praised as stoicism but I now, too late, reject. Weemo and Evelyn indulged themselves until their feelings were spent. That is one destination of feelings. In the abrupt, modern idiom, use it or lose it. Others seem to have no trouble with the concept. For them it's as natural as October apples falling from the tree. Jeremy seemed to know it all along, and it was he and not I who taught it to Claudia.

I've asked my question of Evelyn. Not in this particular context, of course, though I wouldn't doubt that she knows what I'm thinking. But I've raised it in other ways. Evelyn has encouraged me to try to set aside the rules of the law partnership for my own advantage so they extend the age for retirement. I have declined. When she asked me why I wouldn't, I told her I intended to live my own morality. And she said a curious thing: she said, Charles, outside the religious orders you must be the last remaining man on earth to be doing that.

That is not to say I don't have a few productive years left at the firm. The practice continues to occupy me full time, and after that, I shall devote myself to one or two ideas I have for nature articles. And although I shall step down as a partner and can no longer vote on partnership affairs, I will maintain *an office and keep an active schedule as a senior counsel. The bulk of my practice is estate administration—the process once the testator has died—and I confess that a good portion of that work is done by computers, paralegals, and perfunctories. I too am a supernumerary, but I am the oldest among them and in the system I've helped to create my seniority protects me.*

Still, I'm named in a dozen wills under probate at any given time, either as executor or attorney or both. The firm has that designation to thank for the fees that are generated, and it is the same designation that I drafted into the wills when their makers were very much alive. Estate planning is the one field I know of where one can make provision for his dotage. All one needs to do is to outlive his clients, and it seems that I shall.

Evelyn and I have reached an interesting accommodation. Like minor characters in a great Renaissance painting, we have finally struck postures which balance each other. It was true at the beginning of our marriage that, but for passion, we might have been considerate and easy companions, and that later on, our divergent interests interfered with whatever amity had grown between us. Now, I am sixty-one, and as passions ebb we both recognize the value of a companion to whom no explanation is necessary. We have made one concession to our different points of view. We take our winter holiday apart, I going to a pastoral and usually remote destination while Evelyn enjoys touring the European capitals.

In dentistry, when a new crown is put on a rotting tooth, to anneal the two materials they use a technique called spanning the margin. The tooth is buffed so that the joint between artifice and what is left of the enamel blend together. Time does just that for a couple as different as we are. It spans the margin, and whatever separation there has been, whatever rift or crack becomes imperceptible, unimportant. Neither the conceit nor the observation would be within the vocabulary of a younger man.

I saw Claudia one last time before writing these words. It was only last year, the day after Thanksgiving, a dreadful day in New York because of the crowds of shoppers milling about and the young children on vacation from their schools. I was walking down Fifth, midtown, bumping and jostling my way across the sidewalks. I couldn't find a cab and had only a few blocks to walk from my apartment to a lunch date. I was late and irritable. In front of me strolled two women with large shopping bags, at a speed and breadth that disregarded the pressing mob behind them and marked them as suburban or, worse, out-of-towners. I growled "Excuse me" at the back of one, in a heavy coat of bright red cloth, and as she turned around, she said my name.

"Charles."

It was she. Her hair had silvered, perhaps more than showed, and there were new wrinkles around her eyes. But all to her advantage. She looked as beautiful, and something else as well. It would be saccharine to use the word happy, for I had no evidence of what was going on behind those eyes. They lit in me the same fires they had thirteen years, fourteen years earlier.

"I've never seen you wear red," I said. I cannot explain why that remark came out as we stood in the stream of pedestrians that flowed out of Sak's revolving doors and the first of the Salvation Army bell ringers tried to interrupt our conversation.

"No," she said, surprised. "I've only just started wearing it." She laughed and I did too. I don't recall the rest of the conversation except that she told me she and Jeremy were still together and she'd come here to shop. I'm sure she introduced me to the woman with her. She said that we all must get together and something in my face must have dissuaded her for she added immediately, No, I suppose not, and I nodded my agreement that that was best.

It was only as I stood, looking at her, that it came to me how much of my life she had occupied. Far more than the time we knew each other. My story line had a beginning and an ending, each the mirror image of the other, but no middle. Claudia was the middle, the exposition, terribly brief as it was. Or do I have it reversed? Isn't it that the story is not mine at all, but Claudia's, that she is the player and I am the audience? I came out of the play with as much as an audience can expect. Entertainment, catharsis, even some insight into myself. But insight is another form of measurement, and I think they are both overrated.

My ambition to write a journal of the three signal events in my life also now seems to me misguided. I'll shelve these scribblings in a back closet in the Connecticut house. Manhattan real estate is too valuable for storage. They'll sit with so many other unfinished pieces, on the evolution of the palm, the nesting habits of the phoebe, and the banana in Eden. There were not three signal events. St. Alban's and my marrriage were not points of decision or departure but simply points on a roadway. I passed by but never considered altering the course of my journey. There was only one signal event, and as it turned out it was an event for everyone involved but me.

And in some measure all of us got what we wanted. Weemo and Evelyn had, briefly, each other and they have been left to pursue similar connections if that is where they are led. It is true that Weemo now must do so on a more frugal scale. Jeremy, of course, got Claudia and Claudia got freedom. And I saw the natural order work its way through human selection.

That may be cold justice, but justice is by nature cold. For the sun, one must go south, and in two months I shall do that. I shall holiday at a small island off the coast of Venezuela, where snowy egrets nest and one sees flying fish and whales play, and there are very few amenities for the guests. When the day is cool, early and late, I can walk on the beach with my field glasses and sight wildlife. And in the heat of the day, I can sit in my cabin, or better under the thatched chalapa on the beach. There I shall enjoy the breeze off the ocean and be out of direct heat. There I can sit and sketch, and watch the sun bleach the sand and shell in a light too bright for color, the sun that can be clouded over by time or sound or memory but, when I close my eyes, again appears, floating, first gold then black, elusive, incorporeal.

About the Author

Bruce Ducker's three earlier novels have received critical acclaim. His poetry and short fiction appear in literary magazines including The Yale Review, Commonweal, The Quarterly and Poetry. He lives in Colorado.